D1736325

LINEAR TACTICAL SERIES

GHOST

USA TODAY BESTSELLING AUTHOR
JANIE CROUCH

GHOST: LINEAR TACTICAL

DEDICATION

To my Stephanie...

always more than an editor.
A friend
A sister
An advocate
An inspiration

Not just to me, but to so many

We'd all go play in traffic for you, woman.
But you'd be yelling at us to get off the street the whole time.

I love you.

1

Dorian Lindstrom stood in the icy sleet of a freak March Wyoming storm.

Thundersnow. When Mother Nature couldn't decide what the hell she wanted to do, she did everything: snow, rain, lightning.

Nobody in their right mind would be standing out here in it.

Dorian hadn't been in his right mind for some time. For the six years since he'd gotten out of an enemy prison in Afghanistan, to be exact.

But the good thing about being tortured within inches of your life? Standing out in the middle of a balls-to-the-wall storm didn't faze you in the slightest.

Especially when you were on the hunt for someone threatening your family. Or at least the only family Dorian had left.

Not many people were stupid enough to threaten the men of Linear Tactical, especially on their home turf in the mountains of western Wyoming.

Their years as US Army Green Berets had trained them

to adapt, defend, and survive almost every type of situation. Then they'd left active duty and started their own self-defense, weapons, and wilderness survival training facility for civilians.

So if someone was brilliant enough to think it was a good idea to come after the men of LT—or their loved ones—they'd better have a damned good plan.

Dorian wasn't sure the people he was currently watching for in this crazy-ass storm had *any* plan at all, much less a good one.

He knew his enemy today, and he wasn't afraid of them or any attack they might make. Dorian would prefer a straight-up fight, but these guys weren't going to give it to him. They'd already shown their true colors by bullying a woman who lived alone as well as cutting the brake lines of a Linear guy's fiancée today. *Pregnant* fiancée.

Whether the dumbasses knew it or not, they'd sealed their fate the moment their razor had touched that hose.

With this storm, and until Dorian and his team could hunt down the people responsible, the Linear guys were taking the tactically smart approach: a united front. They were keeping the people who meant the most to them together inside Finn Bollinger's house where the team could keep them safe.

Dorian had volunteered to take watch outside. Nobody had been surprised by that. Everyone knew Dorian didn't do crowds. Even friendly ones.

But as much as he was spoiling for a fight, there had been no sign of a threat out here besides the storm itself. There was nobody out here. Nobody—especially not people with the limited skill level of these guys—got past Dorian in the wilderness.

And he wasn't the only one keeping watch. There were

another half dozen men associated with Linear in vehicles around the perimeter of the house. Some military trained, some not, but all able to handle themselves.

Three of Dorian's closest friends—brothers in every way but blood—had the women they loved inside Finn's house for protection.

This was his family. They had helped him pick up his pieces six years ago when there hadn't been many pieces left to actually pick up. And they continued to help him pick them up every time he broke apart.

He would die for them. Kill for them.

But he wouldn't have to tonight. There was no threat to his family out here right now. Another wide circle around the perimeter of the house confirmed that.

Perhaps the friendly neighborhood idiots had come to their senses and realized an attack would be a suicide mission. More likely, they were cowards and planned to strike when their targets were more vulnerable.

There was no sign of a threat here. No sign of *anything* but a winter hurricane. Dorian ought to move inside too. The guys in the cars could keep watch, and he could come back out every hour or so.

Dorian knew these woods, had spent days—*weeks*—in the surrounding wilderness. The people who had targeted Charlotte's brakes had been careless enough to leave traces behind. There was no way anyone that sloppy was in these woods tonight.

Nobody was in these woods but him.

Yet his eyes were in constant motion, surveilling the woods around him even when he sensed nothing.

Because he felt it.

Felt it *again*, damn it.

Felt *her*.

He stopped suddenly, crouching down. He'd had that being-watched feeling on and off for weeks. There was no danger to his friends out here, but was there danger to *him*?

Was there a literal ghost—*Wraith*—out there? Or was his mind playing tricks on him again?

What Dorian had lived through would've killed most men. But there had been a price for that survival. Reality sometimes became fuzzy.

In this case, the dead coming back to life.

Grace Brandt, codename Wraith, had died a little over six years ago. He'd seen her die in an explosion no one could've survived. He'd been captured and subsequently tortured for forty-one days because he'd been so distracted by her death.

Her being alive was impossible. Her being in the tiny town of Oak Creek, Wyoming, in the middle of a thundering snowstorm, was beyond impossible.

But this wasn't the first time he could've sworn he'd felt her presence recently. He'd always been able to feel their connection when Grace was near.

He ran a gloved hand across his forehead. His mind sometimes couldn't be trusted.

Hundreds of hours with his psychiatrist, Dr. Diaz, had finally enabled him to say that out loud.

So he said it now. "My mind sometimes can't be trusted."

God, it *sucked* to say that. Even worse, it sucked to know it was true. That his body had come out of forty-one days of torture and eventually healed. His mind . . . well, some days were better than others.

Evidently, this wasn't one of the good days if he thought a dead woman was nearby. He stood back up and walked toward the house. There was no way Wraith was alive.

"My mind sometimes can't be—"

His senses picked up on the arrow a split second before it struck him in the waist from behind. He let out a mostly silent curse before dropping low behind a tree, ignoring the pain.

He'd been shot with a damn *quarrel*. There was a reason he knew what the short arrow used in a crossbow was called.

Because it had been Wraith's weapon of choice. Had been for all the years he'd known her.

He didn't touch the bolt—another name for it. He got into position in the cover of the trees and pulled his rifle-scope up to his eye.

Nothing.

Even knowing exactly where the shot had to have come from, he saw nothing. This crazy-ass blizzard didn't help.

Phasing out the pain, he kept his sights on the area in front of him, keeping his head down as much as possible, waiting to see what other attack would come.

None did. Minute after minute . . . nothing.

One perfect quarrel shot had struck his body, letting him know he wasn't alone but without doing any true damage.

And it had come from someone good enough to stalk these woods without his knowledge.

There were very few people in the world who could accomplish the latter. Even fewer who could accomplish the former.

There was only one person in the world good enough with a crossbow to hit him at this distance in a storm like this one.

Maybe his mind *could* be trusted.

The dead didn't always stay that way.

Wraith.

"Is it okay if I touch you, Dorian?"

Two hours later, he sat in one of the curtained-off sections of the emergency room in Oak Creek's small hospital. It was a busy night. Lots of minor accidents due to the storm.

Once he'd determined he wasn't going to end up as a pincushion for more arrows, he'd gotten himself back to Finn's house. Dr. Anne Nichols, Zac Mackay's girlfriend, had immediately brought him here.

"You've already taken the quarrel out, Doc. I think the worst part is over. Plus, I've been through a lot more pain than having an arrow removed."

She smiled at him, then moved behind him to look at the wound. "I know you have. I'm not worried about your pain threshold. But I also know you don't like to be touched, so I didn't want to assume it was okay."

Didn't like to be touched was an understatement. *Could barely stand to be touched* was closer to the truth.

Anne Griffin had walked back into Zac Mackay's life nearly a year ago. Despite a rough start and a difficult history between the two of them, Zac had quickly realized what a treasure the quiet, insightful doctor truly was. Any other medical professional probably wouldn't have realized Dorian's discomfort the first time, much less asked about it.

"I know it's you, Annie. I'm okay."

"I want to check the stitches before we release you. Honestly, you couldn't have been hit in a better place. No organ damage, minimal muscle damage—you did the right thing by not yanking the *quarrel* out, by the way." He'd already taught her the proper terminology.

Dorian shrugged. "We were all trained in basic field

medicine in the army. Not yanking out an impaled object is Field Med 101."

"Well, that and the fact that whoever shot you used a really small arrowhead means you should be back to fighting shape in no time."

"Small arrowhead?"

Annie reached around him to the table and lifted a bag. "This needs to stay in the bag in case it becomes a piece of evidence in a criminal case. But I knew you'd want to see it, so here it is."

He studied the bolt through the clear plastic. "It's a practice head."

Annie nodded. "Yes, that's actually what I thought too. A hunting arrow would've done significantly more damage to your flesh, no matter where it had struck."

"Believe me, the person who did this—"

"Your Wraith?"

Dorian nodded. "If she'd wanted to maim or kill me, I wouldn't be sitting here right now talking to you. This was a message."

"The note? I mean, I appreciate the woman letting us know that Jordan's house was on fire, but couldn't she have just picked up a phone?"

The note attached to the arrow had allowed them to help save a friend in need.

Dorian shrugged. Yeah, a phone would've worked, or a knock on the door, or stepping out from behind her cover and talking to him.

He turned away from Annie to look out the small window in the treatment room. Any of those things could've worked. But they would've led to questions.

First and foremost . . . how the hell was Grace alive?

Annie fooled with the evidence bag behind him.

"Having that note attached to the arrow had to have made her shot much more difficult."

He nodded without looking. "It did. She would've had to compensate for both it and the storm. It's a testament to her skill."

Annie, generally so mild and kind, scoffed. "It's a testament to her recklessness. I know we have our hands full with the people trying to hurt Jordan, but I think you need to hunt this Wraith down, and we need to make sure she's put behind bars."

Dorian didn't waste his time explaining the futility of trying to arrest Wraith. She would never allow herself to be taken alive.

He turned to face Annie. "I'll deal with her."

"Dorian, we all respect the hell out of you, you know that." Annie's eyes were steady on his. "Zac loves you like a brother. But are you sure the person who shot you is who you think it is? I know that sometimes . . ." She faded off.

"Sometimes I can't tell reality from fantasy?"

She gave him a delicate shrug. "Sometimes we all need a little help deciphering what's dangerous when we can't see it for ourselves."

"I think that's my cue to enter."

Both Dorian and Annie looked up at the woman standing in the doorway.

"Hey, Doc," Dorian said. He wasn't surprised Annie had called his psychiatrist, especially since she had an office here in the hospital.

Hell, half the town of Oak Creek probably thought he was crazy, although none of them ever said it to his face. He certainly had plenty of symptoms of mental deterioration.

Unable to be around people for long periods of time? Check.

Unable to stand most physical touch? Check.

A tendency to stay in the wilderness for days, sometimes even weeks, at a time? Check.

Putting two of his best friends in the hospital during an uncontrollable bout of violence? Check.

Dorian shrugged. "I don't blame anyone for thinking I'm crazy."

Dr. Diaz leaned her head against the doorframe. "I prefer a different term than *crazy*."

"Prone to chronic distress, delusional proclivities, and neurotic tendencies, as well as suffering from acute post-traumatic stress disorder?" Dorian was well aware of his own psychological diagnosis.

Dr. Diaz raised an eyebrow. "I was going to say 'cuckoo for Cocoa Puffs,' but, you know, whatever."

Dorian laughed, and even Annie chuckled. This was why he'd made more progress with this young psychiatrist, who'd happened to set up practice in Oak Creek, than any of the other PTSD *specialists* who'd tried to work with him over the years. She always made it her priority to see he stayed connected to his humanity. Humor had been one of the best ways to do that.

Annie turned back to him. "I don't think you're crazy or cuckoo, Dorian. None of us do. But we're all aware that you've been through a severe—the *most* severe—trauma. Nobody comes out of that unscathed."

Dorian looked down at all the scars covering his chest and arms. Both women had already seen them. Different sizes, lengths, thicknesses. Some, he could remember distinctly what had given him the mark—and he had discussed many of them with Dr. Diaz. The one on his shoulder was from a soldering iron. He had a matching one on his left calf.

The scars around his wrists matched the ones around his ankles. They were from the first two weeks of his captivity, when he'd fought against his metal restraints, tearing the flesh of his wrists.

After two weeks, he hadn't had the strength anymore to waste on futile attempts at escape. All he could do was put his energy into merely surviving each day.

But most of the scars that riddled his body were a complete blank. At some point, his mind had blended them all together in a cauldron of agony. Dr. Diaz had gently suggested that was probably for the best.

No need to constantly relive what had nearly killed him the first time.

Annie moved toward him with a bandage, looking at him for permission, and he nodded.

He held his arm up out of the way as she covered his wounds. Dr. Diaz was still keeping her distance at the door.

"As much as it might not look like it, since I'm sitting here in the emergency room, that arrow wasn't a threat. It was a message."

Annie nodded. "About Jordan's house burning. Sure."

"No, the message was for me. The message was to let me know that it was definitely Wraith."

Now Dr. Diaz took a few more steps into the room, eyes narrowed. "Wraith is dead, Dorian."

They had talked about Grace before. "I thought that too. I was wrong."

Dr. Diaz stared at him, not saying anything further, concern in her brown eyes.

Annie finished attaching the bandage and stepped back. "Why do you call her Wraith? I know your codename in the military was Ghost. Don't ghost and wraith mean the same thing?"

He began slipping on his button-up shirt, careful of his stitches.

"Yes, close." They'd all had similar codenames in Project Crypt: Ghost, Wraith, Shadow, Phantom, Vision. The government black-ops group that had assigned them their names had been nothing if not consistent.

"You worked with each other in the military?"

"In a roundabout way." That and so much more. More on every possible level.

Annie took off her gloves. "But you thought she was dead until today. Why?"

Dorian looked down at his shirt. "I watched her die in an explosion in Kabul. Trying to get to her was how I got captured in Afghanistan."

Wraith shouldn't have been there in the first place.

She shouldn't be here now.

Dr. Diaz studied him without speaking as he finished buttoning up his shirt. Dorian knew she wanted to talk further about this, but she wouldn't in front of Annie.

Annie turned to walk out the door. "Well, dead then or alive now, I think that this woman is dangerous. You need to find some answers, Dorian."

He couldn't agree more.

2

"I think we look pretty good for dead women, Grace."

There were only a few things Grace Brandt knew for certain in this life. The fact that she could not be further from her namesake was one of them.

"Ray. I don't go by Grace anymore, Angela, I go by Ray now." Grace had been dead for a long time.

The two women sat at a table in a small coffeehouse in Reddington City. Ray had chosen this place because of its three separate exits, all of which would allow her to disappear into the crowded streets of the Wyoming city within moments. She sat with her back to the wall at a corner table with four different weapons strapped to her body within easy reach. And that didn't count the ways she could kill someone with her bare hands if she needed to.

It still took all of her self-control to stay seated and *normal* in the café.

Too many people. Too much chatter. Too much *everything*.

Lately, the more she was around people, the more it seemed intolerable. Of course, being alone was no picnic either, between the dizziness, nosebleeds, and blinding headaches.

She forced her attention back to the woman who'd spoken to her. Angela Landry. She was another reason Ray had chosen this coffeehouse, and this table in particular. It was easily accessible by someone in a wheelchair.

Ray didn't make the mistake of thinking someone in a wheelchair couldn't be a threat, but in this case, she and the woman across from her had the same enemy.

The enemy of my enemy is my friend.

"I've technically been dead a lot longer than you, so I think I should get the most points for the beauty section of the pageant." Ray forced a smile at Angela, forced not because she didn't like the other woman, but because Ray just wanted to get out of here. Get away from all these people.

And because smiling seemed so completely unnatural to her.

"Are you sure you're okay?" Angela whispered.

Ray gripped her coffee cup with a strength that was close to shattering the ceramic but forced her features to remain neutral. A skill, ironically, her handlers at Project Crypt had taught her.

"I'm okay. Just don't like crowds."

Angela nodded rapidly. "Oh, yeah, sure. That makes sense. A lot of the Crypt agents had difficulty being around crowds. A tendency toward introversion was one of the psychological traits sought after in agents."

Ray wondered once again how much about Project Crypt Angela actually knew. As far as Ray could remember, she hadn't been much more than a glorified intern, fetching coffee and taking notes.

Ray studied Angela with her sunny disposition despite

the wheelchair. The woman was probably a couple of years older than Ray's own thirty-two years. Even at her low clearance level, Angela had to have known about Project Crypt's questionable morality.

But did she know the truth?

Did she know about the brainwashing and the sleeper missions and the fact that, in the end, it wasn't the US government that held Project Crypt's reins at all?

Ray sure as hell hadn't known. Not at the beginning.

Ultimately, it didn't matter now, and if Angela didn't know, Ray wasn't going to tell her. The woman had already paid a huge price for being part of the organization at all.

A year and a half ago, someone had started eliminating anyone who'd ever had anything to do with Project Crypt. Not only the active agents still left, who arguably might need to be eliminated, but *everyone*. The scientists, and even an attempt at Angela, who'd barely been more than an intern.

So now Ray and Angela were somehow mismatched partners—one broken on the outside, one broken on the inside—on a journey to find and stop the killer.

Angela was studying Ray now, completely uncaring that her back was to so many people and potential dangers in the room, something Ray could never have stomached. "I haven't heard from you in more than a month. Not since you went to see Ghost. Are you okay? I've been worried about you."

Ray forced her hands to gentle their grip on the mug, then took a sip of the lukewarm brew she didn't really want. "I'm okay."

She wasn't okay. She wasn't anywhere near okay, and shooting Dorian with that arrow a month ago had made everything less okay.

Why had she done that?

She'd stayed *dead* for six years, giving Dorian no clue at all that she was alive. Then shot him with her crossbow. With a fucking *note*.

She could've notified Dorian of the fire at his friend's house a half dozen different ways. Or she could've done what she was trained to do: mind her own damn business and not worry about a civilian fire where no one was getting hurt.

Instead, she'd shot Dorian with her crossbow.

Why had she done it?

Because she'd wanted him to know without a shadow of a doubt that she was alive.

But *why*?

Angela was still staring at her. "I thought you had planned to stick around Oak Creek to see if Ghost might be the killer," the woman said.

"He's not."

"Are you sure? After what he went through in that Afghan prison, he's the most likely to have incurred the damage necessary to alter his psychological state. The most unstable."

"Dorian isn't the killer." Ray kept her tone even and her hands relaxed on the table.

Angela took a sip of her own coffee. "I know you two were close back in training, and I don't want to believe he's capable of this sort of thing either. But—"

"Dorian didn't do it."

Not only did Ray believe that because Dorian was one of the best human beings she'd ever known, but also because after watching for more than a month, she didn't think he was actually capable of successfully carrying out the attacks against the Crypt members. Particularly not the agents who had exceptional skills when it came to detection and defense.

Maybe that was part of why she'd shot him with her crossbow. It had been a test.

She should've never been able to get the drop on Dorian. He should've sensed her and taken her out. No, his skills were no longer good enough for him to be the killer she and Angela were hunting for.

"It's not him," Ray said again.

Angela held her hands out in a gesture of surrender. "Okay, I'll take your word for it."

"Look, Angela." Ray fought against the urge to rub her forehead at the pounding starting there. "Maybe we should just get out. Everyone thinks we're dead. Why don't we keep it that way?"

Ray would disappear. She wasn't sure where she would run to, but she'd get the hell out of Wyoming. Away from Dorian and the life he'd built.

She wasn't sure what Angela would do, but honestly, that wasn't her problem.

"I was thinking that too. But then this happened last week."

Angela pulled out a thin file that had been stuffed between her leg and the edge of the wheelchair. She opened it and slid it across to Ray.

It was a newspaper clipping dated from last week, the stabbing death of a scientist in Los Angeles.

"Dr. Holloman," she whispered.

The face that starred in her nightmares. Project Crypt had been the brainchild of Timothy Holloman—a genius in his own right, with multiple doctorates in both the medical and behavioral sciences.

He'd been the one to recruit them. He'd been the one to

put them through all sorts of mental and physical tortures in order to make them into more perfect agents. He'd looked right into their eyes and lied as he told them it was all for the good of their country. That they were heroes.

He'd been the one who'd brainwashed them. Made them into sleeper agents stripped of free will.

Ray had found out about the sleeper missions by sheer accident. And she'd still allowed herself to be Holloman's puppet for too long.

So seeing him dead didn't exactly disturb her. She should've killed him three years ago herself rather than only destroying as much of Project Crypt's labs and computer files as she could.

"If you're expecting that to upset me, it doesn't. The world is a better place without Holloman in it."

"This also happened." Angela pulled back the newspaper clipping to show the rest of the story. Not only had Holloman been killed, but his wife and two small children had also been brutally murdered.

Even Ray flinched at the photograph of a four-year-old lying in a pool of his own blood.

"Whoever's doing this has to be stopped," Angela whispered. "Those children were innocent."

Ray stared at the pictures.

Did the person doing this *really* need to be stopped?

Obviously, killing preschoolers wasn't acceptable. But wiping out the rest of Project Crypt? Destroying the monsters Crypt had created—including her—and the people able to create more . . . Was that a bad thing?

There was something to be said about wiping the slate clean.

But that would also include Dorian.

"Whoever did this is just going to keep going," Angela

continued. "More innocent people are going to get hurt. All of this points to an agent. Someone trained to do this sort of killing."

Ray nodded, sliding the paper back over to Angela. They'd talked about this possibility before, and with every death it looked more and more likely.

Of the twelve Crypt agents who'd started ten years ago, only four remained.

Three had died in active missions before Ray had found out what Project Crypt truly was.

Five more had died in the past eighteen months, systematically eliminated, along with at least three scientists—now four, including Dr. Holloman—involved with the project.

All the deaths had been made to look like accidents or random acts of violence. Only people trained in Crypt's ways would see the workings of another Crypt agent.

"I'm not trying to guilt-trip you, but as one of those trained agents, you might be the only one who can stop the killer."

Everything in Ray—from the pounding in her head to that little voice in the back of her mind—told her to get out. To stand up right now and walk away.

That this was the only chance she would get if she wanted to get out of this alive.

But she already knew she wouldn't.

Dorian. The killer would eventually come for Dorian.

"Fine." Ray finished the last of the cold coffee. "We need to get as much information as we can on Phantom and Shadow. One of them has to be the killer."

Angela raised an eyebrow. "Are you sure? Nothing I've been able to find on Shadow suggests he's alive at all. And Phantom was always one of the more calm and rational active agents. Almost cold. The psychological profile of this killer would suggest mental deterioration."

"So you think it's Ghost."

"He's the only one who was ever taken off of active-duty status because of psychological damage, due to his . . ." Angela waved a hand in front of her.

"His torture," Ray finished for her.

"The torture the leaders at Project Crypt knew about and could've taken measures to prevent. That gives Dorian a lot of motive for killing everyone."

"He doesn't know about that."

"Are you sure?"

"Relatively." If Dorian knew Crypt had been able to do something about his capture and subsequent torture six years ago, he would've demanded answers. He would've pulled at Crypt's strings until it had all unraveled.

He would've found out the truth, and the truth would've destroyed him.

A truth Ray would take to her grave to make sure he never found out. Watching him the past few weeks in Oak Creek had only reaffirmed that for her. Those people were his family now.

But was Angela right? Had something snapped in Dorian's mind and made him the killer? She hadn't seen anything that suggested so, plus Dorian was no longer in the top form it would take to bring down other Crypt agents like the killer had.

But it was possible.

It was time to find out how possible.

"You focus on Shadow and Phantom, but be careful," Ray told Angela. "Whoever the killer is, if he finds out you're snooping around, he's going to know you're alive. He won't make the same mistake the second time and let you live."

"What are you going to do?"

Ray pushed her coffee cup to the edge of the table. "I'm going back to Oak Creek. It's time for me to figure out who my enemies are."

Ghost was either the killer, which meant she was going to have to make some really hard decisions, or he was an over-trained civilian caught in a situation he wasn't aware of or prepared for.

Either way, it was time for her and Dorian to have a *talk*.

Hopefully, they would both come out of it alive.

3

Ray wasn't surprised to find Dorian in the woods when she went looking for him three days later, after finally recuperating from her meeting with Angela.

More headaches and nosebleeds. Another blackout. Each time, it took a little more out of her.

But today she was feeling better and had caught up with Dorian teaching some sort of wilderness survival class. The Linear Tactical website had provided a course description.

Even a dead woman could stalk the internet.

It was absolutely pathetic how many times she'd studied Dorian's picture on the Linear website. How often she'd watched the video where he demonstrated a self-defense move while someone else narrated.

It had been one of the few things that had kept her sane three years ago when she had discovered what an utter fool she'd been with Crypt. She'd known their methods were morally corrupt, but until then, at least she'd thought the hell she'd chosen for herself benefitted her country.

Nope, sorry, Ray, no such luck. You've been selling your skills, your mind, and your body *to your government's enemies! Thanks for playing, better luck next time.*

The knowledge had cost her the last piece of her soul.

So watching a video of Dorian teaching a basic *o goshi* hip throw—and maybe or maybe not pausing on his tiny little grin at the end—had become a basic part of her survival for a while.

Not that she'd deserved survival.

The class Dorian was teaching now wasn't self-defense, it was wilderness survival. It included elements of the SERE training—survival, evasion, resistance, and escape—they'd gone through for Crypt.

Not so much the resistance and escape part; the half dozen high school–aged boys Ghost was teaching probably didn't need to know how to survive torture. But shelter building, fire craft, plant edibility, preparing animals for consumption, water purifying . . . A lot of the training elements were straight out of the SERE handbook. And good, useful information that everyone should know.

She'd been watching them for two days. At first, she'd stayed far enough back that detection would be nearly impossible. She'd mostly studied Dorian and his teaching partner. The other adult male from the Linear Tactical team was a tall, handsome man with a lithe swimmer's build, unlike Dorian's in-your-face strength. Like Dorian and all of the Linear Tactical men that she'd seen, Swimmer Guy had well-developed situational awareness.

The teenagers tended to be a little boisterous and unaware of what was happening around them, but Dorian and his friend definitely weren't.

So she kept her distance.

She circled widely and silently around them so she could observe from different vantage points. But what she saw was always the same: the kids responded to Dorian. He was patient with them, friendly. She couldn't hear what was being said, but it was obvious from the body language she caught in her binoculars. These kids respected Dorian, and he respected them.

He also took this training gig seriously, on occasion leading the boys somewhere so that finding the food or water they needed would be more difficult, teaching them to think for themselves.

More than once, she'd thought the boys had been assigned a task they couldn't do.

More than once, she'd been wrong. Dorian seemed to know when to push them and when to help.

Now, on day three, with a storm approaching from the southwest, Ray decided to get a little closer. Dorian had been out here for more than forty-eight hours, his attention split between the needs of the group and what he was trying to teach. The storm would give her even more cover.

He wouldn't be aware she was here.

In Dorian's defense, there was no reason to think any sort of enemy would want to infiltrate his group. They were no threat to anyone.

But the Ghost she'd known would've detected any sort of infiltration regardless of whether the party was an enemy or not.

She'd never been a wilderness specialist like Dorian. He used to tease her about how much she hated the cold. That was still true, although over the past six years, she'd learned to love the outdoors a lot more, since being around people had become increasingly difficult. Not to mention the importance of staying dead and off the grid.

So being out here now, knowing she was about to sit through a storm, didn't bother her.

Even if this was a waste of her time.

Ghost wasn't the killer. She'd known that before talking to Angela a few days ago, and it was more obvious to her now. Dorian was capable of killing, had certainly been trained to do it effectively in multiple ways. His brutal natural strength and intelligence had merely made him better at it.

But Dorian wasn't like her. The killer instinct didn't come naturally to him.

Dorian Lindstrom was a protector first and foremost.

He didn't kill people in cold blood. Even if he'd figured out what Project Crypt really was and what they'd almost made him do, she couldn't see him murdering Dr. Holloman in such a heartless way.

And she couldn't imagine him killing Holloman's four-year-old son under any circumstances.

The storm neared; she worked her way closer. As expected, Dorian and his friend were spending their time preparing their charges for how to best survive a storm of this caliber in the wilderness. It was probably something anyone who lived around here should know. A damn sight more useful for teenagers than sitting at home playing video games.

She worked her way in until she could actually hear snippets of the conversation between the boys and the men.

She found a cluster of trees that made a good place to stop. She climbed low into the back of the cluster careful to keep the trees between her and Dorian's camp. She couldn't see them, but at least she could hear a little.

The boys were excited about the storm, as only teenagers probably would be, all of them ready to test their mettle against Mother Nature. They were talking all over each other about what they needed to do.

"What's the best plan for surviving a storm in the wilderness?"

Something inside Ray's chest clenched. God, Dorian's voice. Deep, strong, confident.

It had been six years since she'd heard it last, and that had just been a panicked shout in her direction not to enter the building.

A shout that had saved her life and gotten him captured.

Hearing his voice now definitely shouldn't affect her in this primal way. Yet she found herself leaning closer.

The boys argued amongst themselves about storm survival. Was it better to stay closer to the trees or farther away? Higher ground or lower? What general terrain would be best?

Dorian let them talk for a few minutes before finally reining them in. "The storm is like a fight. And I know every single one of you knows the best way to ensure you survive a fight. Because if you don't, I'm going to make you take the elementary school self-defense class next week."

"The best way to survive a fight is to not get in one in the first place." All six of the boys said it in unison with varying degrees of enthusiasm.

Ray couldn't help but smile. The philosophy of the statement was sound but certainly not sexy, especially not to a bunch of teenagers.

Dorian chuckled, the sound causing that weird clenching in her chest near the vicinity of her heart. Again.

"That's right. It's not sexy, but it's the truth. When we have the option, we walk away."

"And if we don't have any other option?" one of the boys asked.

"Then you damn well make sure you know what you're doing. Let's get started with the basics."

He began to show them how to build a low shelter.

Ray kept herself hidden behind the tree, remaining motionless for long periods at a time—something she'd mastered over the past few years.

She squashed the desire to break from cover to look at Dorian, to see him with her own eyes rather than through a telescopic lens.

What would that accomplish?

Yet here she was, digging her nails into her palms to stop herself.

She listened instead. She allowed herself that—the sound of his voice.

She was too far to make out all his words, only the deep timbre of the sound itself was enough for her. Enough to calm the deepening chaos that had been building inside her for months with no apparent cause. The anger. The despair.

The sound of Dorian's voice drove it all back.

She leaned her head back against the tree. She'd been alone too long if she thought her ex-boyfriend's voice, talking to a bunch of teenagers no less, was keeping her demons at bay.

The longer she listened to him patiently work with the kids, the more she realized he couldn't possibly be the killer. No matter what Angela had suggested about his psyche being fractured, Dorian wasn't a killer.

It always came back to that. Dorian wasn't a killer.

But sitting here also confirmed another fact: Dorian was no longer the warrior he'd once been. This was twice now she'd been able to get way too close without him realizing it.

If the killer came looking for Dorian, he'd be a sitting duck. His skills were obviously no longer what they'd been before his capture—not that that wasn't understandable.

She caught part of some corny joke Dorian told the boys about building shelters. They groaned and laughed.

Ghost had made a life here. She didn't try to fool herself into thinking she wasn't jealous.

He may have forgotten his lethal skills, lost his edge, but he'd found an existence that didn't seem to require either.

Dorian seemed . . . happy.

And that was what she'd wanted, right? The reason she'd sold her soul to the devil? To give Dorian that very thing: happiness. Even if it was without her.

She'd always known it would be without her.

It was time for her to go. Leave this place for good. She'd allowed her sentiments to rule her for too long.

She'd made a mistake by shooting Dorian with that arrow last month, but if she disappeared now, maybe he'd chalk it up to some insane coincidence. It couldn't have been Wraith that had shot him during the storm. Wraith was dead.

It was time to leave Ghost to the life he'd built here. Not Ghost, *Dorian*. Ghost had died in an enemy prison camp.

She would slip out during the storm while he was teaching others to survive.

And she would find someone to come in here and protect him. She'd made enough contacts over the years to find someone who could be trusted to protect a civilian and his family.

Ray would hunt the killer.

And Dorian would never need to know that she'd been here at all.

4

Dorian's waist itched right where that damned arrow had hit him a month ago. It had itched all weekend.

Not the literal itch that had come with the stitches. The same itch he'd had before Wraith had shot him that day.

She was here.

He ought to be concerned. And he was. But more than that, he was *relieved*.

He'd searched for her every day since that quarrel had hit him and hadn't found a single sign of her. Nothing.

With every day he hadn't found any evidence of her and she hadn't shown up, with or without more arrows, he'd begun to doubt himself a little more.

Five days ago, he'd sat across from Dr. Diaz and forced himself to admit *out loud* that it was possible Wraith hadn't been the one to mark him in that storm.

That sentence had been one of the hardest damn things he'd ever said. One, because it meant that his mind really was more out of touch with reality than he wanted to admit.

And two, so much worse, was accepting that maybe Grace hadn't shot him because Grace was *dead*.

She'd been dead for six years, and she was dead now and was going to be dead forever.

And accepting that all over again had been worse than being hit by a thousand quarrels or bolts or whatever anyone wanted to call them.

Dr. Diaz hadn't tried to force him into saying it. She'd seemed more than willing to talk about the possibility that Grace was alive.

But Dorian didn't want to talk about it. He'd barely survived losing Grace the first time. Chatting about it seemed unbearable.

But now, Grace was back. It was all he could do not to smile.

He'd known there had been someone watching them all weekend, but they hadn't come close, so he'd left it alone.

Today, they'd come closer.

She'd come closer.

Grace was here and tracking them. To what end, he had no idea. Hopefully, no house fires this time. He didn't want another damn arrow in the waist.

The boys were busy building their shelters, working together, talking amongst themselves about the best overall plan.

Dorian stood facing the storm as if he were studying it. Really, he was keeping his back to where he was pretty damn sure Grace was currently perched—about 150 yards back in a cluster of trees.

Gavin Zimmerman, the one man who probably knew Dorian better than anybody in the world, approached from a diagonal to make sure Dorian knew exactly where he was. Dorian appreciated the consideration, although it wasn't necessary. He was well aware when anyone was within touching distance.

Controlling the urge to lash out was a little more difficult.

"Everything okay?" Gavin asked.

Dorian nodded slowly. "I'm going to need you to take the boys farther in toward town and have them set up shelter there."

Gavin looked out at the weather front that would be on them in less than an hour. "Storm more dangerous than we thought?"

Oh yeah, the storm was about to be a hell of a lot more dangerous than they'd thought. But not for these boys.

"She's here." The words were so low they wouldn't travel beyond Gavin's ears.

A testament to their friendship, Gavin didn't ask who or if Dorian was sure. "Do you want me to call the team?"

They always traveled with a short-range communication device when they had civilians out in the wilderness since cell phones were useless out here.

"No, she and I are going to have a chat one-on-one."

Gavin crossed his arms over his chest. "You sure about that, brother? She's dangerous to you in more ways than one."

"She had the upper hand when I thought she was dead. That won't happen again."

Grace. Was. Alive.

And, by God, Dorian was going to see her with his own eyes today. Get some damn answers.

Gavin glanced over his shoulder. "How do you want to play this with the boys?"

"The truth."

"That the love of your life who caused you to be

captured and tortured for weeks, pretended to be dead for six years, then showed up alive, recently shot you with her crossbow, and is now stalking you nearby somewhere? *That* truth?"

Dorian smiled and turned back toward the boys. "No, a more important truth than that. In order to survive, you have to adapt."

Evidently, Dorian was still learning that too.

A few minutes later, the boys were not excited at the announcement that they had to leave their hard work behind.

Gavin played it perfectly. "Let's go, guys. This is a lesson in adaptability. What if you discover your shelter is no longer in a stable location, or there's an animal threat, or any number of things that might mean you have to move and set up again rapidly? Let's see what you can do."

Once the boys saw it as a challenge, they quickly began working the problem.

These were all boys Dorian had gotten to know well over the past four years since he and the guys had started Linear Tactical. Being old enough and skilled enough to come on one of the advanced weekends was now a rite of passage for a lot of the local kids.

Dorian couldn't think of many reasons why Grace would be following him while he was with a group of teens, and none of the few reasons he could come up with were good.

Gavin continued to utilize the situation as a teaching exercise, leading the boys back toward town and finding a more barren section of the woods for them to camp in, making shelter building even harder. The boys definitely bought it as a greater challenge.

Once they were hard at work building a shelter again in a race against the storm, Gavin walked over to where Dorian was standing and observing it all. "Are you sure she's not going to have her crossbow again?"

"If she was going to shoot me with that thing, she would've already done it. Once I leave you guys, I'm going to make sure she doesn't get another chance. She's already heading away from us." He hadn't felt Grace's presence as strongly since they'd left the other campsite.

"So you're going to track her. What are you going to do once you find her?"

"We're going to have a little chat."

Gavin crossed his arms over his chest and looked over at the boys. "And if she doesn't feel much like talking?"

Dorian didn't answer. He wasn't sure what lengths he was willing to go to to keep his family here in Oak Creek safe. But he had to get answers. Starting with why Grace was here and how she was alive.

"You're sure it's her?" Gavin asked, not pressing when Dorian didn't answer his previous question.

"That's the *only* thing I am sure of."

That and the fact that he would not be sitting in Dr. Diaz's office again struggling to know whether or not Grace Brandt was dead. Today, he would get his proof.

"I've already radioed Zac. He's on his way out here. He should get here right about the time the storm hits. You owe Annie a bottle of wine for taking Zac away from her on her day off."

Dorian winced. "Done. Be sure to tell her I won't be cheap in my wine choice."

Dorian didn't say goodbye to the boys, not wanting to distract them from what they were doing—and just in case he was wrong and Grace was closer than he thought.

And then he went hunting.

There was a lot he could teach others about wilderness

survival. Things to look for, things to run from, things to run toward. He could teach people how to navigate by the stars, how to tell what plants were edible, and how to avoid predators. He could show them how to cover their tracks if someone was hunting them.

He could even teach people how to track others. To a degree.

Part of what Dorian did in the wilderness was pure instinct. It had always been. Maybe it was the fact that he'd been lucky enough to have been raised in a group foster home on a ranch in Colorado. Pete and Jennifer hadn't had much money, but they'd had lots of knowledge and more than enough room for Dorian and the other boys to learn about nature and the outdoors.

Dorian had always had a natural instinct for wilderness survival, an instinct that had been honed over the years. His wilderness skills had been the reason he'd been chosen for both the Green Berets and Project Crypt.

Moving silently, he backtracked to the area where the boys had built their first shelters. It didn't take him long to find where Grace had been sitting in a tree. The markings weren't obvious, a slight scruff where she'd hoisted herself up, some broken pieces of leaves on the branch where she'd been sitting. She obviously hadn't thought that he'd been aware of her presence.

"Tsk tsk, Wraith. First rule of engagement is to never underestimate your opponent."

Following her from there in the opposite direction of the town was difficult, but not impossible. She was moving carefully enough not to make any trail noticeable, but no matter what, she was never going to be as good as he was.

He saw her for the first time a little less than an hour later. She was crouched by the river, filling her water bottle.

He breathed past the pounding in his chest.

There she was. So very alive.

Only for a second, nothing mattered but that. For the first time in six years, he could take a breath without splinters of grief slicing into his heart.

But he tamped that emotion down. Just because she was alive didn't mean Grace wasn't his enemy.

He was damn well going to get some answers from her. And getting them wasn't going to be gentle. Sitting down and talking wasn't an option. Until he knew for sure why she was here, he couldn't accept anything she said as the truth.

It was going to take drastic measures. He'd been preparing for them.

He took a moment to study her while she was distracted with her actions. Her long blond hair was pulled back into a braid. She looked up and closed her eyes, soaking in the small patch of sunlight that had made it through the thick trees before the storm hit.

God, she was breathtaking. Her blond hair, icy blue eyes, angular features, and tall, trim build all spoke to her Nordic heritage. Everything about her was strong and focused. That had been true since the first day he'd met her ten years ago when they'd been brought in together as part of the Project Crypt team. Those blue eyes had been bright with laughter and life then. Her face focused but relaxed.

It definitely wasn't anymore. Now, her face was exhausted and tense as she enjoyed a moment of sun—God, how he remembered she loved the sun; the image of that lithe body in a bikini in Capri would be burned into his memory until the day he died.

Guilty conscience, Grace?

He didn't look at her long, knowing that would tip her

off, subconsciously at the least. Instead, he eased back, returning the way he'd come and swinging wide so he'd be able to cut her off a half mile up.

She'd go straight up the river—it offered her the most options if she needed to change course.

He wasn't going to give her that option.

He knew the exact outcrop of rocks where he would attack. He wouldn't make the same mistake she had: he would not underestimate her abilities.

She might weigh nearly a hundred pounds less than he did, but that didn't mean she didn't know a dozen ways to kill him in under five seconds. And that was without using a weapon.

He could kill her right now if he wanted. Just like she could've killed him a month ago with that quarrel and no doubt many other times this weekend.

Why was she here? *How* was she here?

The questions would have to wait. He moved quickly and got into position behind the large rock outcrop. He'd only get one chance to take her by surprise, and even that might not be enough.

She moved closer, deeper into the water as she came around the rocks, as he would've done, unwilling to take the rocks blind from the other side. As soon as he knew she was there, he pounced.

Surprise flared in those blue eyes as he tackled her and sent them both flying into the chilly water. Surprise didn't hold her in its grip for long. She bucked, using their momentum in her favor, bringing both her arms up in between their bodies and pushing away, rolling before he was able to grasp her again.

They both used their core strength to kick up out of the water, landing on their feet in fighting stances. Neither of them spoke, and Dorian didn't wait to attack again. His chances to win in hand-to-hand combat against her lessened the longer the fight went on. She had an unnatural stamina that would always work in her favor.

Of course, Dorian had a few new tricks. She wasn't going to like them.

He swung in a right-left combination, not holding back. His blows could knock her unconscious—hell, they could knock someone twice her size unconscious—but he didn't think they would land.

They didn't. She blocked them both, then came in toward him, ramming a knee up into his ribs twice before jumping back out of reach of his arms. She spun her body around in a roundhouse kick that would've knocked him on his ass if he hadn't blocked it.

Overhead, the storm decided to get in on the mix too. Rain fell all around them.

She flew at him again with a sliding side kick. She had always loved putting those long legs to good use in a fight. But this time, he was ready for her. He stepped to the side and wrapped an arm around her waist.

Grace twisted, halting for a second, trying to figure out her countermove. A grasp around the waist wasn't a good attack, and he'd caught her off guard for a second.

But that was all he needed.

He jerked the syringe he'd had in his hand, bringing it into the fleshy part of her waist, releasing the special concoction he'd had on him for thirty-four days, ever since she'd shot him with that damn quarrel.

Because he'd always known this moment was coming. Even when he'd been forced to say she might not be alive, his mind had known this was coming.

Once he'd injected her with the fast-working sedative, he let her go.

For the first few seconds, she wasn't aware anything had happened. She flew at him again with a kick-punch combo, snapping his head around when her fist found his chin. That was going to leave a mark.

When she spun around for another kick, she wobbled slightly.

She knew immediately something was wrong.

"What did you do?" she whispered.

That voice. That voice had been part of every sensual dream he'd had for the past ten years.

"You shot me in the waist last time, I just returned the favor."

She swayed more heavily on her feet as the drugs kicked in. "Cheater."

He chuckled. It was so like her to say that.

She threw one more punch at him. It was so easy to dodge it was almost comical.

He caught her as she fell. He didn't want her hurting herself.

He planned to do that.

She pushed him away as her legs gave out from under her.

"It's time for us to have a talk, Grace." He lowered them both into the icy water as she lost more and more control of her body. Rain plastered her hair to her face as she tried to talk.

"Don't— Don't—"

Don't what? Don't hurt her? Don't kill her?

Those blue eyes fluttered closed. Her words were slurred. "Don't call me that."

5

Ray woke up naked, tied hand and foot, with her arms stretched overhead.

On a tarp.

She kept her eyes closed, her breathing even, refusing to give in to the panic clawing at her gut. She was inside a structure somewhere, but she had no idea where. Everything was fuzzy.

Dorian had jumped her. Caught her unaware. Injected her with something.

Fuck. Tied naked on top of a tarp was probably the worst possible scenario. There was only one reason you put an enemy on a tarp.

Easy cleanup.

She'd been wrong about Dorian. Had underestimated him on so many levels.

Unbeknownst to her, he'd obviously sensed she was out watching his little camping group, then tracked her.

She'd seen what she'd *wanted* to see rather than the truth.

A deadly error for someone in her line of work.

She'd mentally accused Dorian of forgetting his training, of losing his edge, becoming barely more than a civilian.

Lying here in the cold, bound hand and foot—*on a goddamned tarp*—she realized that was the reality she'd *wanted* for him. That he'd gotten out, become soft and happy, found a place to live the rest of his life in peace.

She'd wanted that for him. Paid for that for him.

Now she had to face the fact that he was likely the killer, and she had just handed herself over to him with her own complacency and nostalgia.

"I know you're awake."

She didn't open her eyes. His voice came from the corner, near the only heat source in this room.

She was so fucking cold. She hated being cold.

"You should've fought me like a man, not drugged me like some pussy." Poking the tiger wasn't a good idea, but she couldn't seem to help herself.

But Dorian only chuckled. "I couldn't take a chance on either of us ending up with a serious injury. We both know that's a distinct possibility in a fight between us."

She finally opened her eyes, giving herself a moment to adjust to the slight spinning of the room. They were in a small cabin. A stone fireplace burned in one corner and a stack of supplies—canned goods, water jugs, what looked like an extensive first aid kit—rested on some shelves opposite the fireplace.

She avoided making eye contact with him and looked around the rest of the room. In the corner closest to her head was a large, comfortable-looking chair and ottoman, no less. A stack of books piled next to it—so definitely Dorian's. The man had always loved to read.

The comfy chair was completely out of place in the rustic cabin, and if they were anywhere near where they'd fought in the river, it had to have been a bitch to get here. The only other furniture was the small eating table and single wooden chair near the fireplace.

"So you wanted to make sure I wasn't hurt before you brought me to your freaky cabin in the woods to . . . what?" She pulled on the restraints on her wrists. "Torture me? You didn't used to be into the kinky stuff, Ghost."

"I spent five weeks naked and tied up in that Afghani prison."

Ray closed her eyes again. She knew the extent of his physical damage when he'd been held prisoner. She'd seen the actual medical report.

Hell, that was why she was tied up here right now. The reality she hadn't wanted to accept: no one could go through what Dorian had gone through and still come out whole on the other side. Angela had tried to warn her.

Ray had no idea if there was any way out of this. What was a mental time bomb with him and what wasn't? What might trigger him into a murderous rage? What might get him to let her go free?

God, she didn't want her last conscious thought to be that Dorian was a monster.

"For what it's worth," she said softly, "I'm sorry for what happened to you."

He stood from his chair at the table and walked closer. She cringed, wishing she could crawl farther inside herself.

Dorian had seen her naked plenty of times, but never once had she been worried that he might use his impressive strength against her. They'd been surrounded by so much violence and psychological warfare during their training with Project Crypt, that the time they'd spent together in bed had always been the opposite: lazy, gentle, slow.

"I got captured because of you, you know. You showed up at that café in Kabul. The explosives were already set, and the only thought in my dumbass head was getting you to safety."

"I know. I'm sorry. I thought . . ."

He held out a hand to silence her. "Did you know about the explosives?"

"I knew something, but—"

"And did you learn about them from somebody on my team? Someone from the US government? Were you there on our side?"

"No. But I wasn't there against you either."

He crouched down beside her, his smile bitter. "You were the last person I expected to see there. I've spent years of my life trying to figure out why you were. I thought maybe we had crossed missions, or that you had come to that godforsaken hellhole to warn me of something, or, Jesus, just to see me."

She closed her eyes again. It was a bad tactical plan to close her eyes when her enemy—and Dorian definitely was her enemy—was so close. But she did it anyways. "It wasn't that simple. Nothing we ever did with Project Crypt was that simple. You know that."

"So you were there officially for our government? Hell, I'll even take *unofficially*."

"If I tell you what you want to know, are you going to untie me? Let me get dressed? Let's talk about this as reasonable adults. Two people with so much history between us— that's the way we should be talking about it."

He leaned forward, resting the weight of his arms on his knees, perfectly balanced. Such a small move, but so telling in terms of strength and agility. He'd be able to fend off an attack from any direction.

How had she missed any of this? How had she underestimated him to such a degree? This Ghost was every bit as deadly as the one she had known years ago. Maybe even more so.

His hazel eyes stared so intently into hers, it was all she could do not to look away. "Yes, Wraith. You tell me that you were there on a mission for the US government, and I'll compromise. I won't release you completely, but you can at least have some clothes. I know how you hate to be cold."

The bastard's eyes raked over her entire body, pausing on her chest, where the evidence that she was cold was more than pronounced.

She wanted to lie. It would be so easy to make up a story about why she'd been in that café. Maybe he'd believe her, maybe he wouldn't. But the temptation to try was there.

But she'd never been able to lie to Dorian.

"Want some clothes? Talk to me. Were you on a sanctioned mission for our government?"

She almost scoffed at that question. None of them had ever been on missions sanctioned by the government. They'd had no idea.

"No, I wasn't." She ignored the part of her brain that was screaming at her, calling her the biggest idiot on the planet for not lying to him.

Tell him what he wants to hear, then figure out the rest when your life's not in danger.

But the truth kept coming out anyway. "I wasn't there on official government business. Or unofficial government business. But neither was I there to betray you."

She'd been there because she'd found out about the sleeper missions and that a Crypt agent in Kabul meeting with the Haqqani network that day had been programmed to kill Dorian's team at some future date.

She'd never dreamed it was Dorian himself who'd been programmed to do so.

He stood, shaking his head, towering over her. "You were there meeting someone in the Haqqani network, the same group that took me."

"Yes. I was trying to get some answers. I didn't know you were casing them too."

He walked over to the fireplace, scooped some of the ashes from around the low-burning fire, and poured the ashes on top of it, effectively dousing the flames.

"You were there trying to get answers?" he said. "Interestingly, that's exactly what I'm trying to do. It's going to get pretty damn cold in here without that fire. Wyoming is like that sometimes, even in April." He reached over to a hook on the wall that held a coat and slipped it on. "I'm afraid you're going to get pretty uncomfortable."

He walked over to the door and opened it, letting the cool storm air in, dropping the temperature even more. He grabbed a canteen that had been sitting outside.

"I went ahead and filled some bottles with river water, since it was still near frozen."

He walked back over to her, methodically opening the canteen. Before she could actually process what he was going to do, he poured the cold water over her body.

After her initial shocked gasp, she forced herself to stay silent. It was only cold. She's been through worse.

"It's only cold—that's what you're telling yourself, right?"

She didn't answer.

"I don't want to hurt you, Grace. Just tell me what you're doing here."

"Don't call me that."

"Call you what?"

"Grace."

His eyebrows pulled together. "Why? It's your name."

Grace was generosity and kindness—the bestowal of blessings. She hadn't been anything close to that in six years. Couldn't stand the thought of the word associated with her.

"No. It's not who I am anymore."

He studied her for long minutes. Shivers already trailed up and down her body as he walked back over and shut the door.

"Well, I'm not going to call you Wraith."

"Ray." She said the word, then gritted her teeth to stop them from chattering. "I go by Ray now."

His eyebrow rose. "I guess it's an appropriate middle ground between the two." He grabbed the wooden chair from the table and brought it close to where she was tied, turning it around backward and straddling it. "So tell me, *Ray*, why are you here? Why are you not dead? What do you want, and are you planning to harm the people I care about?"

She wished her hands were untied, not so she could fight, but so she could wrap her arms around her torso and curl up into a ball against this cold. Telling him the truth seemed like the best possible option.

"I was in Kabul that day searching for intel about Project Crypt. And to warn you about it." She gritted her teeth to keep from chattering, tensing her muscles to stop the shuddering. "I'm here now for mostly the same reason, believe it or not."

His arms remained crossed over the back of the chair as he stared down at her. Those hazel eyes looked empty. "Details."

"Project Crypt wasn't what we thought it was."

His eyes narrowed. "How so?"

"Our missions were never government sanctioned. Someone else held the reins from the beginning."

"What?" He sat up straighter in the chair.

"They chose us as agents not only because of our aptitude and skill sets, but because of who we were—all of us young, most of us without any family. Every single one of us willing to go to absurd lengths to complete a mission." She stopped for a second, sucking in deep breaths as shudders wracked her body once again. "The things they did to us in training, Dorian, both as a group and when each of us were taken off individually . . ."

His eyes narrowed. He knew exactly what she was talking about without her having to say it. As a group, the active agents of Project Crypt had spent weeks in training to make them harder, stronger, more brutal, and less likely to break. They'd been subjected to every sort of physical and psychological test that could be used to make someone stronger.

They'd all also spent periods alone for months at a time with only their trainers. Supposedly, that had been to work out and overcome their individual fears and phobias.

It was also when they'd done most of the actual brainwashing and established the measures needed to turn them all into sleeper agents. Of course, none of them had known it. They'd known they'd been through the most difficult weeks of their lives, but they'd had no idea what had been done to their minds.

They'd gone from agents able to survive nearly anything to agents who could survive nearly anything and also be turned into mindless puppets with only a few trigger words.

Dorian stood and began pacing back and forth. "The

Project Crypt training was what allowed me to survive during the five weeks I was detained. Without it, I never would've survived—physically or mentally."

He was probably right.

But they'd *all* been experiments.

And Dorian's part of the experiment was worst of all, in her opinion. To see if the programming could withstand the greatest cognitive dissonance: killing the people he cared about most in the world. His Special Forces team.

If he hadn't been captured that day in Afghanistan, he would've murdered his team at some point. But the torture had broken his conditioning.

How was she supposed to convince him that Crypt was evil and keep that part out of it? But she had to. The knowledge would destroy him.

God, she was cold. It was hard to make any sense of the thoughts in her head.

"Th-the training was real, but we were still pawns in someone else's chess game. I came across information by accident." A shudder ripped through her body again. "I was in Kabul to confirm my suspicions."

"So what you're saying is that the organization that trained us and sent us out on missions was actually not part of the US government at all?"

She was shaking so badly now she could hardly speak. "Yes—yes. Once I was sure, I got out."

He stopped pacing and stared down at her. "I've thought you were dead for *six damn years*, Grace. Where have you been? Why didn't you contact me before now?"

"D-don't call me that."

"Answer my fucking questions."

Dorian had never been one to use profanity. Had the

torture brought that out of him? Did she bring that out of him? It was hard not to stare at his lips when—

"*Wraith*. Focus."

Right. God, she was so cold. What was the question?

"Where have you been?" he asked again.

"Once I-I got out, I had to hide. Being around you wouldn't have been safe."

That was true too. Just, again, not the entire truth.

He stared down at her for a long minute before turning to the supply shelves. He grabbed a towel, then picked up a thermos by the fireplace.

"Are you telling the truth, Wraith?"

"Yes. I promise, yes."

She whimpered in relief when he took the towel and rubbed it briskly all over her body. Warmth. Blessed warmth. His deep, firm rubs began restoring feeling to her body, and her shudders subsided.

He didn't say anything as he did it, but Ray couldn't stop watching him. Watching his big hands on her body. Nothing about what he was doing was sexual, but her body couldn't seem to grasp that.

After not nearly long enough, he stopped. She almost whimpered, but at least she wasn't unbearably cold anymore.

His hand slid behind her head, and he lifted her gently, bringing a cup of warm water he'd poured from the thermos to her lips. "Warmth from the inside will help too."

She drank greedily before collapsing back into his hand. He set her head back down on the floor and crouched on his haunches again. For long moments, he just stared down at her with those hazel eyes.

All she could do was stare back. The shivering had taken everything out of her.

"Tell me the real reason you're here, Grace. Let's start all the way back at Kabul and go through it again."

She closed her eyes, sucking in a breath. He didn't believe her. She didn't even try to correct her name.

"I'm telling the truth. Project Crypt was actually run by enemies of the United States. We were all specially trained to do . . . certain missions. Missions that seemed like they might be helping the United States at the time but long-term were not."

She stopped, not sure what else to say. Explaining the sleeper missions might give more credence to her argument, but then he'd want details about the particulars of his sleeper mission.

"What are you thinking about? Trying to remember what you said? Making sure your story matches up?"

"No. I'm telling the truth. My story isn't going to change."

That was the purpose of questioning a suspect over and over. Eventually, they would trip themselves up in a lie.

He tilted his head to the side. "Here's the thing. I don't believe you. I don't know why you're here now when I was quite certain you died that day in Kabul. But I do know that I will do whatever it takes to keep my friends and family safe."

"Dorian . . ."

He stood up. "Let's start again, shall we?"

He pulled off the towel he'd left covering her body, and she cringed. It hadn't been providing any warmth, but she was consciously aware of how naked she was without it. He hung it neatly over the back of the chair, then walked toward the door. This time he brought in two large jugs of the icy water.

No.

"Ghost." She shook her head franticly. "Dorian. I'm telling the truth. I swear, I—"

She sucked in a breath as he doused her with the icy water once again.

"Let's start at the beginning. Why are you here? And I'm going to need you to tell me the truth this time."

6

"I'll be back tomorrow after you've had a chance to think."

Dorian had thrown those words at Ray four hours ago when he'd left her in the cabin at sunset.

Shit. It had been a long day.

She'd lain there silently as he'd dried her off a little. He'd even given her some warm broth to get some calories into her system.

She would be fine. He'd been keeping careful track of her body temperature and the water temperature, which after the first couple of times hadn't been nearly as cold, not that her mind had been able to tell. He'd made sure he wasn't doing any real damage.

He knew what real damage was and would never have the stomach to inflict it, especially not on Grace.

Ray.

What the hell was that about? He had no idea.

No matter what she wanted to call herself, using her dislike of cold against her had been difficult enough. He knew what it was like to be naked and freezing and not have any idea if it was ever going to stop.

Dorian looked down at the slight tremor in his own hand. It was possible that he was the only person who'd been truly damaged during those eight hours of inter-rogation.

The storm had already moved past by the time he'd left her. That particular cabin was one he'd built himself. He'd built or found dozens in the hundred miles of wilderness that surrounded the Linear Tactical property. This one, about five miles north of town, was the one he used most often.

Or had been. He wasn't sure he'd ever be able to sit in his favorite reading chair again without envisioning Ray's shivering, naked form over in the corner. Or remembering what her body had felt like as he'd rubbed her with that towel over and over.

What sort of sicko, perverted bastard did it make him that he was going to be able to remember the soft feel of her curves under his hands for the rest of his damn life?

While he was interrogating her under duress.

He opened the door to the Eagle's Nest, one of three bars in Oak Creek and the one most frequented by him and the guys. Or as often as Dorian frequented anything where there were groups of people.

He'd gotten home about two hours ago, showered, and changed, and he had known he needed to get out of his house. He couldn't be at home alone, his normal MO, or he'd head back to the cabin where he'd left Ray.

That was the worst plan possible. In order for this to work, he needed to stay away from her. If he didn't stay away, then the past few hours torturing them both had been for nothing.

And he definitely couldn't be trusted if he went back to that cabin. For more than one reason.

A text from Gavin had let Dorian know that the Linear boys were at the Eagle's Nest, not an uncommon occurrence for a Sunday evening.

So Dorian was joining them.

He tensed automatically as he walked through the bar's door, even though it was all friendly faces, Oak Creek's townspeople giving him their greetings or waves. He pulled in a breath and let it out. This was a safe place. His friends, sitting at a booth in the back corner, had had his back a hundred times over.

There are no enemies here. There are no enemies here.

He repeated it as a mantra, reminding his brain—already wound up from today's activities—of reality. The *real* reality, not the reality his mind sometimes lent itself toward.

His hand was still shaking as he stuffed it into his pocket.

"Dorian. What's up, brother?" Finn gave him a small salute and stood, grabbing a different chair so that Dorian could sit where he'd been sitting rather than have his back to the rest of the bar.

And that was family, wasn't it? They did what you needed without making a big deal of it.

"Everything okay?" Zac asked. "Gavin thought you might be taking a couple of days on your own after that high school trip. Not that any of us would blame you."

"Yeah, and thank you for taking over for me. I might be going back out. Just needed to come in town and be around people for a little bit."

To make sure he was centered in his own humanity and

had everything locked down before dealing with Ray again. For both their sakes.

All four men around the table actively stared at him now.

"What?" he asked.

Aiden laughed. "I don't think any of us have ever actually heard you say you *wanted* to be around people before."

Dorian grunted. He couldn't blame his friends for being shocked. His ops normal was staying as far away from people as possible. But he wasn't ready to go into all this with them yet. His conversation with Ray was between just him and her.

He still wasn't sure if she was telling the truth. God knew she could withstand a lot and still keep a lie intact.

She would break under real torture, of course. Torture wasn't like movies, where the hero could withstand anything forever.

Everyone broke eventually, would say whatever they had to say to make the pain stop. Dorian certainly had.

To this day, he still didn't know exactly what knowledge his captors had hoped to gain from him. He'd known a lot, details about specific upcoming missions, locations of safe houses and meeting points. But as soon as he'd been captured, all of those details would have been immediately changed.

He'd been useless to them.

That hadn't stopped the agony. Hadn't stopped him from becoming more animal than man inside that cell.

"Beer?"

Dorian gave a little nod to the waitress. "Yeah, thanks." He needed it. The guys were still staring at him. "Isn't it past your bedtimes?" He looked specifically at Zac, Finn, and

Aiden, all of whom had wives or girlfriends waiting for them at home.

"Zac had something he wanted to tell us, like the pretty princess he is." Gavin smirked.

Zac flipped him off good-naturedly and leaned back farther in the booth. "Don't be a hater because you can't get any women to put up with you full-time, Redwood."

Everyone laughed at that. Gavin, codename Redwood when they'd been in the army together, was arguably the most stand- up and well-liked of them all. Attention from the opposite sex had never been a problem for him, although he'd rarely taken advantage of it since his divorce and move to Oak Creek three years ago.

"Don't try to change the subject. Spill the beans, Cyclone."

Zac grinned. "I asked Annie to marry me, and she said yes."

Everyone raised their beer up in a toast. Dorian reached out to shake his friend's hand.

"We've got the psychiatric exam scheduled for tomorrow," Finn chuckled. "Obviously, the good doctor is not in her right mind if she agreed to become a Mackay."

Aiden rolled his eyes. "Don't even start. You and Charlie getting all pregnant and married is what started this whole process to begin with. Everyone's falling like dominoes."

Aiden tipped his head toward one of the dancing couples on the other side of the bar, swaying to a slow song. Jordan Reiss and Gabriel Collingwood, another newly engaged couple. Dorian was glad to see Gabe was forcing his young fiancée to get out of her house more and interact in town. After what she'd been through, she deserved to know people welcomed her here.

"You and Violet are next," Gavin told Aiden with a grin.

Aiden shrugged. "Any day of the week she'll have me. Violet gives the first indication, and I'll drag her to the closest church immediately."

"It's like a Hallmark movie around here," Dorian muttered.

Gavin chuckled. "Watch many of those, do you?"

Finn stood up, saving Dorian from having to answer Gavin's question—and lie. "I've got to head out." Finn slid the chair he'd grabbed back to the nearby table. "Charlie will cry if I'm not there to rub her back when she's trying to get to sleep."

Zac slid out of the booth, laughing. Charlie, even four months pregnant, wasn't the crying type. "More likely she'll knock you on your ass."

"I'd prefer to avoid either. They're both equally scary." Finn gave a wave, and Zac and Aiden joined him, saying their goodbyes and following him out, leaving Gavin and Dorian.

They sat for a long moment without saying anything, both sipping their beers.

"You were looking a little shaky when you first came in."

Dorian ran a hand over his eyes. "Believe me, I was feeling shaky."

"You catch your Wraith?"

His sip turned into a gulp. "I did."

"And am I going to need to help you hide a body?"

Dorian rolled his eyes. "Don't be ridiculous."

The other man shrugged. "Given that she shot you last time she saw you, and what I know about your history with her, it's not a completely unreasonable question."

No kidding it wasn't. "Oh, it's totally plausible that one of us might kill the other. I'm talking about getting *you* to help hide the body. There's at least half a dozen people I'd call before you."

Gavin was too honest for his own good. Hell, it was how he'd gotten the codename Redwood.

Gavin chuckled. "Fair enough. So, there's no body?"

"No. She and I had a . . . talk at one of my cabins."

"A talk. Find out anything interesting?"

Only that a huge part of his existence had been a lie, if he could believe Ray. "I've mentioned the covert sector that trained me."

Dorian had only ever talked about Project Crypt in passing, and not ever by name. He'd been an active Crypt agent during part of his time in the Special Forces.

Gavin nodded. "Sure. We all knew you were working with some other covert government team. We had bets about if you were doing blended ops with the SEALs or Force Recon or something."

"No. I was part of a black-ops group. Temporary, short-term, one-man missions. Getting into and out of places and situations undetected. Precision work."

Gavin shrugged. "Small missions are often the most effective. Agencies know that."

"Well, if I can believe Wraith, it seems that the agency I worked for went rogue at some point, and the missions they sent me on weren't US government sanctioned. I always knew the organization was black ops, but now it looks like I wasn't playing for the right side."

"Are you sure? That's pretty farfetched."

Dorian took another sip of his beer. "It's not impossible to believe that the people calling the shots weren't on the up and up. I never questioned my assignments out loud, but I definitely ignored some warning bells in my head."

And then he'd gotten captured, and it hadn't mattered

anymore. By the time Dorian had gotten out, he'd been broken to the point that Project Crypt missions weren't an option.

"And Wraith? How does she know all this?"

"She was trained by the same organization I was. Had her own active missions like I did."

Gavin pushed his empty mug toward the edge of the table. "This Wraith—"

"Grace Brandt. But she goes by Ray."

"Okay, Ray. She's the woman you told me about, right?"

The one who had meant everything to Dorian. The love of his life. "Yes. And yes, until recently, I thought she was dead. That she died the day I was taken captive. Actually, she was the reason I got captured at all. I was distracted by her and got careless."

Gavin sat back and stared, obviously sorting through all the information and trying to make sense of it all. Dorian didn't blame him for needing a minute. It was a lot to take in.

Gavin grimaced. "I've got to ask the hard questions, man. Why is she here six years later? I could understand her finding you long before now, and I could understand her staying away for good. But why *now*? And why tell you the truth about your covert-ops group? You're out—so of no use or threat to them."

Dorian scrubbed a hand across his face. "I've been out since my capture. Project Crypt marked me as ineligible for missions after what happened. Hell, I could barely do anything but work a desk for the army."

Crypt had written him off. That had hurt at the time, but if what Ray had said was true, he should count his blessings.

"Are you sure she's telling the truth about all this?" Gavin asked.

"Eight hours of interrogation under duress make me think that yes, she's telling the truth."

Gavin whistled through his teeth. "Jesus, Dorian. Are you okay?"

"I just admitted to torturing *her* and you're asking if *I'm* okay?" But he wasn't. He wasn't okay. His hands were shaking again.

"All right, I'll bite. Is she okay? But you're my first priority."

"She doesn't need medical attention, don't worry. I used repeated dousing in cold water. Not very hard-core in the greater scheme of things, but effective, especially with her. Plus, it was just part of my bigger plan."

An important plan. Because he damn well hadn't wanted to hurt Ray, but he had to know what she was doing here. Even if they both had to pay a steep price to get the information.

"What can I do to help?" Gavin asked. "Where is she now? I don't know what your plan is, but getting more gruesome in an attempt to get answers out of her is not going to sit well with your psyche, brother."

"Most of today was to make her think that I wasn't really willing to hurt her. That I wasn't capable of doling out more pain than she could handle."

Which was the absolute truth. Merely the thought of putting Ray through a fraction of what he'd endured sent a river of revulsion up his spine. Today's actions had been at his very limits, even knowing he wouldn't be truly hurting her.

"So you're not going further with your interrogation methods?" Gavin asked.

"I knew not getting the truth from her was a probability from the moment I went after her. Her words can't be trusted, but her actions can. I placed a tracking monitor on the back of her neck before I left. I'll be surprised if she's not already out of the cabin by now."

"So, no torture."

Dorian scrubbed a hand down his face. "It's about knowing my strengths and weaknesses. And hers. I couldn't hurt her, Gav. Not like that. Not in the way I would have to in order to make sure I knew she was telling the truth."

His friend nodded. "Then this sounds like the next best plan."

"Yeah. I'll follow and see where she leads me." He took the last sip of his beer. He hoped this plan worked. Because he had to know what was going on.

"Your Ray . . . she's blond, right? Five foot eight, athletic build, could put the fear of God into you if she's angry?"

"Yeah, that's her to a T. Why?"

Gavin shook his head. "I'm not sure your plan to track Ray is going to work, man."

"Why?"

"Because she just walked in the door, and she's headed this way."

7

"I think this belongs to you. I didn't want to take a chance on it getting lost." Ray slammed the tiny tracker down onto the table.

She'd found it on the back of her neck; Dorian had undoubtedly put there during one of the times when he'd been playing good cop, holding her head up and feeding her warm water or broth.

Ray wasn't even pissed.

Or maybe she was a little bit, because she'd underestimated Dorian *again*. But she wasn't mad because of the tracker. Looking at the day holistically, she realized her first instinct about him had been correct. Dorian wasn't a killer. And while the past ten hours had not been comfortable, they could've been much, much worse.

After he'd left, when she'd first realized there was a little bit of give in the tie binding her right wrist, she'd thought Dorian had miscalculated again. But none of it had made any sense. He was good enough to track her, capture her, and interrogate her, but not smart enough to check her restraints before he'd left her alone for an extended period of time?

He didn't say anything, just sat there at the table with the same friend who'd been on the camping trip with the boys.

"Was the entire day an extended setup? Or did you plan to go further with the torture but lost your nerve?"

Dorian leaned back in the booth, regarding her almost lazily. "Let's just say I lost my taste for torture after being tortured to within an inch of my life multiple weeks in a row." He held out a hand toward the man sitting across from him. "Ray, meet Gavin Zimmerman. Gavin, Wraith."

She nodded briefly at the other man, who pinned her with his eyes. "We've met before, right?" Gavin asked.

They had. Briefly. But Ray had looked much different on that occasion, and talking about it now was only going to lead to Dorian asking questions she really didn't want to answer.

"I don't think so." She glanced back at Dorian, relieved when Gavin didn't push the matter.

Dorian tilted his head toward the bar. "The kitchen is still open. You've had a long day. Want me to get you something to eat?"

"Are we going to act like you didn't have me tied up naked in your cabin a few hours ago?" She raised an eyebrow.

"Are we going to act like you didn't shoot me with your crossbow rifle a month ago and pretend to be dead for six years?"

Gavin cleared his throat. "Alrighty, then. When we start talking about kinky stuff, that's my cue to leave." Gavin slid out of the booth. "You kids play nice."

She didn't miss the look the other man shot Dorian. No

doubt Gavin wouldn't go far. He might be on his way to get backup.

The smart plan would be for her to get out now. But she couldn't. Not yet. Not without the answers she needed. She slid into the booth seat that Gavin had just vacated. "Sure. I'll have steak and eggs."

Dorian chuckled, and Ray did everything in her power to ignore what that sound did to her. How many nights had the memory of that soft sound and the vision of his smile gotten her through?

He called the waitress over and ordered her food as well as a beer for them both.

They stared at each other from across the table.

He was the first to break the silence. "I was out of the game completely. I thought you were dead. Even when you were here before, I thought I was going crazy, that it couldn't be you. You had to have known that quarrel would confirm for me that it was you. You wanted my attention, now you've got it."

It was a fair point without an easy response.

Why had she contacted him now?

Maybe because of that itch at the back of her neck that meant her time was running out. That whoever was killing the people associated with Crypt would be coming for her soon.

Maybe it was the damn headaches and nosebleeds all the time—some sort of tumor.

Or maybe because she was selfish. And if this really was the end, she just wanted one more chance to be with the man who had always meant everything to her.

But how the hell was she supposed to explain all that?

They waited in silence until her food arrived, then she all but pounced on it. Dorian sipped his beer as she finished the eggs first before starting on the steak. She was three bites in when he shifted his weight, pulling his head over to one side like he was stretching his neck, then rubbing his thumb across his forehead.

To anyone else, it would've seemed like the gesture of a tired man waiting for his companion to finish her meal. But not to her.

He'd just signaled to his team.

She placed her fork down on her plate and slid the steak knife a little more firmly into her hand. She was on the edge of the booth without saying a word, eyeing both possible entrances.

The kitchen was a third. She couldn't keep an eye on all three.

"Easy there, Wraith."

She tilted her head without stopping her study of possible attack routes. "I'm not interested in spending any more of this day held against my will, *Ghost*."

He nodded slowly. "That was to call them off, not bring them in. Gavin only wanted to make sure I'm okay."

She tilted her head slightly. "And the big guy over there? He's definitely trained and has been eyeing us. The woman too—I remember her, the one whose house burned last month—although she doesn't hold herself as though she has any training."

"Gabriel Collingwood. Former SEAL. And yes, his fiancée, Jordan, has no military background whatsoever. Both are watching us because they've probably never seen me sitting here with a woman before."

She ignored the way her insides melted at that news. "Are you telling me the truth, Lindstrom?"

"I am. About all of it. Nobody's coming after you. At least, not my people. Eat your dinner."

It would be so easy to make the choice to trust him. That scared her more than anything that had happened today.

"I need to go to the restroom." She was up and out of the booth, knife still in hand, before he could respond.

She used the bathroom, came out of the stall, and washed her hands, thankful no one else was around. She caught sight of her reflection in the mirror.

She cringed immediately. Not only because she looked like she'd been put through a day's worth of low-grade torture. But because she couldn't stand to look at herself in general. This face and body and what she'd allowed them to be used for.

Genetics had blessed her with a beautiful package on the outside—too bad it encased something so shriveled and broken and ugly.

What was she doing here? Dorian wasn't the killer—she knew that for a fact now. Why hadn't she left the tracker in the cabin and run?

Why had she shot him with that damn arrow in the first place a month ago?

The only thing coming back into his life would do was taint him. Why didn't she have the courage to leave him alone?

She could do it now.

Without looking at her reflection again, she left the bathroom, taking an immediate left to cut through the kitchen rather than going back toward their booth. She forced herself to put one foot in front of the other, past the waitstaff and cooks who were looking at her funny, until she reached the kitchen's door to the outside. It was already wide open.

Ray grit her teeth and walked out, not looking back.

Focus on the mission.

God, she didn't want to. Didn't want to leave. But she forced herself to keep moving.

She would need to get to her car, parked a couple miles outside of town. It was better to walk rather than steal a car for that short amount of distance. She'd concentrate on—

"You didn't finish your dinner."

Ray stopped walking but didn't turn around at Dorian's words. "It's better for me to go."

"I can't let you do that."

Now she turned to face him. "I'd like to see you try and make me stay. Especially if you don't cheat this time."

They stood face to face, staring each other down. Fighting would mean they'd both end up hurt. Bloody.

But they were probably going to end up that way whether they fought or not.

"Dorian—"

"You came back for a reason, Gra— Ray. Last month. This weekend. Was that because you intended to harm me?"

"No."

"Then I'd like you to stay so we can both actually get some answers."

She rubbed her hand across her aching forehead. The answers weren't simple. The truth—even the parts she was willing to give him—was ugly. Staying might not be the right answer in the long run.

But he was right. He deserved to know more about what was going on. To be aware of the danger so he could protect himself and his loved ones. "Okay."

He didn't say anything else as they walked inside together and sat back down at the booth. He had the waitress warm up Ray's steak so she could finish it.

"Were you telling me the truth today about Project Crypt?" he finally asked.

She chewed a bite of her steak, then swallowed. "Yes, unfortunately."

"And you're not here to harm me or the people I consider to be my family?"

"No, definitely not them, and only you if you try to pour freezing water on me again."

He took another sip of his beer and shrugged. "I actually believe that, but only because if you were trying to take me out, you could've done it many times over."

He could've too. They nodded at each other, a tentative truce established.

She finished the last of her steak. "I was in Kabul that day because I stumbled across some pretty incriminating evidence about Crypt. I knew you were in Afghanistan, but I had no idea you were on a mission against the Haqqani network. I went off half-cocked, thinking I could get details I needed to prove what Crypt was up to on my own. Instead of doing that, I nearly cost you your life."

At the time, she'd only known about the sleeper missions, not about Holloman's—and Crypt's—true face.

He shrugged. "Seeing you there that day threw me. But I should've been more focused. You've always been able to take care of yourself. I should've known you'd take care of yourself then too."

"I didn't die in that explosion, but I did get thrown away from the building. I was unconscious for more than twenty-four hours. As soon as I heard you didn't make it out with the rest of your team, I swear I used every source I had to figure out where you were being held. Crypt wouldn't put any effort in. As a matter of fact, I think they might have known where you were being held the entire time and did nothing to stop it."

Dorian stiffened in his chair. "What?"

She couldn't answer all his questions to the best of her ability without straight-up telling him about his sleeper mission.

"We were cogs in a much bigger machine," she said. "Project Crypt had its priorities, and we as agents were not one of them."

She should've done more. Should've forced Holloman to give her whatever information he had on Dorian's location. But at the time, she'd still been reeling from discovering the sleeper missions.

And had still believed they were working for the good guys. Dorian had paid the price for that.

"I can't believe you survived." She grabbed her beer and took a sip. "Jesus, Ghost. You always were the strongest man I ever knew, but no one should've survived that."

He gripped his mug with both hands. "Sometimes it feels like I didn't. At least, not whole."

"The fact that you are able to have a normal life, able to sit here and have a regular conversation with me means you're whole enough."

He shrugged. "I was so pissed when Project Crypt dropped me like that after what I went through. Yeah, looking at it now, I realize I was never going to be an active agent again. Hell, I was barely a soldier after that. But they should have at least spoken to me. Acknowledged my existence. Not just written me off. I was already feeling pretty damn useless lying there in that hospital. Being silently disavowed certainly didn't help."

Should she tell him that she'd bought his freedom with a price? One higher than she'd ever thought she'd be able to pay?

"Dorian . . ."

"But actually, their abandoning me was the best thing

that could've happened, wasn't it? How about you? Did you use dying in Kabul to get out from under their thumb?"

Also tricky to answer while still trying to be honest. "I got out eventually, once I had proof they were rogue." Unfortunately, it had taken three years to get that, and she'd lost her soul in the process.

Their waitress walked up to the table, her worried eyes shifting between the two of them. "Dorian, I'm sorry to interrupt," the pretty young woman said. "We're closing up for the night, so I was wondering if I could go ahead and close your bill out."

He gave her a smile that spoke of comfort and ease. He'd once given Ray smiles like that too.

"Yeah, Peyton, no problem. I know you want to get home to Jess as soon as possible." He pulled out his wallet and handed her some cash.

Peyton smiled. "She better be asleep or the sitter is going to absolutely kill me. I'll catch you later." She gave Ray a smile before turning back toward the kitchen.

They both stood and walked toward the front door. The place was empty.

"Thanks for dinner."

He made a wry face. "Least I could do after today. Why are you back, Ray? Why did you make yourself known now?"

It was time to tell him about the killer. They walked through the door together. "There's trouble. Honestly, I wasn't sure if you were part of it or not."

"What sort of trouble?"

"People who were involved with Project Crypt are being killed."

Out in the parking lot, they walked toward Dorian's

truck. "I thought they were defunct. Crypt is still operational?"

"No. They're out of commission." She'd seen to that three years ago when she'd destroyed everything she could about the organization—their headquarters, files, research. "But someone has decided to come back and take out anyone who's ever had anything to do with them. Active agents, scientists, and, as of a few days ago, even the children of people who'd been involved."

Dorian let out a curse. "Can't be sanctioned government hits if the killer is taking out children."

They both hoped not.

"I think we have a vigilante killer on our hands. Somebody trying to wipe out all of Crypt's existence." She stared into Dorian's hazel eyes. "The people most able and likely to do that were the active agents."

He didn't flinch from her gaze. "You thought it might be me."

She shrugged. "There's only four of us left. You, me, Shadow, and Phantom. Honestly, I didn't think it was you, but evidence suggests the killer is mentally unstable."

He gave a short bark of laughter. "I guess my actions today didn't do much to help you think I'm mentally stable."

Her fingers itched to trace along his jaw. To step closer to him. She'd never thought she'd be this close to him again. "We both know you could've done much, much worse. If anything, what happened today proved to me you're *not* the killer. Plus, it cleared up some other misconceptions I had."

"Like what?"

"I thought you might need protection. If someone was coming for you, I wasn't sure you still had the skills to protect yourself."

He leaned back against his truck, chuckling. "I'm not sure if I'm offended or honored. Both, I guess."

She was making a mess of this. "I mean—"

They both looked up as a car came squealing down the road, its speed way too high for this area of town. It raced by, swerving like someone was drunk or fighting for the wheel.

"What the hell?" he muttered.

"You got a drunk driving problem in your little town, D?" At least it was late and nobody else was out on the street.

"Not generally. But that car's not going to make it around the curve or the—"

The unmistakable sound of metal screeching on metal assaulted them.

"—bridge."

Ray was already racing toward the crashed car as Dorian pulled out his phone and dialed 911.

He gave the operator the necessary information, then took off toward the bridge himself. He arrived in time to see Ray leap to the edge, stripping off her jacket as she slid down the embankment.

"Ray!"

"They hit hard, Dorian," she called back, not slowing down. "The windshield broke, and there's already water pouring into the car."

He followed her down, stripping off what clothes he could, both of them speeding into the water. The car was pointed straight down, trapped in rocks or something. Now that he could see it clearly, he knew exactly whose car it was.

"Damn it. This is Sheriff Nelson's car."

Dorian waded into the water, the same water he'd used on Ray, grimacing at its icy bite. He ignored the cold and inched his way toward the front of the car. She was right, it was completely submerged.

"They must be unconscious. I'm going to see if I can pull them out through the windshield."

She was right behind him in the roaring flow. "Don't let the current suck you away. If we let go of the car, we're going to get washed downstream pretty fast."

He gave her a brief nod, then ducked under. The cold immediately tried to suck the air out of his lungs, but he forced himself past it.

Feeling around in the dark coldness wasn't easy. He found the windshield and a little hole, definitely too small for him to fit through.

He could see two sets of arms floating up toward him. The inside of the car was flooded, and the occupants were unconscious. For the car to have filled that quickly, one of the side windows must've gotten knocked out. Maybe he could fit through that.

He shot to the surface, gulping air. "Windshield is mostly intact, so I can't get through. Two people inside, both unconscious, fully submerged. One of the front windows must have shattered on impact."

She nodded, and he sucked in a gulp of air and dove once again, this time for the driver's side window.

Damn it, it was still intact. He didn't go back up for another breath—every second he wasted was more time the sheriff and whoever else was in the car didn't have.

If they were still alive.

He grabbed the hood of the car and pulled himself down, struggling not to get washed away with the river's current. Finally, he reached the open passenger-side window—that's what had let all the water in.

But damn it, it was still too small and, at this angle, nearly impossible for him to fit through.

He was about to force his shoulder through the small opening when a fist grabbed his shirt through the opening.

Dorian probably would've automatically punched at the sudden touch if it weren't for the water. Instead, he grabbed the person and yanked them through the window.

Her. Yanked *her* through the window. He could tell immediately by her size and weight.

Keeping a tight grip on her, he propelled them both toward the surface. As they broke through and began gasping for air, Dorian recognized the woman immediately: Susan Lusher, a nurse at the local hospital and Sheriff Nelson's girlfriend.

"Curtis. Curtis is still inside," the woman gasped out. "He had some sort of seizure while he was driving. I couldn't get him out once we were underwater."

"I'll get her to shore. You get him." Ray was already assisting Susan before she finished the sentence.

Dorian dove back down and made it to the window. He tried to cram his frame into the small space, but it didn't take him long to realize there was no way he could do it. He swam around to the front windshield and tried to kick it in but couldn't get enough momentum in the water.

When he burst through the surface again, he was starting to lose feeling in his hands and feet.

"What's wrong?" Ray had already made her way back out to the car.

"I can't make it through the window, it's too small. And the car is starting to shift."

"I'll go through and get him."

Her lips were already turning blue. "No. You need to get out of this water."

She gave a short laugh. "Would've given a lot for you to have said that to me earlier today."

"Even if you can get to him, I don't think you'll be able to get him out against this current."

"Then you pull me out. We don't have time to argue about this. Let's do what we can do, Ghost. We're this guy's only chance."

She was right. They'd trained for stuff like this. How to push their physical discomfort to the background and work the problem. But damn it, she was already shaking visibly in the water.

He let out a growl. "Fine. You get one chance. If you can't get him out the first time, we have to leave him. He won't last through a second round anyway."

She nodded, sucking in a deep breath as he did the same. She grabbed the waistband of his jeans, trusting him to lead her where they needed to go.

Finding the open window this time was easier. He grabbed Ray's wrist at his waist and propelled her through the window, keeping a hand on her ankle so he could pull her back out.

The woman was risking her life for someone she didn't know. This was going a long way toward assuaging whatever trust issues he had with her.

Dorian cursed as the car shifted again in the raging river. He was forced to let go of Ray's leg in order to firm up his own grip and keep from being washed downstream.

But the car continued tipping. If it fell over any farther, it would be completely on its side, trapping Ray and the sheriff inside. Planting his feet against a large rock on the river bottom, he wedged his shoulder under the doorframe and pushed up as hard as he could. The exertion sucked out more of his oxygen. He wouldn't be able to hold this for long.

But damn it, he was not leaving Grace in there. The

whole world was going gray when he felt something bump against him a few seconds later. Ray was trying to get the sheriff out the window.

Using the last of his strength and oxygen, Dorian reached for the sheriff and yanked him through the window.

Where was Ray? Dorian fought with everything he had to stay conscious, every instinct telling him to swim to the surface.

No. He wasn't leaving this car without Ray. He wasn't leaving her behind.

He didn't think he could get the sheriff to the surface anyway. The urge to suck in a breath was overwhelming though he knew it wouldn't provide air.

How many sessions of waterboarding did you survive? Survive this.

Dorian locked his legs against the rock, holding the sheriff with one arm, and reached down toward the window with the other.

Come on, Wraith. Where are you? He was about to let the sheriff go to look for her when a hand yanked at his arm, pulling him upward.

She was out.

They clawed their way toward the surface, hauling the sheriff between them. Once they were up, Dorian could hear the sound of rescue workers over his own frantic breathing.

"Here! They're here!"

Someone took the sheriff out of their arms and thrust a lifejacket attached to a rope at them. Dorian held on to his with numb arms. Ray did the same.

High-powered flashlights pointed in their direction. He

looked over to make sure Ray was all right. She looked as exhausted as he felt, but her eyes were open.

The rescue squad pulled them to shore, then immediately yanked their clothes off down to their underwear. They were wrapped in Mylar blankets and led to an ambulance where they sat silently watching as the rescue workers continued CPR on the sheriff.

After a few more minutes, the paramedics were able to stabilize the sheriff's heartbeat and breathing. Ray and Dorian got out of the ambulance so it could take the sheriff to the hospital.

"Thank you, Dorian." Susan, also wrapped in a blanket, said as she climbed into the back of the ambulance. She turned to Ray. "And especially you, honey. You went way above and beyond what would be expected for complete strangers."

The door closed and the ambulance pulled away.

Half the town of Oak Creek had heard about the crash and had worked their way down to the riverbed. Somebody had offered Ray a jacket, and she was currently sitting against a tree, sipping on some sort of hot beverage. Riley Wilde, also a nurse at the nearby hospital, was taking her pulse.

Dorian stood with his friends. Aiden tossed him some clothes.

"If I had a nickel for every time I had to grab the extra pair of pants in my car for you because you were running around town in your skivvies . . ."

Dorian chuckled and took the pants Aiden held out, slipping them on.

Gavin was there too. Both men lived in town.

"What the hell happened here?" Gavin asked.

"Looks like Sheriff Nelson had some sort of seizure and

ran off the bridge. We happened to be coming out of the Eagle's Nest when he zoomed past us like a bat out of hell."

Dorian spent the next twenty minutes talking to more people, explaining to the sheriff's deputy what had happened and generally accepting a lot of attaboys. Zac and Finn showed up, Annie and Charlie in tow.

Annie reached out to him, then pulled back.

"I need to take your pulse. May I?"

He nodded, she did so, and then began touching his chest.

"Um, excuse me," Zac said with a raised eyebrow. "Just because we are now engaged doesn't mean it's okay for you to start groping other guys."

Annie elbowed him gently in the stomach. "Just doing a layman's check for Dorian's body temperature to make sure it's coming back up like it should."

Dorian kissed the top of her head. "Thank you for asking. But I'm fine. Too much mass to worry about my body temperature dropping that much. You ought to check Ray. She was in the water as long as me and has a lot less meat. She's with Riley over there." He looked around, but there were so many people here now, he didn't have a clear line of sight to the tree where she was sitting.

"The woman who shot you with the arrow is the same one who helped you save the sheriff?" Annie asked.

Dorian nodded. "Damn well risked her life to do it too."

Charlie—all five foot two of her—cracked her knuckles. "I'd still like to have a couple words with her about archery safety. Where is she?"

Finn wrapped both arms around either side of his wife's slightly protruding belly and lifted her off the ground. "Whoa there, mama. I think the archery queen has been through enough trauma for one night without going ten rounds with you."

Including what she'd been through already today with Dorian, Ray had been through more than enough.

It was time to get out of here. Get *her* out of here.

He answered a few more questions for the deputy before telling him he would come by for any follow-up tomorrow. The crowd was wearing on him. He wanted to get Ray out of this. Hell, he wanted to get himself out of this, but he was taking Ray with him. He didn't know where she had been staying—definitely not here in town—but tonight he hoped to convince her to stay at his house. They had more to talk about. And he wasn't ready to let her go yet.

"Dorian." Annie walked back up to him. "Where did you say your friend was sitting? I can't seem to find her anywhere. I asked Riley, but she said she only stopped to take Ray's pulse and give her a cup of coffee, then moved on to talk to some other people."

Dorian looked around, his height giving him an advantage, but it didn't take long for him to realize the truth.

Ray was gone.

9

Ray was running on the last of her reserves, and she wasn't out of Oak Creek yet.

Even including her steak dinner, she hadn't taken in enough calories to combat the amount of time she'd spent shivering her ass off the past twenty-four hours.

Hopefully, the sheriff was going to make it. A heartbeat was a good sign, but he'd been in the water a long time.

The sheriff obviously meant a lot to Dorian. This town, these people, they were all his family. She'd already known that from watching him, but tonight—the way they'd all flocked around Dorian to make sure he was okay—had proved it.

It had been enjoyable to watch. Right up to the point where that woman had started running her hands all over him.

Ray knew the woman was one of the town's doctors. Knew that she was dating one of Dorian's friends. But when he pulled her close and kissed the top of her head, Ray had to look away. She had no right to be jealous. Had no claim to Dorian at all.

She had no place in his new life. She'd done what she'd come to do: figure out if he was the killer and find some way to warn him about the danger if he wasn't. Dorian was more than capable of taking care of himself. The best thing she could do for him was to get out of his life and stay out.

She stumbled along the side of the road before righting herself. She had emergency provisions in her vehicle. Two and a half miles was nothing. She'd made that distance in much worse shape than she was now.

So why did she feel worse with every step she took? If her subconscious dared suggest that she felt worse because she was getting farther away from Dorian, she would punch herself in the face.

She'd lived without him for six years. She could live without him again.

Headlights came from behind her, and she moved smoothly into the tree line. It wasn't the first car to come by, but none had stopped. Most of them had been heading toward town, probably hearing about the excitement and wanting to witness it firsthand.

Nobody was looking for her. Dorian might not have noticed she was gone yet. And if he had, he might not care.

The vehicle passed, and she stepped back toward the road.

She realized her mistake as soon as she saw the brake lights. It was a truck.

Dorian's truck.

He threw it in reverse and came barreling back toward her. For just a second, she considered running. She had a head start. It was possible she could escape him. But if Dorian really put effort into it, he would catch her.

She wasn't sure she could handle finding out if he was willing to put effort into it.

She stood there in wet cargo pants and someone else's jacket, staring at him as he stopped the truck and got out. His eyes pinned hers from over the bed of the truck.

"You didn't run."

She shrugged. "I'm tired. And honestly, I wasn't sure you'd chase me anyways."

He eased around the truck, every bit the hunter—the *predator*—he could be.

"I would've chased you, Grace. To the ends of the earth, I would track you down and hunt you."

From anyone else, those words would be a threat, one she wouldn't tolerate.

From him, they were a promise.

"I'm tired, Dorian."

Not only physically because of what she'd been through today. She was tired of it all. The running, the headaches, the constant battle to watch her back.

He took a step closer. "I know you are." He held a hand out toward her. "I know after today I have no right to ask this, but come rest with me. We've always had each other's backs. Come rest with me, just for a little while."

Hoping she wasn't making a mistake that would cost one or the both of them their lives, she took his hand.

HER HAND LANDING in his was a simple gesture, but Dorian didn't pretend that it didn't change everything. Nothing was ever going to erase what had happened in the past, and he knew full well there were still things she wasn't telling him, but this was the start of something new.

He wanted to scoop Ray up into his arms, partly because she looked so fragile with her oversized jacket and nappy wet hair. But more because he wanted her close to him.

But since she would probably karate chop him in the teeth, he just brought the hand resting in his up to his lips and kissed it on the palm.

"Let's go home."

They rode silently to his house on the edge of town. He didn't ask her where she'd been walking to. No doubt she had a vehicle stashed somewhere nearby.

They were still quiet as they entered his house, Ray waiting by the front door as he silently checked his simple security measures. He had no electronic alarm system; he and Ray both knew how easily those could be bypassed. Dorian wasn't necessarily trying to keep anyone out, he needed to know if anyone had been here. Strategically placed string or tape over doors and windows let him know that well enough.

"Clear," he said after he returned to her.

She was still standing at the front door, almost in a daze, although Ray's daze would probably still allow her to attack or defend herself in an instant. He didn't plan on putting it to the test.

"Shower first or food?"

She stared at him for a long moment before finally giving a tiny shrug.

"How about you take a shower and I'll make us something to eat?"

He led her back to the master bedroom. His place wasn't all that large, only two bedrooms—neither very big—and one bathroom.

But what a bathroom it was. The shower was ridiculously large, taking up an entire corner. It was made out of some ceramic tile he'd laid himself with stone benches running along each wall and two showerheads.

She gave a tiny gasp when she saw it.

He turned and smiled. "I thought you might like this."

As he spun back to turn the water on for her, he realized how true that statement was. He hadn't consciously thought about her when he'd been remodeling this bathroom, but looking at it now, he realized everything in here had been for her.

How had he missed that?

"You used to pick hotels for vacation based solely on the shower," he muttered. He hadn't thought about that fact in years. But evidently, his subconscious had thought about it plenty.

Jesus, he'd never gotten over this woman.

He backed out of the shower, not meeting her eyes. "There are the towels." He pointed to the stack on the shelf. "I'll leave some dry clothes outside the door."

He left without another word, walking immediately into the kitchen.

He made sandwiches and warmed up soup, too tired himself to do much more. And he absolutely did not think about Ray's naked body inside his shower.

Twenty minutes later, she shuffled into the kitchen looking a little less gray with exhaustion. His sweatpants and T-shirt were absurdly large on her slender frame. She had her own wet clothes balled up in her hand.

He took them from her. "I'll throw those in the laundry."

"Thanks."

"Are you sure you're okay? You would tell me if you were hurt, right?"

She shrugged. "Probably not. But I'm not hurt. Only tired."

She seemed so much more than tired. But he didn't pursue it, just pushed food toward her.

They ate in silence, not something Dorian usually minded, but now it made him wonder if she was planning an escape attempt.

As he finished his food and took his dishes over to the sink, he realized it didn't matter. If she wasn't going to stay, she wasn't going to stay. Outside of tying her up again—correctly this time—there wasn't much he could do to keep her here.

She was still staring down at her food, even though most of it was gone, when he walked out of the kitchen. "I'm going to take a shower."

He stopped at the doorway.

"Ray, don't run. Just for tonight, stay. You can go back to fighting the world on your own tomorrow."

He didn't look back as he walked to the bathroom. She was either going to be here when he got out or she wasn't.

She wasn't. He knew that but forced himself to keep walking.

He left his clothes in a pile on the floor and entered the shower, turning the water as hot as he could stand.

He put his arms up on the wall and let the spray from both showerheads hit him. The hot water wasn't going to wash away the knowledge that Ray wouldn't be there when he got out. But at least in here, he could pretend she wasn't going to run.

The shower door opened behind him; he looked over his shoulder. Ray stood there, still fully clothed, obviously unsure of what to do.

"I don't want to run. Not tonight."

Thank God. "Interested in taking another shower?"

He didn't turn around to face her. Displaying the hard-on that had hit him as soon as he'd heard her voice wasn't going to do anything but make this more awkward.

He tamped down his disappointment when she shook her head. "No, I don't need another shower."

"Okay. I'll be out in—"

"I am interested in making love to you in the shower, if that's a possibility."

He turned around to face her. "That is very definitely a possibility. Except for the fact that you have too many clothes on."

She untied the string at the waistband of his sweatpants, then snatched the sweatshirt over her head. The clothes found his in the pile on the floor.

"Is this naked enough?"

He didn't answer, only snaked an arm around her waist and pulled her up against him.

She didn't hesitate, her arms brushing up his chest, across his shoulders before gripping the back of his head and pulling his lips down to hers.

A groan—desperation? relief? pleasure?—escaped both of them. Dorian never thought he would feel this again. Just this, the simple act of his lips against Ray's. He moved gently, almost reverently. Her tongue licked along the seam of his lips, and he let out another groan.

But there was something he had to say before this went any further. He eased back enough to gain a little distance.

"I'm sorry for today. I shouldn't have started with those sorts of extreme measures. It wasn't healthy for either—"

She brought her fingers up to his lips, stopping his words. "We're okay. I'll let you apologize properly to me in bed in a couple hours. But right now . . . I need you, Dorian. Inside me. As close as we can possibly be."

He knew exactly how she felt.

He pushed her up against the shower wall, the heated spray hitting him on the back. He slipped his hands over her neck and pressed his thumbs under her chin, lifting her face to his. He nipped at her bottom lip, chuckling as she attempted to suck his upper.

Their tongues met and danced, then became more frantic as they clutched each other closer. Not breaking the kiss, Dorian reached down and lifted her by her hips, shifting her legs around his waist.

Her fingers threaded into his hair as he reached between their bodies and found her breast. He played with her nipple and smiled against her mouth as a shudder, so much different than the ones from earlier today, racked her body.

Some things didn't change. The way his body knew Ray's was one of them.

Groaning himself now, he rolled his hips against her as her lips kissed along his jaw and up to his ear.

"I need you inside me, Dorian. *Please.*"

He didn't try to stop the growl that escaped him. He kept an arm under her hips and reached behind him with the other to turn off the water. He wasn't sure if it was all the way off, and he didn't care.

Her legs were still wrapped around his waist and her arms around his shoulders as he opened the shower door and walked her over to the long bathroom counter.

"Here," he muttered, setting her down. "I can't make it to the bed."

They were both soaking wet, making a huge mess, but, again, he didn't care. Her legs unwrapped from around his hips, sprawling open on the counter as he trailed his lips down her neck, nipping and sucking.

He reached into the top drawer under her and grabbed a condom. A condom that before last month, when he'd discovered Ray was alive, would never have been in the house.

He'd had no need for them.

There was so much he wanted to do to her body—was definitely *going to do* to her body—but he couldn't wait. Not this time. It had been too long.

And this was Grace.

Grace spread out in front of him, ready for him to devour her.

He slipped on the condom.

"I'm sorry," he whispered.

"I thought we already covered that you could make up for the torture later." Her voice was breathy, rough. Jesus.

"No. This apology is because I can't make this what I want to. I'm not going to last."

"You don't need to last. You just need to fuck me."

"Yes, ma'am."

The counter situated her at the perfect height as he grabbed her ass and pulled her closer.

Watching himself slide inside her waiting, open body almost pushed him over the edge. The way she felt. Her heat. He was going to lose it right now.

"Ghost. Look at me, soldier."

He dragged his gaze up her body. Her chest was flushed, and she was breathing hard. He wasn't the only one affected. Those blue eyes pierced him.

"You can't imagine how many times I've dreamed of this," she whispered.

Oh, he could. He *really* could.

Her legs hooked back around his hips and pulled him the rest of the way into her body. They both let out a hiss as her body stretched around him.

For a moment they stayed there, connected in every possible way.

"Where have you been, Grace?" The words were torn from him, the question rhetorical.

Her face clouded over. Maybe because of the name she refused, maybe because of something more. "I've been too far away."

She hooked an elbow around his neck and pulled him in for a kiss. The second her lips hit his, he lost all control, slamming into her over and over. He would've worried he was hurting her if he couldn't feel her nails scoring into his shoulders and her hips meeting his thrust for thrust.

It was way too soon when streaks of heat spiraled through him, up his spine. He clutched Ray's ass, pulling her as tight against him as he could get.

Her milking him like a hot little fist blew the last of his control straight to hell. Her name slipped from his lips—a curse, a prayer, a promise.

10

Dorian woke instantly at the movement beside him. He didn't open his eyes as Ray slipped out of his bed.

Honestly, it was a miracle he could feel anything or was even conscious at all this morning.

They hadn't been able to get enough of each other all night. After that embarrassingly quick first time in the bathroom, he'd carried Ray to the bed and proceeded to prove that he more than definitely remembered how to do slow.

Worshipping her body the way he'd dreamed of. Using his mouth to nip and lick, suck and kiss over every inch of her. Spending quite a bit more time on some parts than others. She'd always teased that if she wasn't pulling his hair out by the roots, he wasn't doing it right.

He might have a couple of bald patches now, but hell, it had been worth it.

After he'd had her so sated she'd barely been able to lift her head, he'd snuggled in beside her, ready for them both to get some sleep. But less than an hour later, *her* hands had been running all over *him*.

He'd tried to be sensitive to what her body had been through—the interrogation, the river rescue. He'd tried to tuck her back against him and get her to go back to sleep.

But Ray had always had a mind of her own, and when she wanted something, she wasn't one to deny herself.

And if he was what she wanted, he wasn't going to deny either of them. Not after six years of thinking he'd never have another chance with her.

And now she was leaving, sneaking out without saying goodbye. He knew it for a fact by the lack of noise she was making. If she'd needed to go to the bathroom or get some water, she wouldn't keep herself so quiet, the way they'd been trained to when necessity arose.

Her silence gave her away.

It wasn't long—hell, she probably wasn't completely dressed yet—before he heard the front door click closed behind her. Nobody else would've heard it.

He was out of bed an instant later, dressed and out the door less than half a minute after that. Ray was already deep into the woods surrounding his house by that time, which was fine. He already knew what direction she was heading and had a good idea where she was going overall.

She'd been walking southwest out of town yesterday. There wasn't much in that direction. Clearly not the best plan if you were trying to hitchhike.

But it was definitely the place he would've parked a vehicle if he were looking for a central location between Oak Creek and Linear Tactical's main facilities. And, like it or not, he and Ray had been trained by the same people.

Once he was sure she wouldn't hear him, he started his truck and drove in the opposite direction than she'd gone. He traveled along a separate road, where Ray would be sure not to see him, and waited. If he was right, she'd come to him. If not, he wouldn't be able to find her anyway. Today, at least.

He kept his truck parked out of the way, still able to see the road but out of view of other drivers unless they were specifically looking for him.

Why had Ray run? He'd expected it last night before the lovemaking. But why this morning? What had spooked her?

Besides the huge secret she was still keeping.

He didn't know what it was, but he definitely didn't have all the information concerning her.

He was damn well going to find it.

It was another thirty minutes before she finally drove by his hidden parking spot in a Honda Civic—one of the most nondescript, popular cars in the country. She would blend in almost anywhere.

He let her pass and get a safe distance ahead of him, then pulled out after her. He wasn't sure where she was going or how long he'd be following. But his truck was full of gas and stocked with a bug-out bag filled with supplies, food, and cash that would allow him to do what he needed. He always had his vehicle prepped, and beyond that, he could live in the wilderness indefinitely if needed.

As long as Ray wasn't taking him to a mall or some sort of theme park where he was supposed to make small talk with others, Dorian was pretty confident in his ability to handle it.

If he had to guess, traveling in this direction, she was probably headed toward Salt Lake City, or maybe she would turn west to Idaho Falls.

But just over twenty miles later, she pulled off onto a nearly nonexistent dirt road.

Dorian smiled. "Gotcha."

He knew exactly where she was going.

He spent weeks at a time out in this wilderness. There was a cabin about four miles from the turnoff. She'd be able to drive almost two miles, then would hike the rest.

It was a good choice for her—two more roads led near the cabin, but not close enough for most people to know about it. Undoubtedly, she had other getaway vehicles parked there if this was a longer-term base.

Again, it was one he would've chosen, a place not on anything but unofficial maps, and Ray would know where to look for those.

And now, knowing where she was going, he also knew how to beat her there.

He sped up, passing the place where she'd turned off without a glance. Driving another three miles, he turned onto a secondary road. This one would get him closer—less time needed on foot.

Driving as far as he could, he parked his truck next to the other vehicle already waiting there. He didn't touch it, sure it was Ray's and not knowing if she had set up any sort of booby trap.

He secured his Glock at his waist and a knife at his ankle, then grabbed a few more supplies he might need.

He double-timed it to the cabin, sacrificing silence and stealth for speed. He wanted a chance to look around before Ray got there. When he arrived not long after, he knew he'd beaten her.

The cabin itself was functional but not at all fancy. It had basic plumbing and solar power—more than what most cabins in this area had. It wasn't big, only one room, like where he'd held her yesterday.

Most of the hunters' cabins scattered across the Wyoming wilderness were barely more than manmade caves created to provide shelter in dire emergencies. This one had a little more. It had real walls and two sets of windows. The windows were probably what had appealed to Ray: multiple exit routes.

Walking up to the front door, he noted the same strings and tape on the door he would have used to indicate someone had been here. That didn't stop him from opening the door anyway. He wanted her to know he was here from the moment she arrived, which wouldn't be long now.

He pushed open the door and walked inside. It took a moment for his eyes to adjust, but when they did, he could hardly believe what he saw.

Ray had been here a long time. Definitely longer than the past few days. The amount of supplies and how the cabin was set up all signified long-term use. She'd been here right under his nose for months.

But that wasn't the biggest problem.

Photos and papers were pinned everywhere, all over the walls. He walked in for a closer look. Maps, pictures, print-outs of data he couldn't decipher at first glance.

If he were anybody else, he would've mistaken it for a crime scene board in a homicide office somewhere. But Dorian knew what this was: a Project Crypt mission board.

This was how they'd been taught to profile and target their intended victims. But Dorian had never seen one on this scale before.

And it was damned scary.

Pictures of all twelve of the original Crypt agents. Most were coupled with another photo of said agent, dead. Then the scientists—Dr. Holloman, Angela Landry, the other dozens of doctors and scientists who had poked and prodded at them, who had forced them to confront their deepest fears during their long months of training.

Some of them, too, were accompanied by a second photo of their deaths.

Dorian walked farther along the wall. More pictures of the agents again, this time with strings attached to other pictures, ones that didn't make sense to Dorian. His picture was attached to another one of his team when he was in the army. The string on Ray's picture was attached to a man in a suit standing in front of the Brazilian capital building in Brasilia. All the other agents had strings to different government officials, business leaders, and one to a now-deceased actor.

It didn't make any sense. At least to him.

But this had Crypt all over it. A Crypt that, according to Ray, had been defunct for years now. That she wasn't a part of in any way.

This wall said otherwise.

11

S omebody else was here.

The closer Ray got to her cabin, the more she was sure of it. She was absolutely sure no one had seen her get into the car she'd stashed. She'd spotted a vehicle behind her once she was out of town, but it hadn't been Dorian's truck.

And no one had followed her down the dirt road when she'd turned off Highway 191. It was one of the reasons she had chosen this place. Nobody could follow her down that road without her being aware of it.

She'd considered not coming back to the cabin at all. But if it was some hiker or hunter out here, maybe she could get rid of them before they actually saw anything.

Not that she could stay anyway. She was too close to Dorian here. He was much too familiar with these woods. She'd taken a huge chance by making this her residence for the past year.

She'd wanted him to catch her. She could admit that now. She'd wanted him to find her and . . . everything they'd done together last night. Every breathtaking second of it.

But it was morning now, and that was over. It was time to move forward, to find the killer.

She'd missed a few messages from Angela—evidently, she'd found someone who could locate Phantom. He was the next step.

Ray refused to let herself believe that Phantom could be the last stop. That if he was the killer, and she could stop him, she would be free to come back here. To Dorian.

If he would still have her.

But first, she needed to get rid of whoever was here.

She swung around wide, coming up to the cabin from the south side, the opposite direction from where she'd parked the car. Her hand rested on her Viper pistol crossbow—her weapon of choice, although she had her Beretta Pico at her waist if her crossbow wasn't an option. When she saw someone walk past the window of her cabin, she actually relaxed a little. The people she was most concerned about coming after her would not make the mistake of walking past the window when she could be nearby.

Still, explaining all that shit hanging on the cabin walls to a civilian wasn't going to be easy. Not that any of it would be around by the time someone could bring anyone else here to look.

Right now, the best plan was probably to back up and wait until whoever was poking around inside the cabin got bored and left. Normally she wouldn't have any problem waiting out whoever it was. Sitting alone in the quiet wilderness had been much more difficult for her when she'd first joined Project Crypt. She'd wanted to do, go, make things happen.

That was a young person's game.

Now if she could spend the rest of her life in the quiet

woods, not being hunted, not running from anyone, not having to look over her shoulder? It would be nothing short of paradise.

Or it would be usually. Today, she didn't want to sit in the quiet. Didn't want to think about the man she'd left sleeping in his bed. She didn't want to think about the sore places in her body; places that hadn't been used for years.

Then he opened the front door of her cabin.

Her Viper was up and pointing at Dorian in a split second. He must have a weapon too, but he didn't draw it on her. Instead, he raised one eyebrow on his ruggedly hand-some face.

"Really? After everything we did last night, we're back to the crossbow?"

She'd underestimated him again. Maybe not his skill, but his desire to follow her. "What are you doing here, Ghost?"

"I think the real question is what are *you* doing here? What's going on? What the hell is all this stuff inside? What are you not telling me? Are you still working for Crypt? Because when I look inside this cabin, I see someone profiling a mission. And it's got Crypt written all over it."

She lowered her weapon and slipped it back into the harness on her back. She walked up to the door, not meeting his eyes. The inside of that cabin said way too much about her to anyone who knew how to read the details. Dorian did.

"You're not supposed to be here."

"Yeah, obviously you're not set up for company."

She brushed by him, refusing to acknowledge the little rush that coursed through her body from being near him. That shit had to be tamped down. "Sorry, D. If I'd known you were coming, I would've broken out the fine china."

He gripped her elbow. More ignored tingles. "If I'd known you were going to make a run for it, I would've tied you to my bed."

Now it was her turn to raise an eyebrow. "Better than a tarp, I guess."

He winced the slightest bit, and she almost felt bad. But she was going to need all her defenses to navigate this conversation.

"Are you working for them, Ray?"

She wanted to yank her arm out of his grip, but his thumb rubbed gentle circles on that soft patch of skin by her elbow.

Her whole world felt anchored to that touch.

She sighed. "No. I'm not working for Crypt. But I didn't tell you everything about them either."

The thumb trailed down again, and Dorian leaned in closer. She could feel his breath in her hair.

"Then tell me now. Whatever it is you're doing, we'll do it together."

Now was the time to tell him about the sleeper missions. He didn't need to know the specifics, but he needed to know what Crypt was capable of. She gave him the slightest nod and moved through the door. She couldn't help but cringe as she walked inside the darkened room. This had to look damning at worst, borderline psychotic at best.

"Walk me through this," he said. "Help me understand."

"I didn't tell you everything before. Crypt was brain-washing us."

A beat. Another as he tried to wrap his head around what she was saying. "*What*?"

"Dr. Holloman specifically. Every agent had a sleeper mission programmed into his or her subconscious. Crypt could trigger it whenever they wanted to."

Dorian scrubbed a hand over his face. "I don't under-stand. They brainwashed us into killing people? Why do that? We already assassinated the people they told us to."

"This was all Holloman's baby. He sold the government on the project by convincing them that he could teach agents how to access parts of their mind that would make them better and more effective soldiers. He took it to the next level once he had control of Crypt."

Dorian began to pace back and forth in the small cabin. "Holloman could've used us to kill anyone he wanted."

She shook her head. "No, it's not like that. I've seen the research myself." Destroyed it all herself. "One sleeper mission. That's how it worked. It would take too long to 'reprogram' us for more than one. But the targets themselves weren't as important to Holloman as what it taught him about human behavior."

"Like what? Give me an example."

She walked over and pointed to her picture on the wall and the other picture it was attached to with a string. "This is Manuel Cuellar. I assassinated him seven years ago."

"Okay." Dorian didn't blink that she'd assassinated someone.

"I spent a week with him, getting close enough to kill him." A very intimate week. Sleeper mission, indeed.

Dorian's lips tightened. He knew exactly what she meant. "Okay."

"I have no recollection of this mission at all. None of it from beginning to end."

Dorian whistled through his teeth.

"Dr. Holloman wanted to learn as much as he could about the human psyche from our sleeper missions and how well we performed them."

"What was mine?" Dorian whispered.

She lied to him without batting an eye. "I don't know. You were tortured and your conditioning was broken before you could complete your sleeper mission. According to Crypt's research, your torture became the research they were interested in—the fact that the conditioning could be broken."

He let out a bitter laugh. "I guess I should be thankful I was captured."

If he knew the truth, he might actually be thankful.

"I'm glad that bastard is dead," Dorian whispered as he turned back to look at the walls.

"Yeah, I definitely didn't lose any sleep over Holloman's death either. But killing his family? That crosses a hard line. Whoever the killer is has to be stopped. That's what I've been working on here."

He nodded without looking at her. "Go on."

God, she respected this man so much. She'd dropped a huge mental bomb on him, but he was moving forward, concentrating on the issue at hand instead of dwelling on it.

"Five of the nine remaining Crypt agents have been killed in the past eighteen months. Hit-and-run accident, heart attack, drowning, and a couple of stabbings. But there was no tie between these people except Crypt, so law enforcement never linked them together."

Dorian walked from picture to picture, studying them.

"Five doctors or scientists have also died in the past year and a half. Again, no overt ties to one another, so no one was looking for a killer."

"How did you find out about it?"

"Angela Landry brought me in."

He turned from the data on the wall. "The soft-spoken assistant? I don't remember her very well. How did she find out about it?"

"She was one of the killer's targets. Lost the use of both legs when she was run off the road and over a sharp incline. The killer thought she was dead, but she made it out. She accidentally discovered I was alive and figured I was probably her best chance at stopping the killer."

"Because only someone pretty well trained could kill other Crypt agents."

She wasn't surprised Dorian had already put it together. "Exactly."

Dorian turned back to the pictures. "And Holloman and his family were the most recent victims?"

"Yes. I was going to walk away, but . . ."

"But kids," he said softly, looking at their picture.

"Yeah. Somebody has to stop this guy, D. And if it's an active agent, and it's not you or me . . . then it has to be either Phantom or Shadow."

"We should concentrate on Phantom."

"Why? Is Shadow dead? Angela hasn't been able to find anything on him at all."

"No, Heath works for us at Linear Tactical in some of our more covert overseas dealings. He's not officially listed on any documents. Having a dead man at our disposal works pretty well for us in some situations."

"What sort of situations?"

Dorian shrugged. "Our bread and butter is what we do here in Wyoming: survival and weapons training. But we also take on some corporate and covert assignments: K and R, private security."

Corporate kidnap and ransom was a big issue in many less stable countries. An intermediary working between the two parties often allowed the situation to be handled without anyone dying. "And that's the sort of stuff Shadow does for you guys?"

"Yes. I'll double-check some of his assignments against the dates of these murders, but I'm pretty sure he wasn't in the country for most of them."

"Okay." She turned and pointed to one of the pictures. "That leaves Mason Wyndham. Phantom. We haven't been able to find any information on him either. Don't guess he works for you too?"

"No, sorry. I never knew the guy very well."

Ray shook her head. "None of us did. Mason never really talked much to anyone else or tried to bond with anyone. He was a complete loner."

Neither of them needed to say that those characteristics were consistent with a murderer.

Dorian studied his picture. "I do remember he always got the job done. I never wanted to hang out with him during downtime, but I never worried whether he would do his job either."

Efficient. Focused. Cold.

"Yeah. Talking to him is my number one priority," she said.

Dorian turned to her. "*Our* number one priority."

"Dorian . . ."

He was reaching for her with concern. "Your nose is bleeding. Are you okay?"

She smiled quickly and wiped it with the back of her hand. Being back in this room wasn't helping her head, obviously. "Yeah, don't worry about it. Happens every once in a while."

He didn't look convinced. "Jesus, Ray, is this from yesterday?"

She touched his arm. "It's not. I promise. It's a reaction to . . . something. Pollen or something in the air. It's been happening on and off for a while." Plus blinding headaches, tunnel vision, and blackouts.

None of this was happening because of fucking pollen. But she needed to finish this one last mission, to find the killer, then she could worry about whatever was happening in her body.

His eyes narrowed as he studied her, but he didn't push it. She turned away and grabbed a tissue from her backpack. Hopefully, this wouldn't be one of the bad bleeds.

Her phone chirped, saving her from having to say anything else. "It's Angela."

He turned to her from the pictures. "Does she have a location on Phantom for us?"

Not for us, Dorian.

Ray nodded. "She has a computer expert I can meet with. Access to some files that should give us a location."

"Good. Actionable intel. When can we meet with the computer expert?"

Ray needed to be at a bar in Salt Lake City by midnight tonight. That was about an eight-hour drive.

"I need to do this alone, Dorian. There's no indication whatsoever that the killer is coming after you. Besides, you need to stay here and take care of the people you care about, just in case the killer does come in this direction."

"No."

She crossed her arms over her chest. "*No*? That's it? I'm supposed to accept whatever you decree as law? You haven't been part of my life for six years."

"And whose fault is that? If I had known you were alive, I never would've stopped looking for you. I would've scoured the entire planet."

She'd known that. On some level, she'd known he

would've given up everything to be with her if he'd known she was alive.

"I don't want to fight with you." She reached out and touched his arm. "Last night was . . . everything."

His fingers threaded into her hair at the nape of her neck, tilting her face up to him. "For me too. So you've got to understand that I'm not going to let you do this on your own."

"Dorian . . ."

"Phantom has to expect you're coming, Ray. Honestly, I'm surprised this many active agents have been picked off without someone turning the tables on him. He'll be waiting for an attack. Both of us working together gives us a much better shot."

He was right; she wasn't willing to risk him. He'd suffered enough because of her. She'd seen the literal scars all over his body, testaments of what he'd suffered. She wasn't going to put him at risk again.

She could find the killer—Phantom or not—eliminate the threat, and maybe, just maybe, she could return here and be a part of what Dorian had built.

But she had to get away from him first.

She turned to kiss the palm of his hand so she wouldn't have to look him in the eye as she lied. "We've got a couple of days before Angela can confirm the meeting. We'll have to go to Los Angeles. Will you be all right with that?"

"It's not my favorite, but I'll survive. Now, how about if we go back to my house and wait for the information? No more living like you work for them, Ray."

She was tempted for a moment, so tempted to go back with him, make love to him again, sleep in his arms. She had a few more hours before leaving was critical.

His eyes narrowed. "What? What aren't you telling me?"

Damn him. He'd always been way too perceptive when it came to her. She had to make her move now or she wouldn't be able to.

"Nothing. I've had a lot of years of being on my own. Being part of a team takes a little readjusting."

She smiled, then knelt down by her pallet and grabbed the few belongings she had—packed and ready for a quick getaway, as always.

She also grabbed the vial of flurazepam with its injection trigger.

She'd had it here in case she needed to tranquilize any civilians who happened to find her. She hadn't planned to use it on Dorian. But then again, the pansy had used something similar on her when they'd fought in the riverbed.

He was going to be as pissed as she had been.

"Okay, I've got what I need. I'll leave this other stuff for right now. Except for you, I haven't been discovered yet, so I'm not too worried about it."

He nodded. "How long have you been here?"

"Almost a year."

Before she expected it, he had her back pressed up against the wall. He moved so damn quickly for a man his size.

"Never again," he growled, his lips millimeters from hers. "Never again do you hide from me in that way."

She couldn't answer. She was about to leave him again, and she didn't know when, *or if,* she'd see him again.

He kissed her with a furor that hadn't been there last night. But even in his anger, he was gentle.

He'd always been gentle with her.

She flicked the tip off the needle and pressed it into the back of his neck before she could change her mind.

He tried to pull back from her, but she dropped the

empty vial and dug both her hands into his hair to keep his lips against hers.

He didn't stop kissing her.

But it didn't take long for him to realize something was wrong.

She expected anger as he drooped against her, already a little wobbly on his feet.

"Aw, hell, Grace."

She didn't correct him, just helped ease him down, the same way he had helped her in the riverbed. She was glad he didn't try to fight. She didn't want to hurt him. She cradled his head in her arms.

"I'm sorry, Dorian, but I have to do this on my own. Your people are here."

He reached up and cupped the back of her neck with one of those big, capable hands. She was almost surprised at the strength behind it.

"You're not alone. Not this time. Don't do th . . ."

His eyes pinned hers as he tried to stay awake, but his arm fell away as he gave up the fight.

She kissed him softly one more time, then laid his head on the ground.

It was time to go.

12

J ust because Ray didn't choose to wear a dress and heels all that often didn't mean they weren't weapons in her arsenal.

Nearly fifteen hours after she'd left Dorian lying on the cabin floor, she walked into an illegal warehouse club on the wrong side of Salt Lake City. Her black dress hugged her figure, plunging low at both her back and chest before flaring into a short skirt. The skirt was flirty, with the added bonus of enough room to hide her favorite throwing knife along the outside of her thigh. A second knife was built into the heel of her stilettos.

A stiletto inside a stiletto had a nice ring to it.

Ray had been trained to run, fight, or flirt with a mark in an outfit exactly like this one. And she could do any of it perfectly.

But God, she was definitely too old for this shit. Maybe not in actual years, but in every other way.

She would never set foot in a place like this without good reason. First, because strangers bumping and grinding up next to her, most of them completely inebriated and living in a fantasy world where it was okay to leave their guard down like that, was not her idea of a good time. Second, because if you were going to do stuff like that, why do it in an illegal warehouse where the cops might bust in any second?

Ray had seen more than enough violence in her lifetime. If she wanted fun, she wasn't going to choose a place where she had to have someone watch her back.

Especially when she'd left the perfect person to watch her back unconscious on a cabin floor.

Coming here without backup was a mistake, but Ray hadn't had any other option. Taking care of herself wasn't the issue—she wasn't afraid to fight men twice her weight. But fighting them would cause a scene, one that would, in this day and age, end up on social media almost instantly.

Once that happened, her greatest asset—being dead—would be gone.

She wasn't exactly sure who she was supposed to meet. Someone who went by the name Neo, which made Ray roll her eyes. Angela didn't know what he looked like or where in here they were going to meet.

Ray was at every tactical disadvantage. She'd wandered around as much as possible earlier, in a different outfit and hairstyle, trying to scope out the place.

The exits were few.

Hidden areas and blind corners were many.

And now the bar was loud and packed with people everywhere.

Every single one of them was a potential threat.

And her head was pounding—making everything around her seem more jarring.

"Can I buy you a drink, sweetheart?" A hand landed way too low on her hip.

Ray forced herself not to break any of the frat boy's fingers. Instead, she gave the guy a tight smile and shook her head, stepping out of his reach.

But that put her closer to the dance floor. More hands groping anyone near. More bodies writhing.

The inside of her head felt like it was trying to jump out of her skull. Every flash of light from the dance floor, every beat from the techno music, made it worse.

Swallowing against the nausea pooling in her gut, she made her way toward the stairs that led up to a small balcony. At least there she'd have some sort of vantage point. Although what good was a vantage point if she didn't know what she was looking for?

She didn't give a shit about any of it.

Upstairs was more of the same noise, lights, and people. She could see more of the club from here, but it was also pretty obvious that she was looking.

When a hand grasped her hip once again, a big body pressing up behind her, she was done. She grabbed the knife strapped to her thigh before she could stop herself.

To her surprise, a hand covered hers over the weapon.

"Tsk tsk, Wraith. You don't want to do that. You've already drawn more attention to yourself than you should have."

Dorian?

She tried to turn, but he placed an arm on either side of her on the balcony and pressed even closer.

"Of course, that dress and those heels pretty much mean no one with eyes is going to miss you anyway."

"How did you find me?"

One of his hands trailed up her arm and across her shoulder to the back of her neck, where he tapped his finger.

She raised her fingers to feel where he'd touched. Sure enough, there was that same type of tracker he'd put on her the first time. She couldn't believe she hadn't found it. It hadn't occurred to her that he'd put another one on her.

"During that last kiss? Pretty sneaky, Lindstrom."

"No more sneaky than you drugging me."

"Why are you here? I thought we decided you were going to stay in Oak Creek to protect your family while I handled this."

His soft chuckle in her ear sent shivers down her spine. "Just because that was what you decreed doesn't mean I agreed to it. You're not the boss of me, Sunray."

Was he actually being playful?

She threw her weight backward with her hips, moving him back enough that she could spin around and face him.

Good God. Dorian was always handsome with his rough-cut face. A carved jaw made softer by lips that were so full they were almost luscious. Strong, broad cheekbones. Those clear hazel eyes that took in everything around him. He was sexy as hell in his usual cargo pants and T-shirt.

But in this open-collared, button-up dress shirt rolled up at the sleeves and tucked into black jeans, he was downright devastating.

Ray fought for words. "I thought being in public places like this made you panic."

His features were already pinched.

"Look," she continued. "I can't do what I need to do and worry about whether you're going to have some sort of emotional breakdown."

It was an utterly unfair, emotional bitch-slap of a statement, and she regretted the words as soon as they left her mouth. Dorian had every right to not want to be around people, and she was not handling this well.

To her utter shock, his arms came fully around her, swaying the two of them to the sultry beat now coming through the speakers. Her hands flew up to his chest.

"What are you doing?"

His head dropped closer to her ear. "Dancing. For the past hour, you've been close to blowing the whole mission—studying everyone like you were trying to pick them out of a lineup. Looking like you were going to break the fingers of anyone who came anywhere close to you. Not exactly blending in with the nightclub crowd."

Damn it, he was right.

"Here are the facts whether you want to hear them or not," he continued, "I don't need a babysitter. Yes, being around people isn't easy for me, and I'm never going to choose to do it long-term. But neither is it impossible."

His hands dipped lower on her hips, pulling her tighter against him. Ray didn't try to fight it.

"I'm more than capable of taking out anybody in here, including you, so don't forget that. I can compartmentalize and get a job done."

For the first time since she'd entered this bar, her brain wasn't slamming against her skull. Dorian was here. Miracle of all miracles, he wasn't mad at her, and she finally had someone who had her back in this fight.

He reached down with one hand and tilted her chin up so they were looking eye to eye.

"I forgive you," he whispered.

"For drugging you in the cabin?"

He smiled. "For that too."

"For sneaking out of bed this morning?"

"That too."

She rolled her eyes. "For shooting you with my crossbow?"

He chuckled. "I can see we might be here all night." All the humor fled his face. "I forgive you for being there that day in Kabul."

She closed her eyes, feeling like a thousand pounds of brick had fallen on her chest. "No. You can't. You went through hell because of me."

"I went through hell because of my torturers, not because of you. And who knows what my sleeper mission might have been?" Guilt flooded her. "What happened to me in Afghanistan broke the Crypt conditioning, so if nothing else, I'm glad about that."

"Dorian . . ."

His lips pressed gently against hers. "And you're not the boss of me, so I can forgive you. Hell, I already have. But more importantly, you're going to have to forgive yourself."

"No, there are things you don't know. I—"

"Hey, you Ray?" A woman's voice had them breaking apart.

"Yes."

"Neo's ready to see you now."

THE PETITE WOMAN who had interrupted their conversation led Ray and Dorian to the back of the club and into a VIP booth separated from the rest of the club by a thick velvet curtain.

Dorian kept his hand at Ray's waist the whole time they walked, relieved when she didn't try to pull away.

For one, they needed to be a united front for whatever was about to happen. But more importantly, because he wanted her near him.

He wasn't surprised by her stunt at the cabin, although

he'd been plenty pissed when he'd first woken up. Mostly because she was so determined to do this alone.

This place was a nightmare, and in more ways than one. He knew she had a knife strapped to her right thigh—he'd never known her to wear a dress without one—and she probably had another one stashed somehow in those shoes.

She still shouldn't have been trying to do this alone.

The VIP area was pretty standard—a large table with plush bench seating on two sides of it and chairs on the other two. A large man, his head shaved completely bald and earrings running up both ears, sat in the middle of one of the benches. He easily weighed as much as Dorian but with more fat than muscle. Another, younger man sat on the second bench, flanked by pretty girls.

Men standing on either side of the table were obviously Neo's security guys.

How the hell had Ray thought she could handle this on her own? Even she couldn't take out this many people with two knives.

Everyone stopped their chatting as the messenger led Ray and Dorian up to the table. She immediately took a seat next to the big, bald guy.

"Ray?" he asked Dorian.

Ray shook her head. "I'm Ray. And I'm assuming you're Neo."

The guy grunted and turned to Dorian, ignoring Ray. "Why do you want the information we've got for you tonight?"

Ray gave Dorian a slight nod. If Neo wanted to be an asshole, so be it. Ray only wanted the information about Phantom's whereabouts; she didn't care who did the talking to get it.

Dorian tilted his head to the side. "Why do you care why

we want it? You're going to get paid." Everyone shifted a little uncomfortably. Neo shrugged and glanced over at the woman who had escorted them in for a second. She gave a tiny nod too, just like Ray had.

Dorian almost chuckled. Evidently, he was also an asshole. They'd both assumed the men were in charge.

They. Weren't.

"How about you and I shut up and let the real bosses talk?" Dorian said to the big man. He turned to the woman who'd walked them in. "Neo."

Everyone around the table stiffened. Beside him, Ray's gaze shifted to the woman. "We're not here to play games."

"Fine," the woman responded. "I'm actually Neo, but most people don't get past Smith here."

Ray shrugged. "People see what they want to see. Honestly, I probably would've missed it too. Ghost is a little more observant than I am."

"A good person to have around, then." Neo held out her hand and one of the security guards placed a hard drive in it. "The information you wanted was more tricky than I expected."

Ray nodded. "Government files can be that way. I'm sure you had to dig deep into the DoD database to find the location of the person we're looking for."

Neo smiled. "I've been hacking government files since I was in middle school. That's not the problem."

"What *is* the problem?" Ray crossed her arms over her chest.

"Most people assume hacking is like traveling through some vast wasteland, picking up information here and there where one can find it. It's the opposite. There's information everywhere and the hacker has to decipher what's valid and useful while leaving the rest alone." Neo rolled her eyes.

"The government tends to be the worst when it comes to excess information. Damn information pack rats."

"Did you get the info or not?" Ray asked.

"Oh, I got info, all right." Neo leaned back and crossed her arms over her chest. "After having to root through what you destroyed three years ago."

Dorian looked over at Ray. What had she done three years ago?

Neo held out a hand. "Look. I don't care about your little war with Project Crypt—isn't that what it's called?—I stumbled on some information, and I think you better know about it before you go visit the person I was hired to find."

Ray shook her head. "No, location first. The info you've already been paid for."

"Very well. Homestake, Montana. That's where your guy is."

She gave them the coordinates. Neither Dorian nor Ray needed to write them down. They'd both committed the information to memory.

"Do you know where that is?" Neo was studying Ray.

"No. Should I?"

"I guess not. It's a tiny town in the middle of nowhere. I thought maybe you'd recognize the name."

Ray shook her head. "I don't."

A man wearing a jacket, which also meant he had a weapon holstered underneath, rushed through the curtain and bent to whisper something in Neo's ear. The woman immediately stood, everyone around her following her actions.

Dorian really looked at her for the first time. She was young, much younger than he would've assumed, maybe twenty-five at the most. She had long black hair, but now that he was looking at it more closely, he realized that was probably a wig. A couple of freckles showed through the thick makeup she had caked on. This woman wasn't what she seemed.

"We're about to have a little trouble with the law," Neo said. "The danger of meeting at a club with so much illegal activity going on."

Ray held up both hands. "That's got nothing to do with us. We're not undercover cops."

"Oh believe me, I know. Law-enforcement databases are ridiculously easy to crack."

Neo held out her hand, and her companion placed a hard drive in it. "I found some information you should probably see. There's some stuff about brainwashing."

Ray's face paled.

"We already know about the brainwashing," Dorian said.

"It's time to go, boss," bald, earringed, not-Neo said.

Neo nodded, allowing herself to be led out. "The info on that hard drive is going to bring up more questions than answers, I'm afraid."

Someone screamed in the main section of the club. That and SWAT busting in was all it took to ensure panic.

Neo and her team disappeared into the crowd. Dorian grabbed Ray's hand and rushed in that direction too—then came to a halt when someone from inside the club began firing at the police.

That's when all hell broke loose.

Everyone rushed for the main doors near the front. Dorian moved backward against the wall in the opposite direction, keeping a firm grip on Ray. There was an exit near the back. Most people wouldn't know about it.

Dorian breathed through the panic attempting to claw its way into his psyche.

Noise. Smoke. Screaming.

He'd lived in that hell before, and it all just threw him back into that prison.

When two massive guys pushed between him and Ray, separating them, Dorian's control snapped. He threw one guy up against the wall, crashing his fist down on the man's face.

He grabbed the guy's collar and looked at him. He was one of Dorian's captors. The one who had broken his fingers.

Dorian hit him again and again until a small hand caught his wrist and pulled at him.

"D. Dorian! D, look at me, baby. It's Ray. Grace."

"Grace?" What was Grace doing here?

"Stay with me, Dorian. We're going to get out of this."

He looked down at the man now lying unconscious against the wall. That hadn't been one of his captors at all—looked nothing like him.

There was blood on his hands. Just like when they used to cut him.

"D!" Grace had both hands on his cheeks, pulling his focus to her. "Some dumbass knocked me over and damaged the hard drive. We're going out the back door. Keep hold of me and let's get out of here."

He nodded. Yes, he had to get her out of here. There was no way he could allow Ray to be trapped in here.

The things they would do to her.

He grabbed her wrist and almost dragged her through the crowd, using his size and strength to bulldoze people out of his way.

They would not take Grace.

He would not let them take her.

He didn't stop until they were out the small back door.

Stars. Air. They were out.

Grace was out.

"Jesus, D, you were amazing. It would've . . ."

She was saying other stuff, but he couldn't understand it. Saw her lips moving but couldn't hear the words.

Everything was starting to move too slowly. To get sticky like he was walking through molasses.

He was shutting down.

He forced one foot in front of the other as she led him somewhere a few blocks away. When she opened the car door, he got in on the passenger side. When the door closed he flinched.

No.

He wasn't in that prison. He wasn't in that prison.

Breathe.

Breathe.

There was no air.

13

Dorian had been a machine inside the club, focused solely on getting them out. Once they'd escaped the building, she'd taken over and led them to the car she'd parked a few blocks away.

She drove them silently—well under the speed limit so as not to draw attention—dodging the people and cars frantic to escape the mayhem. They were halfway outside of Salt Lake City before she realized something was wrong with Dorian. He sat ramrod stiff in the seat, looking straight out in front of him. His breath was getting more and more shallow rather than returning to normal.

Shit. She recognized the signs of a panic attack coming on.

"D, what can I do? Do you have some sort of medication?"

No answer. PTSD symptoms could take all sorts of shapes and cost all sorts of prices. She had no idea what Dorian would need to get through his. She drove a little farther out of town and down a deserted road until she could pull off safely.

Dorian was barely moving now, breath sawing in and out, trapped in whatever hell was inside his mind.

It wasn't safe for them to stay in this area for long. Too many chances they'd be spotted. The killer could be after them, the cops could be after them, and now anyone wanting to resurrect Crypt's work could be after them, too, now that they had the hard drive, even if it was broken. She had to get Dorian out of harm's way, and fast.

She didn't know what would help and what would hinder him right now. PTSD was a nasty beast. Touching him might comfort or ground him, but it also might trigger him further. The same for talking, music, movement.

He gripped his phone in his hand, and she took a chance, unfurling it from his palm and using his thumb to unlock the screen.

She opened the contacts and clicked on Gavin's name, the guy she'd met at the bar. She pressed the call button.

A woman's voice answered. "Dorian, where are you? It's the middle of the night, I need ice cream and Finn and Gavin are comparing penis sizes."

Before Ray could figure out what to say to that, the woman continued. "Okay, not really, but they are sparring and that's basically the same thing. Why do they have to do this at midnight?"

"Um, may I speak to Gavin, please?" Ray finally got out.

"Who is this? Why do you have Dorian's phone?"

This was the small, blond, pregnant woman. Charlie. Ray hadn't met her but knew her from her surveillance of Oak Creek.

"It's important that I speak to Gavin."

"You're the one who shot Dorian, aren't you? Why do you have his phone? Why don't you come back here to Oak Creek so you and I can have a chat woman to woman? Hey!"

Charlie's voice trailed off as the phone was obviously taken from her.

"This is Gavin Zimmerman."

Dorian was beginning to shake, almost like he was having a seizure.

"Ghost is having a panic attack, and I need to know how to help him."

"Where are you?"

"I'm not at liberty to say, but we are not nearby. Does he have any medication? Triggers I can avoid? Meditation phrases or pictures or anything?"

Crypt had conditioned Dorian's brain to perform a certain way upon hearing certain words. It stood to reason that similar phrases or pictures could also help him.

"Make sure nothing is restraining him in any way," Gavin said. "Get him outside if possible, and as far away from people as you can."

Ray reached over and unhooked Dorian's seatbelt in case he mistook it for a restraint. That seemed to help a little bit.

"Did something trigger him?"

"A shootout at a nightclub. Blood. A lot of noise and violence."

Gavin muttered a curse. "Usually, it's a slow buildup for him, and he can feel it coming. He gets out, gets away for as long as he needs to. But taken by surprise like that . . ."

"He shouldn't have been there at all. He followed me." And if he hadn't, she'd probably be dead right now.

"Dorian is a big boy who can make up his own mind. I hope it was worth it. Look, he should have a number for Dr. Diaz in his phone. Maybe she could talk to him. They've been working on some verbal cues to help him regulate."

"I'm sure she'll be thrilled to get a call at midnight."

"For Dorian, she'll do it. Even better, tell me where you are, and we can get to you faster than you would probably think."

"No. I'll be in touch if I can't get him out of this."

Gavin was saying something as she disconnected the call, but Ray didn't have time to debate this with him.

Ray found the number for the doctor, then stepped out of the car. Voices, even hers, maybe especially hers, might make it harder on Dorian.

The woman picked up on the third ring. "Dorian? Is everything okay?"

"Dr. Diaz, my name is Ray. Grace Brandt." She had no idea if Dorian had ever mentioned her name to the doctor.

"Wraith."

Evidently, he had. "Yes, that's right. I'm here with Dorian now, and he's having some sort of panic attack. Gavin Zimmerman said I should call you."

"Can you get him to my office?" The doctor sounded much more awake now.

"No. We aren't anywhere near Oak Creek." She explained the situation about the bar and Dorian's symptoms.

"Unfortunately, under the circumstances, I can't really provide you with any specifics. Things Dorian and I have been working on are private and privileged."

Ray didn't like it, but she appreciated the security of it at least. "Look. Why don't we do a video chat, and I'll put the phone in the car with him? You can see him, do your psychology voodoo stuff, and help him. I'll stay outside the car."

"Fine." Before Ray could say anything else, the doctor disconnected the call. A couple of seconds later, a video call came through.

"Get in the car and point the phone where I can see him."

Ray did as the woman asked, surprised to see someone so young and attractive as Dorian's psychologist.

"Dorian, it's Dr. Diaz." The woman's voice was even, slow, but not patronizing. "You're safe right now. You're free to move, free to get up and walk around, free to go get a cheeseburger at McDonald's."

His whole body jerked.

"Dorian, there's nobody here. Nobody holding you down or taking away your choices. You're free to move. Free to do whatever you want."

If anything, Dorian got more tense.

"Ms. Brandt, do you mind stepping outside the car like you offered? I need about ninety seconds."

"Sure." Ray propped the phone on the dashboard in front of Dorian. He didn't look like he could see much of anything right now, his hazel eyes glassy and unfocused, but at least that way the doctor could see him.

Ray got outside of the car and counted down the seconds, cringing when she heard sirens in the distance. They needed to move now.

She gave Dr. Diaz two full before heading back around to the driver's side. Whatever the psychiatrist had said, it would have to be enough. Either that, or Ray was going to have to get them out of here and worry about helping him later.

When she opened the door and got inside, she could immediately see that Dorian was doing better. Not great, but at least not catatonic. "Dorian?" she whispered.

He gave her the slightest nod.

Ray grabbed the phone. Dr. Diaz looked out at her. "He should stay with you now. But he's not going to be one hundred percent for a while, and you definitely need to keep him away from crowds."

"Okay."

"Listen, in the past, these sorts of episodes have ended with a heightened need to release aggression. He's always had his Linear Tactical teammates around to work that out, generally with sparring. I don't want you—"

"I can handle it, Doc. Ghost and I have gone toe to toe before. We can certainly do it again."

"Good. Although I'm not sure it's good for his ultimate mental health to be fighting with you the way he needs." The woman cleared her throat. "I don't want to overstep my bounds, but there might be other ways he could work out the same sort of aggression. Maybe more healthy ways for both of you."

The woman's rounded face contorted into an uncomfortable grimace. Obviously, she knew she was recommending something outside of polite social boundaries.

"Sex. Yeah, I get it, Doc. I'll take care of him."

"And he'll take care of you too, Grace. He needs that. You both might, actually."

Ray had no idea what to say to that. "Thanks for your help, Doc."

She disconnected the call and started the car. At least Dorian wasn't shaking anymore. Evidently he and the psychiatrist had worked out some sort of calming trigger word. After all the sleeper-agent stuff, Ray wasn't sure that was a great idea, giving someone that sort of access to his unconscious mind, but it seemed to have helped him now.

She drove out of town, using roads that weren't highways but still had a little bit of traffic on them. Empty back roads could be just as dangerous for being followed.

She headed north—they had to go toward Helena and

Phantom. But first she needed to get Dorian somewhere he could get through this. A hotel wouldn't work. If he came out of this needing to beat the shit out of something, she didn't mind fighting with him to give him the outlet, but that wasn't going to work in a hotel room.

She needed help. She didn't want to take a chance on leading anyone to Angela. Praying she wasn't making a mistake, she pulled over on the side of the road again and grabbed Dorian's phone. He offered her his thumb this time to unlock it.

"I hope your friends can be trusted, and I'm not about to get us both killed," she muttered. Dorian didn't say anything, but she didn't expect him to.

She texted Gavin.

Need a safe house with some space. Heading north out of Salt Lake City toward Montana.

There was a response less than a minute later.

Keep heading north. Will have something for you soon.

Ray restarted the car and began driving up Highway 85. She turned up the heater when she noticed Dorian was shuddering, not the same as before, but still a little scary. She didn't want to talk to him or touch him in case that made things worse.

When an address came through on Dorian's phone twenty minutes later, she didn't stop driving this time. She read the location into her own phone to get the directions.

And then she hauled ass to get there.

Dorian was obviously fighting whatever was happening to his body, trying to stay somewhat present and aware. But it was taking a toll.

She knew some of what had happened to him when he was captured, but mostly the physical wounds: breaks, burns, cuts. Those were certainly bad enough.

But what about the rest? What had it done to someone proud and strong like Dorian to have every bit of power and dignity stripped away from him for weeks on end? That, as much as the torture, had left scars.

Helpless. Hopeless. Not knowing if it was ever going to end.

What would she want if it were her? If her mind couldn't figure out exactly what was happening?

She'd want some sort of semblance of power.

She moved her hand to her inner thigh and unsheathed the ballistic knife she had strapped there. Carefully grasping the sharp end, she handed the blade handle-first to Dorian.

She didn't take her eyes off the road, just held it out to him with one hand. "To protect yourself. You're not helpless here."

She kept the knife stretched out between them for miles. It was only when her arm started shaking slightly with fatigue that he finally reached over and took it.

She hoped she wasn't about to get stabbed with it.

After a couple of more miles in silence, she slowly reached over and opened the glove compartment. She slid out the .38 and held that out to him too.

"Not helpless. Not ever again. I'm not going to let them get you. You're not going to let anyone get you."

She couldn't tell if he could hear her.

"I'll help protect you."

Still no response. She remembered what Dr. Diaz had said about them needing each other.

"And you'll help protect me."

"Yes." The single syllable sounded like it was torn out of him, but at least she knew Dorian was there.

"That's right. You protect me, and I protect you.

Together."

The noise he made was no more than a grunt, but his grip on both weapons solidified—muscle memory taking over and preparing him to use them if needed.

Ray sped on through the night, and within a couple hours, they turned off the interstate and onto some back roads. And not a bit too soon either. Dorian was obviously fighting to stay conscious. He'd beaten back his demons, for now, but the physical cost had been high.

"Hang in there, Ghost. We're almost there, then you can rest."

The small safe house didn't look like much, barely more than the cabin she'd occupied in Wyoming, but Ray didn't care. All that mattered was that it was out of the way and no one was around.

She parked the car to the side and grabbed her secondary weapon from under the driver's seat. Dorian was starting to slump over to the side. Shit.

"D? Hang in there a couple more minutes, okay? Let me check this out, and I'll be right back."

She didn't wait for an answer, just got out of the car. Keeping her weapon trained in front of her, she walked up the steps. She got the key out from under the mat as she'd been instructed, then used it to open the door.

Now they'd find out if Gavin was looking to betray them in any way. Because he was never going to have a more perfect opportunity than this.

She made her way inside, silently moving from room to room. She was starting to feel more secure, relaxing as everything seemed to be what they needed when she got to the back room.

And heard the slightest bump from the front door.

Shit. She'd been wrong; someone had followed her.

Gavin had sent someone to hit them while they were weakened. Had the person already gotten to Dorian? He was a sitting duck out there in the car, even with the knife and the gun. In the state he was in, they were basically props in a play.

Keeping low, Ray eased back down the hallway toward the front door.

She didn't want to spin from around the corner and shoot. What if Gavin had sent a friendly to check up on them? Could he have been stupid enough to send law enforcement?

But the longer she waited, the more any advantage she held was lost.

She turned around the corner, knowing that hesitating long enough to determine if it was friend or foe might cost her her life.

But the form of the man in the doorway was one she recognized right away.

Dorian.

And he wasn't coming into the house, he was facing back out.

Standing guard so someone had her back while she had secured the rooms.

"Dorian?" She lowered the weapon and rushed to his side, wrapping an arm around him as he nearly collapsed against her. She had no idea how he'd gotten himself out of the car and up the stairs.

"Protect each other," he whispered, his breathing labored. Those hazel eyes were cloudy. He'd used the last bit of his strength to get here.

To protect her.

She pulled him inside as he stumbled to the floor.

"Yes, Ghost. Protect each other, always."

14

Dorian woke and leapt to his feet in the same motion, already taking a fighting stance, although he knew it wouldn't help.

They held all the power here.

The first few seconds of waking up, before his mind remembered where he was, before the pain set in, were the best part of his day.

But it never took long for the truth to demolish that fantasy.

He'd long since accepted he was never walking out of here alive. The only question now—like every day—was whether this would be the day he died.

"Dorian?"

No. No. No. No. Nonononono.

The days where he could hear Ray's voice were the worst. It meant he was the weakest. Closest to breaking.

He covered his ears with his hands like he was five years old.

"No. Stay away from me," he told the ghost of the dead woman who still owned his heart.

"Fine. I'll make us some coffee."

She would make them coffee? He hadn't had coffee in . . .

Since yesterday.

The view shifted, and suddenly he could see everything clearly. He wasn't in an Afghani prison cell or the box they sometimes made him sleep in. He was in a house.

He was alive. He wasn't in pain.

He looked around. This wasn't his house. He closed his eyes again, trying to put the pieces together. He'd had an episode. Was he in one of his cabins?

And then he smelled coffee.

Everything came rushing back to him in a second: the club, the shooting, blood on his hands.

The paralysis in the car. It happened sometimes. Dr. Diaz had told him it was similar to sleep paralysis, but he was awake. Asleep or awake, he had been unable to move or protect himself.

He remembered Dr. Diaz talking him through it. Except this time there'd been an urgency, because . . .

Ray.

She was here. They'd been together at that club. He hadn't imagined her.

Adrenaline spiked through his system, but he forced himself to stay calm. Normally, he called one of the guys and they fought for hours after one of his episodes.

That wasn't an option now.

"Ray?"

Her head peeked from around the corner of the kitchen. Her beautiful features were tight. "Does my being here bother you? My voice? My person? Do you want me to leave?"

"No, never. Why would you think that?" An unbearable thought came to him. There was so much he could never remember of his episodes. "Oh God, did I hurt you? Ray, I'm so sorry—"

"No." She took a step closer, then seemed to stop herself. "You didn't hurt me. You didn't seem to like my voice a few minutes ago."

He shook his head. "I was having a flashback. When I was captured I—I used to sometimes hear your voice in my head. That generally meant it was going to be a bad day for me."

"Oh." She turned back toward the coffee maker, but not before hurt flared in her blue eyes.

He grabbed her waist and spun her back around. "Most days it took every ounce of focus I had just to stay alive. On the days I could hear your voice, all I wanted to do was go to you. Give up that fight. To be happy with you wherever you were. You were all that I wanted."

She shook her head. "I spent every single second of every day you were captured trying to find out where you were located and to get you rescued. Your team did too. They didn't know I was around, but they were crazy with worry about you."

He brought his forehead down against hers. God, he wanted to kiss her. Wanted to lift her up and set her on the counter like he had in his bathroom and use up some of this energy that was flowing through him at an almost unbearable rate. "I know you did. I believe you."

"Are you okay?"

His smile was rueful. "I'm always a little . . . itchy after an episode. It'll pass."

After he went ten rounds with someone or stepped outside to run a half marathon.

He stepped away from her. Touching her right now when he was so volatile wasn't a good plan. "Look, after these PTSD episodes, I'm a little . . . high-strung." He looked down at his hands. They were shaking.

To his surprise, she nodded. "Want me to clear the furniture out in the living room so we can spar? Dr. Diaz mentioned you might need some exercise."

The type of sparring he normally did after one of these episodes was ugly and brutal. The Linear guys were used to it. Actually, they tended to like it as much as he did. They spent a lot of time teaching self-defense moves to civilians— good ones that were effective, basic, and in good form. They were all firm believers in knowing and understanding the rules before breaking them. They spent an equal amount of time teaching local boys and girls boxing and a little bit of MMA sparring, again with proper rules and expectations.

So the chance to really let loose with one another and fight with very few holds barred was something all of them looked forward to from time to time. And if it would slay Dorian's demons, even better.

But he didn't want to fight with Ray in that ugly, brutal manner. Not that she couldn't take it.

"I'm pretty sure we'd need more space than that tiny living room."

But shit, he was going to have to do something and fast. Going out for a run wasn't an option. Not when there could still be people looking for them, and he wasn't going to leave Ray alone anyway.

He turned away from her. "Look, I'm going to do some workout moves back in the bedroom. Just give me an hour."

It wouldn't be enough. Even now, it felt like the walls were starting to close in on him. He couldn't breathe, and any second now, he was going to crawl out of his own skin.

Ray said something to him, but he couldn't stop to decipher it over the buzzing in his ears. He gave what he hoped was a lighthearted wave over his shoulder and tried not to bolt toward the back room.

DORIAN WAS ALL BUT TWITCHING. Ray watched him walk back toward the bedroom and knew he was having difficulty with the feel of his own skin.

Even knowing what was happening, she still wasn't sure how to best help him. He was right about the living room being too small for the kind of sparring he needed. And they'd never been good sparring partners anyway, beyond the lighthearted stuff. They'd been too close, knew each other's fears and weaknesses too well to want to use them against each other.

The other choice was sex, and she wasn't sure if Dorian wanted to have sex with her again after she'd drugged him and run out on him.

But damn it, she wasn't going to leave him to suffer through this alone. Not if there was something she could do.

She fried up some eggs and made a couple of pieces of toast, making a mental note to thank Gavin not only for lining this place up in such a hurry, but also making sure it was stocked.

She balanced the plates and coffee mugs and made her way back to the bedroom. She could already hear Dorian working his body. Hard, by the sound of it. She opened the door and stopped in her tracks.

He *was* working his body hard, and he was doing it completely *naked*.

He was doing push-ups at a rapid pace, facing the other direction, and hadn't realized she'd come into the room. Ray couldn't look away from his body. She'd seen him naked a little over twenty-four hours ago—was intimately familiar with his strength and agility and all the scars that covered his skin. And before recently, she'd been intimately familiar with him, known what he could do both in and out of bed.

But this was different.

This was Dorian without any veneer of civility, Dorian stripped down—literally and figuratively—to his most base self.

The warrior.

He turned to her slowly, never stopping his movements, and she realized he'd been aware of her presence the whole time. He'd been waiting to see if she would leave on her own.

"Go, Ray." His voice was deeper, more guttural, than she'd ever heard it.

"This is not giving you what you need. Dr. Diaz—"

"Dr. Diaz isn't here, and this will be enough."

She set the plates and coffee mugs down on the chair by the door and took a step farther into the room. "Dorian, I can help. I—"

"I'm not going to fight you, Ray."

"I don't want you to fight me. I want you to *fuck* me."

The frantic push-ups stopped.

"You need exertion to bleed out the adrenaline," she continued, confident in what she was saying. "But you spar with your boys because you need some sort of human contact with someone you trust. You need someone to touch you, but in a way you can accept."

His eyes narrowed, but she continued. "Your push-ups are only going to get you halfway. You need something else, and we both know it. So you either fight me, or you fuck me."

He was on his feet and had her pinned against the wall

with his big body two seconds later. "I don't want to hurt you."

She didn't touch him, just let him push up against her. "Then we take this to the bed rather than the mat."

"You don't understand, I'm not in control. I'm as likely to hurt you in bed as I am if we fight."

He buried his face in the crook of her neck. His lips brushed along the sensitive skin of her shoulder, then his nose, like he was sniffing her.

As if the animal inside him was that close to the surface.

She wasn't afraid. With anyone else in this situation, she'd have a healthy dose of fear, but not with Dorian. Never with him.

"You're not going to hurt me, D. Hell, I don't know if you *can* hurt me. If your brain would allow you to do it."

He growled, *growled* against her neck. His naked body thrust up against hers harder. "You don't know that."

"What's the last thing you remember about last night?"

Concentration obviously wasn't easy for him. "I don't know. The club, then the paralysis setting in."

"Do you know how I got you from the car to the house?"

He stiffened. "You— I— No, that can't be right."

"It is right. You fought off the impossible and got yourself into the house because you thought I needed to be protected. You weren't going to let anything hurt me last night, and you won't let yourself hurt me now."

She reached out to touch him, trailing her fingers along his shoulders, unsure if he wanted to be touched or held in any way. "I want you, Dorian. I *trust* you."

She barely got the words out before he pushed the skirt of her tiny dress up to her waist and ripped her thong off with a sharp sting.

His big hands grabbed her ass and boosted her up. He growled again as he slammed into her with one hard thrust.

This was so different from the lovemaking that had happened at his house. Primal. Raw. Unlike anything that had ever occurred between them.

This was Dorian without holding back.

She met him thrust for thrust, her own passion building, moaning as he bit a little harder than was comfortable at that place where her neck met her shoulder.

"Yes," she cried.

The encouragement set something inside him free. Keeping her pinned against the wall with short, deep thrusts, he let go of her hips with one hand and grabbed her leg, hiking it higher, her knee almost up to his shoulder.

Her moans turned into sobs—God, he was deeper than he'd ever been—and he paused.

She dug her fingernails into the back of his neck. "Don't you dare stop. Don't you—"

She cut off with a little squeak as he slammed inside her again. Over and over, the sound of them hitting up against the wall brutal and beautiful and obscene.

He didn't stop.

He didn't stop until they were both shaking and panting and calling each other's names. All Ray could do was hold on and survive the magnificent onslaught.

15

A few hours later, they ate cold eggs and drank cold coffee, both of them too physically and emotionally wiped to go back to the kitchen and warm the food. Neither of them wanted to get out of bed.

They sat next to each other, leaning up against the headboard of the bed. The bed Dorian had carried her to, placing her on all fours and pounding into her until the sounds they emitted were hardly recognizable as human.

"Ray, I am sorry—"

She reached over and touched his lips, stopping the words. "There is absolutely nothing to apologize for. In case you missed it, I wanted all of that just as much as you did."

He entwined his fingers with hers and kissed her fingertips.

God, he looked so much better than he had before. More relaxed, not at all like he was about to jump out of his own skin. His eyes were clearer than she'd seen them before. He was more at rest. More at peace.

At least physically.

"Are you sure I didn't hurt you? I was pretty damn near out of control."

Now she brought his fingers up to her lips. "I was right there with you. I know slow and gentle tends to be our default setting, and I have no problem with that. But I've got to admit, I sort of liked frantic and out of control."

"That was new to me."

"Did it work as well as sparring with the guys?"

"Better. So much better."

"I'm surprised you haven't tried sex before." As soon as the words were out of her mouth, she wanted to bite off her own tongue. Was she really suggesting he have sex with someone else? Ray didn't trust herself not to shoot another woman outright with her crossbow if she had to witness that. "I mean, your doctor seemed to suggest that physical touch along with a physical outlet would be most helpful to you."

She should really stop talking. Like right damn now.

"Yeah, Doc Diaz and I discussed different physical outlets, but sex really wasn't an option."

"Why? I'm sure there are plenty of women around Oak Creek who wouldn't mind helping you burn some energy." *For fuck's sake, Ray. Stop. Talking.*

"Yeah, but none of them were you. And if it wasn't you, then, honestly, I wasn't interested. I'd rather fight it out with one of the boys."

It made her feel better that he wasn't running around town with all the women. "Dorian . . ."

He ran a hand over his eyes. "I know we didn't use protection today. Hell, that was the last thing on my mind. But I want you to know that I'm clean. I had every possible type of test done to me after my capture."

She smirked. "You know that would've only told you

about any STDs up *until* then, right? That was six years ago."

Dorian flushed. This big, giant man who could probably throw a small car if he needed to, actually flushed. "Yeah. Well, I haven't had sex since then."

Ray was trying to wrap her head around this conversation. "I don't understand."

"I don't like to be around people. And I can barely stand to be touched. Except for you. It's not that I don't mind you touching me. It's so much more than that. I crave your touch."

"And there hasn't been *anyone* else?"

He shrugged. "Didn't seem like I should force myself to be intimate with someone if it wasn't what I wanted."

Of course. No one would expect a *woman* to have sex after a physical trauma if she didn't want to. What a double standard, to think a man should have casual physical encounters if he didn't really want to. Dorian had never been casual about sex.

She hadn't either. But it had been part of some of her Crypt missions. The Crypt leaders had told them that from the beginning. Like killing, using their bodies as weapons had to be part of what they were willing to give.

What had been labeled "intimate critical missions" had felt a lot more like whoring herself out after she'd discovered Crypt was corrupt.

Thankfully, she'd dodged those bullets.

"I'm clean too." She'd been checked after each mission for any STDs. And then, after a possible pregnancy scare even though she'd been on birth control, she'd had her tubes tied. "And pregnancy isn't an issue for me. Tubal ligation before I discovered the truth about Crypt."

"Grace . . ."

She rubbed her eyes with her fingers. "Seriously, *don't* call me that." She was the furthest thing from grace in the history of the world. "The important thing is the wild monkey love isn't going to result in any wild monkey babies."

"Is that what you wanted? No children ever?"

She shrugged. At the time it hadn't seemed important. Babies, families . . . that had all been so far outside of her future she hadn't had the sense to realize what she was giving up.

She couldn't fool herself into thinking she was any closer to it now. Even if she were biologically capable of having kids, that wasn't her path. She would've been a shitty mother anyway.

She shifted away from him and slid to the side of the bed. "Since you're feeling better, we need to get going. Finding Phantom is the most important thing. Plus, nothing can change the other anyway."

Dorian's eyes bore into her back. But she couldn't turn around. Couldn't let him know how much she mourned a future that could never be.

He didn't touch her, and she was thankful. She might have shattered.

"I guess we better go," he finally said.

RAY WASN'T silent on the trip to Montana, but obviously the topic of her inability to have children was not open for further discussion.

He was trying to wrap his head around how he felt about the news. He'd never really thought about having kids, mostly because he'd thought Ray was dead and there wasn't anyone else he wanted to have kids with. But the idea that she could never have them at all—that she'd given up the opportunity for Crypt, no less—left a gaping hole in his heart.

And she obviously wasn't okay with it, despite how even she'd kept her voice when she'd told him.

He had a feeling this was the tip of the iceberg when it came to the things she wasn't telling him.

He'd known that, of course. Nobody showed up after six years of being *dead* without some secrets. But Ray's seemed to weigh on her—like the whole world would fall apart if she shared them.

He wanted to help her shoulder some of that burden but wasn't quite sure how to do that yet.

While he'd driven, she'd tried to connect the damaged hard drive to her laptop. It was obviously an exercise in futility, and it wasn't long before she was putting it all away. "With enough time, we might be able to get data off of this, but my laptop isn't equipped for that sort of work. Maybe Angela can do something with it."

"Or we've got a guy. Kendrick Foster—he's a certified computer wiz. If there's something that can be salvaged off that hard drive, he'll be able to do it. Maybe he could work with Angela if you brought her to Oak Creek."

She nodded, noncommittal, but at least not saying no outright.

He wanted her back in Oak Creek. Whatever way he had to get her there, he would use it.

Then whatever way he had to *keep* her there, he'd use that too. Short of tying her up again.

Maybe.

"I called Gavin this morning to check in and had him run Shadow's assignments for us against the victims' deaths.

Heath definitely isn't our killer unless he's figured out how to be in two places at once. We've got positive ID of him across the world during some of the hits."

Heath Kavanaugh was a key overseas asset for Linear, although he didn't go by that name very often. The man was a top-notch negotiator and had a way with people that made him effective in situations when others weren't.

Dorian had never thought Heath was the killer but was glad to be able to provide proof.

"Good. I hated the thought that it could be Heath."

"Until we get this figured out, Zac is calling him back stateside. Heath should be in Oak Creek in the next few hours."

"So we focus on Phantom." She pulled up a map on her laptop. "Here's where he lives, almost smack-dab in the middle of the state on fifty acres near Homestake, just outside of Butte. From the looks of it, Homestake makes Oak Creek seem like a bustling metropolis. Since there aren't a lot of places to hide, we're going to have to be careful. If he's the killer, he's got to know someone's eventually going to try to stop him."

The *if* was the problem. *If* they knew for sure Mason was the killer, they could go in and take him out. Providing him a chance to explain himself was more dangerous for them than him. Both Ray and Dorian had rifles that would allow them to surveil Phantom while they decided whether or not to attempt to take him alive.

Dorian had been pissed when he'd woken up on her cabin floor and realized she'd stripped every single bit of her carefully gathered surveillance from the shelter, but now he was thankful she'd brought it all with her in her car.

They arrived and parked near the edge of Phantom's property.

"We'll go on foot from here," he said.

She nodded. "I think we should try to take him alive," Ray said as they got out of the car and prepared to split up. "I don't want to make any permanent decisions, like taking Phantom out, when we don't have all the facts."

She didn't quite meet his eyes as she said it.

"Like what?" The same facts Neo had been referring to at the bar?

Ray scanned the area around them. "With Crypt, you never know what facts you're missing." She positioned her rifle strap more fully on her shoulder. "Okay, I'll come around from the south side. You head in from the northeast. We evaluate and communicate via text."

Damn it, what wasn't she telling him? Unfortunately, now was not the time to push it. Not when they were so close to potential enemy territory.

"Roger that."

She nodded and started walking in her agreed direction. No way. He grabbed her arm and spun her around.

"Hey, you be careful." He pressed his lips softly against hers. "We don't know what sort of shape Mason is in, and let's face it, he wasn't known for his stability even back in the day."

She leaned her forehead against his chest. "Okay. You be careful too. Watch out for potential traps. You have the ones that warn you when people come around. He may have the kind that *kills* people who come around."

"Roger that."

This time when she turned away, he let her go. He trusted her to know what to look out for.

Finding out her secrets would have to wait for another day.

Adjusting his own rifle strap on his shoulder, he advanced

on Phantom's small farmhouse. As agreed, Dorian approached from the northeast, being sure to stay deep in the cover of the tree line. He found ample traps that would notify Mason that someone had been here, but none of them seemed designed to harm. That didn't necessarily mean Phantom was innocent, but at least he wasn't willing to kill or maim complete strangers because they happened to come too close to his house.

Dorian did a thorough sweep of the surrounding acreage—there definitely were no people around—before settling behind a tree and a large cluster of bushes. Using the scope of the rifle, he could see Phantom's house, right up to and including the two dogs lying on the front porch.

Dogs were another possible good sign. Again, they didn't necessarily mean Phantom was okay, but at least they meant he was attached to something.

Dorian winced as he looked at the dogs. He had one of his own, a German shepherd he'd raised from a pup when the little fellow's pregnant mom had run out into the street and nearly killed Zac Mackay. Storm was currently staying with Zac and Annie.

There had been times when that dog was the only thing linking Dorian to sanity. Were those dogs the same for Mason? He glanced down when he got the text from Ray letting him know she was in place.

Now they waited.

Normally, waiting by himself in the wilderness wasn't something that bothered Dorian at all. Out here, he was free. Able to exist without the fear or anger that sometimes nearly suffocated him.

But today, it gave him too much time to think about mental deterioration—not just Mason's possible break-down, but Dorian's own. His episode last night. The almost manic sex with Ray this morning. She hadn't asked questions about any of it, but she had to have some. Had to wonder if what she'd seen was the worst of it.

It wasn't.

Ray wasn't the only one keeping secrets. There were so many things the two of them needed to talk through.

Dorian pushed all those thoughts out of his mind. Focusing on things besides the job at hand could get him killed. Worse, it could get Ray killed if he didn't have her back the way he should.

His eyes remained at the scope, the physical discomfort a nonissue for him. That was a positive byproduct of his time in captivity. He was well acquainted with physical pain. In contrast, mere discomfort was nothing.

He held his position for a good two hours. There was definitely something wrong.

Evidently Ray was coming to the same realization.

Something's not right. Going to sweep closer.

She'd seen the same thing he had. *Dogs?*

Haven't moved once in two hours.

That wasn't good. He typed back quickly. *Could be a trap. Be careful. Come in from my angle so I can cover you.*

Roger.

It was another forty-five minutes before he caught sight of her. She'd done like she'd said: swept slowly and carefully.

Those dogs still hadn't moved.

He shot off another text to her. *Got you in sights.*

She walked slowly toward the house.

He watched for movement from all possible directions at the front of the house as she got closer. Like Ray, he didn't think anyone was in the house either. She moved slowly up the front porch steps, looking for potential wires or traps. The dogs still didn't move.

Dorian stood, breaking cover as she took the last step toward them. They would have done something if they were okay. Lifted their heads, wagged their tails, growled . . . *something*.

Ray crouched down beside them, shaking her head, then turned and looked out at Dorian, even though she didn't know exactly where he was. He zoomed in on her face. Every bit of color had leached out. A few seconds later her text confirmed what he'd already figured out.

Dogs dead.

Dorian swallowed a curse. Dead dogs could mean a number of things. Could mean that the killer had already found Phantom and he was dead inside the house.

Or it could mean that Phantom *was* the killer, and he'd snapped and killed his own dogs.

We need to go inside, she texted.

Wait for me. There was no way he was sending her into that house alone.

She picked up a rifle and began searching through the scope, covering him as he moved toward the house. She kept up the coverage until he made it to the stairs.

"Both have been shot," she whispered. "They've been here a while."

They met each other's eyes. Nothing about this felt good.

"I think we might've been wrong about him being the killer. And I think we might be too late." Ray still looked a little shaken.

Dorian nodded. "We go in. But slowly, and with every precaution. This has trap written all over it."

"Do you want to take entry or lookout?"

"I'll take lookout, but I think we ought to double-check each other."

She nodded, obviously not offended. They both knew this place could be wired to blow.

Dorian kept a look out as Ray searched the front door for any signs of explosives or danger.

"I found a notification measure—string—but I don't think the door is wired. Switch with me."

She replaced him, looking out the scope of her rifle for any potential threats as he double-checked her work on the door. He wasn't surprised to find the exact same thing she had. A tiny piece of string had been attached to both the doorframe and the door itself. It wouldn't do anything to stop someone from entering the house, but it would notify Mason that the door had been breached. Dorian used similar measures himself at his house.

"I concur. It's clear." He tried the handle. "And it's unlocked."

Ray looked over at him from her perch, her features tight. The door not being locked could mean nothing or everything.

She stood and joined him at the door. "Let's do this."

The rifles didn't make for great close-quarters weapons, but they were better than nothing.

"I'll go high left."

She gave a sharp nod. She would cover low right.

He counted it down with his fingers. *Three, two, one . . .*

He threw the door open and pulled the rifle to his shoulder in one motion. They both moved silently in their agreed-upon directions.

There was no one in the combined living room and kitchen. He tapped Ray's shoulder and they moved toward the small hallway, then into the bedroom.

She took the lead, covering him while he checked the small closet and bathroom.

Nothing.

Nothing in the second small bedroom that didn't even have a closet.

There was no one here. There was no sign of any sort of struggle and there definitely was no Phantom—dead or otherwise.

"I really thought we were going to find his body in here."

Dorian nodded. "Honestly, I did too."

"Just because he's not here doesn't mean they didn't get to him. He could be lying dead somewhere else."

Dorian looked around the small house. Everything was neat, orderly, much like his house in Oak Creek. Messiness had been trained out of them.

"Or he might've had a breakdown. Shot his own dogs and taken off. He could still be our killer."

Ray looked around one more time. "Either way, we need to get out of here and come up with a new plan."

16

They'd backtracked to their car. Dorian hadn't liked leaving those dead dogs on the porch, neither of them had, but there was no way around it.

They'd stopped by Homestake, the small town about five miles from Phantom's house, to see if they might find any useful information.

And weren't surprised that almost nobody in the town recognized the name Mason Wyndham. He obviously hadn't moved to this area to make friends.

The couple of people who did recognize his picture were wary enough not to talk to strangers about him.

The only positive indication they got that he lived there at all was from an older woman who worked at the small hardware store. They told her they were passing through and had stopped by to visit but couldn't find Mason.

"No, I haven't seen him for a couple weeks now. Not that that's unusual. Mason is a quiet and private fellow."

Ray had given the woman a friendly smile. "Yup. That sounds like him. He hasn't gotten into any trouble around here, has he? Lost his temper or gotten into any fights?"

The older woman looked like she wasn't sure she should say anything else.

Dorian gave her a solemn nod. "PTSD. We all served together, and we all suffer from it." It was nothing less than the truth.

The woman's face softened with compassion. "I don't think he's been in any fights, but sometimes he comes in here looking like he's been through the wringer, you know? Sunken cheeks, eyes darting back and forth like he's not sure who to trust. I don't know how to explain it, but PTSD makes sense."

"Does Mason have any friends around here we could talk to? Anyone he hangs out with?"

The old woman laughed. "You won't be able to talk to his friends unless you speak dog. Mason has two dogs that mean the absolute world to him. I've never seen him without them, never seen him actually talk to anyone else unless he had to."

Dorian met Ray's eyes. Knowing how much Mason loved the dogs provided more questions than answers. He could still be dead, or he could still be the killer.

They took turns driving back to Oak Creek. The closer they got, the quieter Ray became.

An hour outside of Oak Creek, Dorian began to realize what her silence meant.

She was preparing to say goodbye.

There were so many things they needed to talk about. Too much had happened between them too fast. Only three days ago, he'd been torturing her on that cabin floor. And then today, she'd ripped his heart out with some casual words about not being able to have children.

They needed some downtime. They'd gone from one crisis to another from the second they'd reconnected.

And now she wanted to run. It was her default setting.

"You and I need a reboot," he finally said.

That at least got her attention. She turned from the window she'd been staring out for the past hour. "What?"

"We've been running ragged since the moment we got reintroduced to each other. We've had more happen between us in the past three days than most couples would see in years."

"In a lifetime," she muttered.

At least she was talking. "We need to regroup and figure out a way to find Phantom."

"Maybe we can get something off the hard drive. Plus, I still have all my stuff from the cabin. I took it down, but I should be able to re-create the boards and see if there's anything I missed."

"Good." He nodded. "You can do that in the spare bedroom at my house."

"It would be better if I had it with me at the cabin. Sometimes I don't sleep well, and I'm able to study things at night."

She still didn't get it. "You can study it whenever you want to. Because you'll also be at my house."

She went back to staring out the window again.

Dorian's knuckles were white on the steering wheel. How could he get through to her? "What's your plan, Ray? After we stop whoever's doing this, what are you going to do?"

"I don't know," she finally whispered.

He backed up. No point in trying to talk to her about the future. She could barely commit to sticking around for today. "Look, Shadow is already back in town. We'll let Kendrick look at the hard drive. If Phantom is the killer, you know he's off the chain. Instead of working on your own, let's try a united front. And anything from the hard drive would only help."

He glanced over; her face was shuttered once again. Whatever progress he'd made with her had been lost with what he'd just said.

"You think a united front is a bad thing? That you're better off on your own?"

She shook her head. "No. That's smart. The more tactically aware people around, the more likely we are to spot the trouble before it gets to us."

If it wasn't that, then it was whatever was on that hard drive that was bugging her.

She pulled her long legs up to her chest and wrapped her arms around her shins, laying her head on her knees and looking out the window. God, she'd done that for years. Wrapped herself up in a ball when she needed to think. The sunlight reflected off her golden hair.

What's your secret, Sunray? What is it you don't want anyone to find out about on that drive?

Demanding her secrets wasn't going to get him anywhere. Ray had been alone for too long. He couldn't force her secrets out of her, but maybe he could gentle them out of her.

Maybe he should tell her his own secrets.

He rubbed his fingers across his forehead, then jumped straight in. "That PTSD stuff we were talking about with the lady at Homestake? I've got it pretty bad."

She turned her head so it was resting on her knees, looking at him rather than out the window.

He glanced over at her, then back out to the road. He'd never talked about his PTSD as a whole before. He decided to start with what she was familiar with.

"One of the reasons I was so quick to trust that Shadow

wasn't the killer is because I put him in the hospital three and a half years ago when I went into a psychotic rage. It took all the Linear guys to take me down, and Shadow and Gavin were pretty seriously hurt."

"What happened?"

He glanced at her once again. Her lips were pinched, concerned. "Nothing in particular, that's just it. We'd had Linear set up for a little over a year, and I thought I was doing pretty well. I was never going to be a social butterfly, but I felt like I was handling things okay."

"But you weren't?"

"No. I was repressing everything. I thought that since I was in Wyoming—about as far from Afghanistan as one could get—that I would magically be all right." He scrubbed a hand over his cheeks, which desperately needed a shave. "It was a smell that triggered me. Maybe I hadn't prepared myself for that. I knew noises could be a problem, or being restrained. But a *smell*?"

"D. You don't have to talk about this."

But he did. Not just for him, but for *her*. "No. It's important that you understand." He cracked the window so he could feel the air on his face. "The guys and I were inside doing construction on what was to become our new office. To this day, I still don't know exactly what the smell was that caused me to lose it. Some mixture of the dust, or maybe tobacco and gasoline. And then, I accidentally hammered my own finger."

His grip tightened on the steering wheel. "I was back there, Ray. In that prison. They were breaking my fingers, and I couldn't get out . . . and I totally lost it. I tried to kill them—my team. All of them. I had no idea who *they* were."

Jesus, little Ethan, Finn's son—only five years old at the time—had been there. Finn had immediately gotten Ethan away from what was happening, but Dorian was still surprised that even now, three years later, Finn let the kid around him.

"It took all of them to take me down. Of course, they were expressly trying not to hurt me while I had no such qualms. I broke Gavin's jaw. Fractured Shadow's wrist and nearly took out his knee."

"Oh no."

"Yeah, they finally got me subdued, and I eventually came to my senses."

Only to see his friends—his *family*—lying bleeding and broken around him. Ironically, he'd thought they'd been attacked, wanted to help fight. Hadn't realized *he'd* been the attacker.

She reached out her hand and traced along his shoulder. She was the only adult person on the planet he'd allow that touch from without tensing. "What did you do?"

"I left. I took off for nearly four months. I probably would've stayed gone longer, but they came after me. Gavin, Heath, Zac, Finn, Aiden . . . all of them.

"They stayed out there with me for nearly a week. First, not even trying to talk to me—I was in no shape to talk to anyone anyway, more animal than man. But they just stayed out there with me, letting me know they were there, supporting me in a way I could understand."

"They're your family," she whispered.

"Yes, in every sense of the word but blood." Her fingers caressed his shoulders again, and he couldn't help but lean into it. "Without them, I don't know that I'd be able to stand you touching me now. And I can't help but wonder if Phantom has his own demons and maybe didn't have a family to come pull him out of the woods, literally."

"It's possible. But it's also possible he wasn't interested in coming out of the woods at all."

Dorian nodded. "We finally came back into town together. Dr. Diaz started her practice there not long after that, and I started seeing her regularly. She specializes in post-traumatic stress disorder, luckily for me."

"Does she use hypnosis? Trigger words, stuff like that?"

"No. I brought up the possibility to her, but she was adamantly against it."

"Oh. When she was talking to you last night to try to get you out of your paralysis, she asked me to wait outside the car. I thought maybe you two had some sort of voice or word trigger that you'd worked out."

Dorian didn't remember much about his paralysis episode. He never did. But he definitely remembered what Dr. Diaz had said to pull him out of it enough to be able to function. "There's no secret word or phrase, don't worry. She knew what to say to get me as functional as possible—not that that was of any real help."

"I don't understand."

"She told me that you needed me, Ray. That I needed to fight what was happening enough to get you safe. Sierra is a smart woman. She knows there are very few things stronger than what my mind was trapped in."

Like his feelings for Ray and his need to take care of her.

"That's how you got to the door in the safe house too," she said. "Because you wanted to make sure to protect me."

He reached up and grabbed her hand resting on his shoulder and brought it to his lips. "Always."

They drove in silence for a few more minutes. "That episode with the guys a few years ago was the worst by far, but believe me when I say I'm a virtual textbook of PTSD symptoms. Night terrors. Bouts of rage. Difficulty interacting with people. Taken as a whole, it's not pretty."

"But you survived. And you're sitting here having an intelligent conversation with me about your past and what happened."

"Yeah, but not every day is as good as this one. And I never know when I wake up what sort of day I'm going to get."

"None of us do. But every day you get up, and that's what matters."

17

Ray didn't argue with Dorian about staying at his house. It wasn't like she wanted to be anywhere else anyway.

Joining forces with him and Heath did make a lot of sense. Now all she had to worry about was if this Kendrick computer guy would be able to get the information about Dorian's sleeper mission off the damaged hard drive. Now more than ever, she didn't want Dorian to know. After what he'd told her about the episode where he'd hurt his friends, she knew he would take the knowledge that he might've killed his team hard.

There was no need for him to ever have to carry that burden. Although she had to wonder if the event that had triggered him might have been residual mind control from Project Crypt.

It felt weird unpacking her stuff into Dorian's house on the outskirts of town. Or, she should say, one of his houses. Evidently, he spent a lot of time at various cabins out in the wilderness.

But carrying in all of her personal items didn't faze

Dorian in the least. Of course, her weapons and all the data from trying to catch the killer made up 85 percent of her belongings. No one could accuse her of being a clotheshorse.

He placed her weapons with his in his lockbox. Seeing that was just as unnerving as seeing her clothes hanging next to his in the closet.

Gavin showed up not long after they did to pick up the hard drive and take it to Kendrick. She didn't want to let it go but couldn't think of a reason to keep it in her possession that wasn't suspicious.

Gavin must've noticed her face. "Don't worry. I know how important this is. Kendrick is going to do his damnedest to get as much information as possible."

That's what she was afraid of. But she couldn't exactly tell him that.

"Thank you for the safe house," she said instead. "We would've really been in trouble without it."

"Thank you for sticking with our boy and not ditching him."

"I would never leave him alone when he's vulnerable like that."

Gavin shrugged. "The relationship between you two is pretty . . . complex."

"Believe me, I know."

"Complex isn't necessarily bad, though." He gave her a smile. "Okay, I'm out. They're keeping me pretty busy as interim sheriff until Sheriff Nelson recovers."

"Is he doing okay?"

Gavin smiled. "He's a tough old coot. Had a mild stroke, but it won't be long until he's chasing me out of his office. I'll catch you guys tonight at the Eagle's Nest."

Apparently, Dorian had made plans. She watched as

Gavin jogged to his car, then turned to walk back to the house, frowning when she heard Dorian talking to someone else. She hadn't seen anyone go through the door.

"Ms. Peyton said it was okay for me and Jess to come over. Skywalker needed some exercise, and Ms. Peyton needed to finish cleaning Mr. Smith's house."

Ray walked inside and toward the voices in the kitchen. She stayed back so she wouldn't intrude as Dorian knelt down to talk to a little boy and girl.

"Ethan, you be sure to keep Skywalker on a leash when you walk him back down the path. He's much more cray-cray than Storm and might go bounding off if you guys aren't careful."

Did Dorian just say *cray-cray*?

The little girl, maybe four or five years old, thought it was funny, too, and giggled. Dorian ruffled her hair. "And you let Ethan hold the leash in the woods, Ms. Jess. I know you like to think you're as big as him, but you're not quite there yet."

"I'll protect her," Ethan whispered to Dorian. Kid was obviously dead serious about it.

"It's hard to believe the pups are brother and sister," Ethan said. Both children started giggling hysterically as Storm and Skywalker chased each other around in circles. Dorian chuckled too and reached down, scooping both kids up in his large arms, safely out of reach of the dogs' silly antics.

She watched Dorian play with the kids and the dogs, so patient and kind. Ethan and Jess obviously loved and trusted him implicitly.

Nothing about Dorian's actions suggested he was just putting up with them or ready for them to leave. He wanted to spend time with them.

Ray wasn't sure she had the capacity to love the same way Dorian loved these kids. It didn't matter that she didn't have the body parts in working order to make them.

For all intents and purposes, these two children were his niece and nephew. Part of his extended family.

It was time to do what she could to help make them safe. Maybe she wouldn't be able to stay here in Dorian's life afterward—he needed a woman who hadn't done the things she'd done and who could give him the family he deserved —but she could help make sure the ones he loved were safe.

Leaving the laughing and the barking, she walked outside and called Angela.

"Ray? Are you okay? I heard about that mess in Salt Lake City and wasn't sure if I should contact you."

Ray winced. It had never occurred to her to check in with Angela, that the woman might be worried.

"Yeah, I'm sorry. I got caught up with some things with Dorian and didn't call you."

"Dorian was with you in Salt Lake? Are you guys working together? Are you sure you can trust him?"

Ray wasn't about to get into the whole story with her. "Suffice it to say that Dorian isn't the killer. If he'd wanted to take me out, he's had opportunity and means."

"That makes sense. I never really thought it was him anyway."

"We got Phantom's location from the contact before all the shit went down in the club. We went to Phantom's house but weren't able to find him. His dogs were shot dead and just lying there on the porch. We're not sure if that means Phantom has already been killed or if he snapped and is escalating."

"Dead pets are not a good sign either way.""

"At least there's a little bit of good news. Shadow isn't the killer either."

There was a lengthy pause on the other end. "How do you know? I haven't been able to find any information about him or his whereabouts."

"He's been working for Dorian's company, Linear Tactical, but out of the country under an assumed named. He does contract work for them. They were able to pinpoint his location during some of the killings, and he was out of the country. Couldn't have been him."

Angela let out a breath. "Okay. That's good news."

"I've got better news." Well, better as long as no one told Dorian about the sleeper missions. "Neo didn't only hack the information about Phantom. She got curious and dug much further into Project Crypt. Pieced together a lot of what I destroyed when I left and put it on a hard drive."

"What?"

"Yep. It got damaged in the shootout, but Shadow is working with one of the Linear Tactical guys to try to piece together some of the info. I'm not sure exactly what we'll do with it, but at least it can fill in some of the holes."

"Shadow is there right now? I thought you said he was out of the country."

"They pulled him in to help. Dorian, Heath, and I are going to work on this as a united front. Whether Phantom is the killer or someone else, it's time to go on the offensive. To end this."

"What can I do to help?"

"You've done your part. You've already paid too high a price. You need to stay safe and let us do what we're trying to do. Whoever thought they could create fire-breathing monsters and not get burned is about to find out otherwise."

18

Whether Ray liked to admit it or not, there were a lot of situations her training at Project Crypt had prepared her for.

She could survive torture. She could take out an enemy combatant at fifteen hundred yards with a sniper rifle—or at one yard with hand-to-hand combat. She could survive in the wilderness for months at a time with no provisions and through all seasons. And what she could do with the crossbow and crossbow pistol was damn near legendary. Her skills with the knife weren't far behind.

But nothing had prepared her for this.

Meeting Dorian's family.

Because they may not be of blood relation to him, but that's what they were.

His hand was at the small of her back, guiding her through the door of the same bar where she'd eaten a few nights ago. She might be running if it weren't for that touch.

"This place won't trigger you like the Salt Lake City club?" she asked, well aware that it was a stalling tactic more than anything else.

He was too. "You're going to be fine, Ray. These are the people who care most about me, so they're going to accept you too."

That wasn't exactly how it worked. And it wasn't much of a stretch to argue that Ray had brought Dorian more pain than she'd ever brought him anything else.

Greetings rang out as they made it through the door. Despite the many people, Dorian didn't tense at all.

Unlike her.

"Just be yourself," he whispered in her ear before kissing her hair and leading her toward the group of tables his friends had near the back.

As she and Dorian moved closer, all his friends stared at her while trying to hide that they were staring at her. Especially the women. Nobody said or did anything unwelcoming, but none of them looked welcoming either. They already had her pegged as someone who wasn't good for Dorian.

And the worst thing was, they weren't wrong.

Dorian stopped their progress to respond to a waitress who'd wanted their drink order. He had no idea about the animosity his friends, or at least the wives and girlfriends of his friends, were feeling toward Ray. Not that she was going to do anything about it. They didn't have to like her or accept her. The fact that they weren't trying to kill her was enough.

She could accept social shunning with no problem, and she damn well would never let Dorian know that it cracked a tiny piece of whatever was left of her heart. These people may be Dorian's family, but they weren't ever going to be *hers*. So be it.

Ray plastered a smile on her face as they walked the rest of the way to the table when Dorian was done with their order. It didn't escape her notice that his friends had left him a seat that put his back against the wall and gave him visual access to both exits.

These were good people, and they cared about Dorian. They didn't have to care about her.

Everyone was openly staring by the time they got to the tables. Dorian either didn't realize it or didn't care.

But with his next words, she realized she'd been wrong on both counts. Again.

"Everybody," he announced, wrapping an arm around her waist. "This is my Ray."

My Ray.

There was no hesitation, no awkward moment where he tried to categorize what their relationship was. Just a simple, declarative sentence.

This is my Ray.

She could actually see the faces around them change at his words. He'd officially declared her as part of him. So if they were going to accept him, they were going to have to accept her.

There was silence for a few moments, but Dorian just smiled down at Ray like he didn't realize it at all.

"Is this the chick who shot you with the arrow?" asked the small, blond, obviously pregnant woman sitting in the crook of the arm of a hugely muscled man.

Ray forced herself not to tense. It was a fair question.

"It is, Charlie," Dorian answered for Ray before she could do it.

The silence drew out again. Ray wasn't sure if she should say something. Apologize. Explain.

Run.

Finally Charlie nodded. "Okay, good, because I was

wondering if maybe you could teach me how to shoot Finn next time he pisses me off."

And with that, the tension broke. Everyone laughed and the other women started making comments about different lessons they wanted to keep their men in line. The guys merely chuckled good-naturedly.

Everyone talked, and Ray just folded into the group.

The rest of the evening was surprisingly normal. Ray sat by Dorian for most of it, sipping on her beer and getting to know his friends. She met Dr. Diaz, who was much younger than Ray had expected, given how poised and collected she'd been on the phone during Dorian's episode.

The plump and pretty woman didn't look like she could be much older than her mid-twenties. But like Ray, Dr. Diaz —Sierra as she insisted on being called—wasn't part of the inner circle of friends. Some of these people had known each other their entire lives. And the men had all served together in the Army Special Forces, so their bond was almost tangible.

The doctor seemed to spend most of her time observing rather than really interacting, although she had a friendly smile for everyone. Perhaps it was an occupational hazard.

When Shadow walked in, the guys welcomed him with friendly smiles and waves. The ladies obviously appreciated the view, although Charlie was the only one who actually whistled and then immediately blamed it on pregnancy hormones. Her giant husband picked her up and tucked her under his arm on his lap as everyone laughed. Charlie may not be the most polite of the group, but she knew how to break the tension.

Ray stood up to hug the man she'd spent so much time with during their Project Crypt days.

"Hey, Heath."

He smiled and winked at her, so typical for him. "Hi, Wraith. You're looking good."

She dropped her volume, not that anyone was really listening to them. "I'm glad you're here to help out with this Project Crypt mess."

He glanced behind her at Dorian for only a second. "We probably need to talk about what's on that hard drive."

Shit. Had he and Kendrick cracked the hard drive this quickly? She grabbed his arm.

"Listen, Dorian can't know about—"

She cut off immediately when Shadow gave a tiny shake of his head.

"Hey, you two. It's like having the old gang back together." Dorian's arm slipped around her shoulders.

Heath chuckled. "Well, let's try not to get into quite that much trouble."

Dorian looked down into Ray's face and tucked a strand of hair behind her ear. "You okay?"

She summoned a smile. "Yeah. This was not nearly as dramatic as I thought it was going to be. As a matter fact, I might be able to make a full-time living teaching the women of Oak Creek how to shoot their men with a crossbow."

Dorian chuckled, then walked off as someone called his name.

"You and Kendrick have already fixed the hard drive?" she asked as soon as she was sure Dorian's superior hearing wouldn't pick out her words.

Heath didn't quite meet her eyes. "It's complicated."

She had no idea what that meant. "Listen, there's stuff on there I don't want Dorian to know about."

"Ray, listen. Those missions you took . . . Dorian will understand."

"That's on the drive?"

The thought of everything she'd done, the intimate details of those missions before she'd known Crypt was an enemy organization, being made available for anyone—especially Dorian—to see made her sick.

"We need to have a long talk about the drive. There are things you need to know. But this isn't the place."

She nodded. Those years had been ugly, but there wasn't much she could do about it now. "You're right. Just . . . if you could possibly keep the info as private as possible, I'd appreciate that."

Heath grimaced. "Yeah. I understand. We'll talk soon."

Shadow moved closer to the tables to talk to everyone, working the crowd like he'd always been so good at. Dorian was talking to Zac Mackay and Annie Griffin, Annie showing off her new engagement ring.

Ray sat down at a small table close enough to the others to still be part of the group but not necessarily requiring her to talk to anyone.

Until Gavin sat down across from her with his beer a couple minutes later.

He nodded over at Dorian still talking to Zac and Annie. "Our boy is happy."

Ray studied Dorian's face. He was happy. Relaxed. "He trusts the people here. Knows they'll have his back if it's needed."

Gavin nodded. "That includes you. He trusts you too."

"That goes both ways. He and I had a nontraditional restart of our relationship, but I've always trusted him, even when it didn't feel like I should."

"Dorian told me a little bit about what he did to you at the cabin. That was hard on him too."

Ray shrugged. "Believe me, it could've been much worse.

He wouldn't have needed to stretch his imagination to make the questioning much worse."

"Dorian doesn't have it in him to hurt you."

Of course, once he knew the truth about everything she'd done, she wasn't sure he would still want her around. "I don't want to hurt him either."

Gavin took a sip of his beer. "Yesterday, I finally remembered where I knew you from."

Ray fought to hide the tension rising in her body. "Knew me from? I'm pretty sure that didn't happen. Maybe Dorian showed you a picture of me or something."

"Ramstein, Germany. The air force base. You had black hair cut short in a bob. And some sort of padding around your middle, unless you've lost thirty pounds in the past five years."

Shit. "Nope. It's always been blond, and I've always been on the thin side. Good genes. You must be thinking of someone else."

Gavin wasn't buying it. "Dorian had been transferred to Ramstein after his rescue. He was finally starting to come around a little bit. Was saying a few words, could eat and move on his own. He fought hard for his recovery."

She'd been there. She'd seen him. She pushed past the emotion in her throat. "He's always been a fighter."

"There was a civilian doctor there working with Dorian. Guy ended up being assassinated in his sleep. Caused a big brouhaha on base. There hadn't been a lot of action in Germany for a while."

"That's a shame that a doctor was killed like that."

Gavin shrugged one shoulder. "It ends up the good doctor was impersonating someone else. Wasn't authorized to be on base at all. Even had some connections with the Haqqani network."

"Wow. Sounds like someone did everybody a favor, then."

"Yes, I think she did."

"Gavin—"

"I don't know why you're sitting over here by yourself, Ray. Maybe that's just how you roll. God knows we're all used to Dorian needing to be alone. But whatever has that look on your face, that look that seems to say you have some sort of history that Dorian's not going to be able to accept? You need to leave that right here at this table."

She shook her head. "It's not that simple. There are things I've done that you don't know. Dorian definitely doesn't know."

"Let me tell you about the things you've done that I *do* know. Or at least I highly suspect were you.

"That original doctor was specifically there to help Dorian. The terrorist who took his place was specifically there to *hurt* Dorian. You made sure that didn't happen."

She shrugged, not committing one way or the other.

"Dorian was held for forty-one days. We searched every location we knew, shook down every informant we had, and we still couldn't find out where he was. Then on day forty, we got an anonymous tip. The only thing we were ever able to find out about who'd left that anonymous tip? It was a woman. A *blond* woman."

Ray wasn't sure what to say. She'd found out where Dorian was, but she hadn't had the means or the firepower to get him out herself. So she'd gotten the information to the people who could: his Special Forces team.

"It's not as simple as you think," she whispered. "There are things I've done of my own volition, not because someone made me, that anyone would have a problem with."

"Dorian has done some things he regrets too."

"Yeah, he told me about putting you in the hospital."

"And do you think less of him for that? For that loss of control? Do you think less of him because of his episodes or his night terrors or the fact that he has to go live out in the wilderness a couple times a year just to get his head on straight?"

"Of course not."

Gavin stood up and tilted his beer toward her. "Then do me a favor. Respect our boy enough to give him the chance to be okay with your past too."

19

When Dorian woke the next morning, he was a little surprised to find he wasn't alone in bed. Ray was still right there with him—curled up into a little ball at his side for warmth.

God, she had always slept like this when they'd been together. Like she was defenseless and needed someone to protect her. Nothing could be further from the truth.

But also . . . nothing could be *closer* to the truth.

Seeing her last night with his friends—his *family*—he knew there was nothing he wanted more than to fold her into his life.

Secrets be damned.

Yeah, she had them, but he was going to have to accept that she might never be willing or able to share them with him. If she could accept that his mind was broken, that there might be times where he wouldn't be able to sleep in this bed next to her because he couldn't stand to have anything or anyone touching him, that he may be frozen in terror from the past . . .

Then he could damn well accept that she had some

things she wasn't prepared to share.

He pulled her closer, smiling as she unwound her naked body and stretched, lying half on top of him, her head on his chest. He pulled her closer and kissed her hair.

"You're warm," she muttered.

"Your own personal heating service any time you want it."

She rubbed her foot up and down his leg. "I'll take it."

He slid his hand down her naked back, squeezing her waist. "If you keep that up, you'll be taking a lot more."

She chuckled, the sound fading off as she traced a scar— his most recent one, from *her*—on his waist.

"You must have so many questions about me," she whispered.

"I won't lie. I do. But you're not ready to give me the answers right now, and it's okay. It's not a deal breaker for me, Sunray."

"I-I want to tell you. But it's not pretty."

He closed his eyes and took in a deep breath. "Then I want to hear. The past is the past—we're only going to worry about the future."

She was silent for so long, he thought maybe she'd changed her mind about talking. He wasn't going to push it.

"You saved me that day in Kabul. You got captured and were tortured and nearly died because I distracted you."

"Grace . . ." Her name slipped out before he could stop it. "I wouldn't change that. You're alive. And the thought of you being captured . . ."

Jesus. Her being captured, being held in that prison? It would've broken him in every way. There was no way he would've recovered.

"I would be tortured a thousand times before I would have let them take you," he continued.

She rubbed a hand along his stomach, which had tensed at the thought. "I know you would. You saved me that day. It —it's a factor in what I need to tell you now, about the choices I made after Kabul."

That shut him up. He stroked her back instead.

"Like you know, I came to Kabul to tell you what I suspected about Project Crypt."

"About them not being US sanctioned."

She sucked in a small breath. "No, actually. At that time, I'd only found out about the sleeper missions."

"Oh. And you came straight to me with that info?"

Her hand stilled. She was quiet for a long moment. "I-I needed to know what you knew. Needed . . ."

"Needed what?" he asked when she didn't finish.

Her entire body tensed. "Help, I guess. You were who I trusted most. You and Shadow were the only ones I would've even considered going to about Crypt."

There was more, he could tell, but he wasn't going to push. She needed to tell this however she thought best.

"We both would've believed you," he finally said.

"I know. But then you were taken, and my priorities changed. Getting you out became my number one goal."

He shouldn't be surprised. Roles reversed, it would've been his priority also.

"I don't remember much about my rescue. But afterward, Zac and the guys told me they got a tip—that's how they found me." And damn, it hadn't been a moment too soon. He wouldn't have made it another week. "Was that you?"

She shrugged against him. "I had resources they didn't and wasn't afraid to put pressure on the right places."

"Another handy trick Crypt taught us."

"Believe me, I've never been more thankful for my

training than when I was trying to get you out. But then . . ."
she stalled again. "Then, while you were recovering at
Ramstein, I discovered the unthinkable. Crypt had known
your location all along, or at least way before I found it.
They wanted to see if the torture would break your conditioning. They left you in that hellhole as a goddamned
experiment."

Damn Holloman. Damn all of them for messing around
with people's lives.

"Then after—Dr. Flagon at Ramstein? The psychiatrist
who was working with you?"

Dorian nodded. "I remember. He wasn't around for long
though."

"He was Crypt. They sent him to see if you were still
viable as a sleeper agent."

"Jesus. I was barely viable as a human being."

"I know," she whispered. "I was there."

"*What*?"

"When I found out Crypt had sent Flagon, I came to get
you out. I realized Crypt wasn't ever going to leave you
alone. They would push you until you died one way or
another."

"Why didn't you talk to me? I had no idea you were alive,
much less that you were there."

It would've meant everything to him. Given him something to live for. To fight for.

He shifted, sliding out from under her, and getting up
from the bed. He couldn't have any more of this conversation without looking at her. Without understanding why.

For the first time, he was thinking maybe she would've
been better off keeping her secrets.

He slipped on the jeans that he'd dropped haphazardly
over the nearby chair last night. When he turned back to

Ray, she'd scooted herself back against his headboard and wrapped her arms around her legs. He rubbed a hand across his face.

That stance meant she was expecting an emotional blow.

One from him.

Fuck.

Pull it together, Lindstrom.

He sat down at the corner of the bed and pulled in a breath. "I want to understand, Ray, okay? It's just . . . knowing you were alive would've meant everything to me."

Her blue eyes met his. "I killed Flagon. I assassinated him. Without orders."

He was more upset that she hadn't let him know she was alive than that she'd killed the doctor. He should probably feel bad about that, but it wasn't even close. "You did it because you knew he was going to harm me. Roles reversed, I would've done the same."

She nodded, arms still wrapped around her shins. "I've never lost a second of sleep over killing him. But I realized his death wasn't going to stop Crypt. As long as they could get to you, they would keep sending someone."

Her eyes shifted to the window where a storm had been raging all night and rain was still falling. She laid her head on her arms. "I couldn't get you out, Dorian. They were going to hunt us if I did that, and with you, the shape you were in, there was no way we would have made it. I had to find another way."

Those blue eyes closed.

Ice formed in his gut. "What did you do, Ray?"

"I cut a deal with Crypt. At that time, I knew about the sleeper missions, but not that they were rogue. I knew enough to make life difficult for them if I went public, and I made sure that would happen if you or I were killed." She opened her eyes and unwrapped her arms from her legs, stretching them out, covering herself with only a sheet, leaving herself vulnerable. Open for the blow she thought was coming from him.

"I worked for them, Dorian. Willingly. Agreed to take on whatever missions they wanted as long as they left you alone and kept the sleeper-mission shit out of it. It was all I could do to keep you safe."

Whatever missions they wanted? Now it was his turn to close his eyes. "Ray . . ."

"My only defense is that I thought I was working for the US government. I did what they told me, but I thought it was at least for the good of our country. It wasn't."

He opened his eyes to find her staring back out the window. He had to know the extent of it. "What types of missions?"

Her gaze didn't move. "All of them, Dorian. Every single ugly one you can think of, I did. Wet work. Seduction work. Whatever they wanted. I was their good little pet."

Wet work meant assassinations. Which didn't seem to bother him as much as the knowledge that she'd slept with people as part of her jobs.

She let go of the sheet and turned her body until her legs were hanging off the edge of the side opposite him. All he could see was her naked back.

"If you're worried about the fact that you and I had unprotected sex, don't be. I really am clean. I had a close call, a late period, in the middle of working for Crypt. That's when I had the tubal litigation. Because there was no way I was going to chance bringing a baby into my fucked-up life. Once I left Crypt, I got tested again, you know, for STDs. I was clean."

She stood and reached for her clothes.

"Jesus, Ray." He wasn't sure what to say. Where to begin. What did you say to someone who'd ruined their own life to save yours?

Thank you?

You're a dumbass?

"I got out three years ago when I found out they weren't working for our government. At that point, you weren't of much interest to them, I guess. Or they were afraid of everything going public if they came at you."

She slipped a T-shirt over her head.

"And what did you do?"

She didn't turn to face him. "I had spent the previous three years working for enemies of the United States. If I had gone public, I would have taken myself down with them. And honestly, I didn't have enough to do solid damage to Crypt or to justify spending the rest of my life in a CIA holding facility. So I faked my death and destroyed as much of Crypt's research and facilities as possible on the way out."

Dorian felt like his world was collapsing around him. "We should've been working this out together. You should've come to me. If you couldn't at the beginning, why not when I got out of the army and moved here? I was strong enough then. Why didn't you come to me, Gra —Ray?"

He rubbed a fist against his heart as he realized now why she hated her name.

She thought herself unworthy of grace.

"You had a life, Dorian. A family." She turned to face him now. "I met them tonight. Would you have wanted me to bring danger straight to your door? I was handling it."

He slammed his hand down on the bed. "You were pros-tituting yourself to whoever wanted to buy your services!"

As soon as the words were out of his mouth he wanted to take them back. Goddammit, that wasn't how he felt.

He couldn't stand the thought that he'd been tortured for forty-one days, but she'd been tortured for more than three *years*.

"Ray—" he began again.

She was pulling on her jeans. "Don't apologize for saying the truth, Dorian. I sold myself, and I wasn't smart enough to realize to whom."

"None of us had any clue. You were the one smart enough to figure it out in the first place."

She turned to him, rolling her eyes. "What exactly did I figure out? I saw one tiny cube of ice when there was a whole fucking iceberg floating around me. And like you said, I was barely more than a hooker. Just one with highly specialized skills."

"I shouldn't have said that. What I meant was that you shouldn't have tried to shoulder all of the—"

The frantic thumps on the front interrupted him; they reached in tandem under the mattress for their weapons.

Dorian motioned Ray to the side, and she nodded, heading toward the south side of the living room where she'd have a line of sight to the front door through the window.

They were only a couple steps in when the banging came again. "D, it's Zac."

Dorian ran for the door. Zac wouldn't be here in person if it weren't an emergency. He snatched it open to find his friend standing there soaking wet, eyes dark with concern.

"Jess and Ethan are missing."

20

At Finn and Charlie's house, Dorian looked into Peyton Ward's frantic face. Charlie was sitting at the kitchen table, looking pale, clutching a cup of tea. Finn stood right behind her, his normally jovial face serious and drawn.

"Ethan came over to get Jess a couple hours ago with Skywalker." Peyton had been pacing back and forth since Dorian and Ray had arrived with Zac fifteen minutes ago. "It's their normal routine, even in the rain. I didn't give it a second thought."

Finn nodded. "You know the kids. They're in the woods on the paths between the houses all the time. Ethan knows them all backward and forward. Hell, Jess knows them too. We didn't think anything about it until Skywalker showed up about forty-five minutes ago covered in mud."

"Shit. The rains," Dorian muttered.

It had been storming all night. The river was high, the soil was loose. There were way too many places where mudslides or minor rockfalls could be trouble for two kids who had chased an overgrown pup out into the wilderness.

"I wouldn't be worried about them if the dog hadn't come back," Finn said. "Those kids can hardly stand to let him out of their sights. I've already done a pretty thorough search in the area around the paths between our house and Peyton's. The rain is making everything more difficult to track."

Which was why they needed Dorian. He nodded. "We need to get organized. This rain isn't stopping, and if one of them is hurt—"

He stopped when Peyton let out a little sob. Charlie got up and put her arms around the other woman.

Finn already knew what Dorian meant. "I've got Baby gathering people now."

Dorian nodded. Finn's charismatic brother would gather the people they needed for an official search. Normally, they wouldn't start this early, but with two children ages eight and four in this weather . . . Everyone would rather begin now.

"I'll go see what I can find and move from there. I'll take the radio. You and the guys start working from the main trail out."

"I'm going with you."

It was the first thing Ray had said since they'd entered Finn's house. Dorian nodded. Anyone else, even his Linear Tactical team, would slow him down. But Ray wouldn't.

Still. "It's going to be cold."

She flipped him off and turned to the packs they'd brought, emptying out what they wouldn't need. They'd want to be as light as possible.

Less than five minutes later, they were on their way out the door after stopping to give Peyton a brief smile and words of encouragement. Dorian didn't say anything further to Finn. They had the radio for communication since cell phones wouldn't work too far out in the woods. If anything changed on either end, they'd communicate.

He and Ray took off at a brisk jog, Ray never more than a couple of steps behind him. Dorian knew the path Ethan liked to use most and started there. But Finn was right, the storm had washed away almost all traces of where the kids had gone.

He and Ray worked silently, looking for anything Finn might have missed.

Dorian didn't like the ugly words that he and Ray had exchanged, but he appreciated her willingness to push her own needs aside in order to work the task at hand.

Which was what she had done for him too, wasn't it? She'd done whatever she'd had to do to work the problem at hand.

What lengths would he have been willing to go to for her if the roles had been reversed?

Any.

He would've done whatever it took to make sure she was safe, especially while she was healing.

So while the thought of her working for those bastards in ways that hurt her both physically and emotionally churned like acid in his gut, he understood it.

He stopped and turned to her.

"What? Do you see something?" She glanced around her, looking for whatever it was she thought he saw.

"I'm sorry for what I said this morning. What you told me caught me off guard, but I understand why you did it."

She nodded but looked away.

This wasn't the time or the place for a long interpersonal conversation, but his careless words had wiped out all the progress he'd made with Ray to keep her here in Oak Creek.

He walked over to her, got so close that it was a direct affront to her personal space.

"What are you doing, Lindstrom?" She didn't look up at him, just stared at his chest.

"Thank you." He moved closer. "That's what I should've said this morning, but I'm a dumbass who has been alone for too long. You saved my life, and you paid a high price to do it. So, thank you."

She tilted her head up to look at him. "Well, you paid a high price to save my life in Kabul. So how about we call it even? Now, are you ready to find some missing children or do you want to sit around and braid each other's hair and talk about our feelings?"

He didn't try to stop his grin. *This woman*. She had been it for him from the first moment he'd seen her.

She would be it for him until the day he died.

Things weren't totally fixed between them, but it was a start.

"Yes. For God's sake, woman, quit your whining."

The exasperated half smile she gave him created an ache in his chest. How many times had she looked at him the exact same way when they'd been together—like she wasn't sure whether to punch him or kiss him? He'd never thought he'd see it again.

With a huge effort, he turned back toward the path. "If the dog was covered with mud, I say we head out toward the river."

"I agree. I know Skywalker is pretty wild compared to Storm, but how far would he run from them?"

"If Skywalker saw a critter he wanted to chase, he might get pretty excited."

The question was, how far would the kids chase the dog?

He and Ray looked at each other. "River," they both said at the same time.

They moved as quickly as they could in the rain toward the body of water. Just as he'd known it would be, the storm had swollen the river, making it even faster than normal. He looked over at Ray to find her studying something downriver, and he knew she was thinking the same thing he was.

Someone as little as Jess wouldn't last long in those waters. Ethan wouldn't have much more of a chance either.

"If I were searching for them without any clues, I'd head downriver," she said. "But you've got a pretty rocky riverbed here, no mud."

He nodded, but the knowledge didn't make him feel any better. "There's a small ravine about half a mile from here that would be muddy. But it's way far from where Ethan knows he's supposed to be. And it's particularly unstable in weather like this."

"I'd be the first to tell you that I'm not good with kids, so I have no idea what they'd be thinking. And who the hell knows what happens to their thoughts when a dog gets thrown into the mix?"

"Ethan is a good boy. Good head on his shoulders, knows these woods pretty well."

"Then we work on the assumption that something happened that Ethan wasn't expecting, but that he's doing his best to keep them both alive."

He grabbed her hand and squeezed it, praying she was right. They ran through the rough terrain, up toward the place Dorian was afraid Ethan and Jess had gone. Ray had no problem keeping up, not that he'd been worried she would.

When Dorian stopped suddenly, she did too.

"There." He pointed to a spot on the ground where the

rocky riverbed had turned to dirt. One small area had remained sheltered from the storm, and in it was a clear paw print.

Ray nodded. "The dog definitely came this way."

"Kids might have followed."

They both looked up in the direction the print was facing. From here they could see the entire ravine that led farther up into the mountains. At one time, it had been the river's path, until it had cut a new route thousands of years ago.

Now the ravine was dangerous and only experienced hikers used it, and that was in dry weather. In this storm, part of it had already collapsed in some sort of mudslide and rockfall combination.

Dorian let out a low curse. "There are some small caves back in the ravine. Ethan knows not to go there without an adult, but in this storm he might have thought shelter was more important than rules."

"The best way to get up there is straight up, right?"

He nodded. "But it won't take much to trigger another landslide. We might ought to go around the long way. It doesn't do us much good if we break both our legs trying to get to them. Especially if we don't know that they're there."

"I'm a lot lighter and more nimble than you are. How about if I go up and call for them? You take the longer way and see if you spot them. We'll meet up at the top."

He didn't like the thought of splitting up, but she was right. She could make it up those precarious wet rocks much easier than he could. And the storm wasn't showing any sign of stopping.

He grabbed her by the front of her jacket and yanked her close. "Those rocks are no joke. Be careful."

"Yes, sir. I like it when you're bossy."

"Don't think that I'm not aware that you're risking your ass for two kids you don't even know."

She gave him a small shrug. "You know them. You love them. That's enough for me."

Without another word, she was gone.

21

Dorian was right, these rocks were no joke, especially in this weather. It didn't help that Ray's head was pounding again. She ignored the pain. There would be time enough to deal with that when the mission was over.

She moved as quickly as she could, cursing as one misstep sent a pile of rocks sliding. She leapt to the side to avoid being carried down with them, staying planted against a boulder when that small avalanche triggered another one farther up.

Jesus. If two kids and a dog had come scrambling up here, they could already be buried under this rubble.

But that was the worst-case scenario. Like she'd told Dorian, until they had proof otherwise, they would work under the assumption that Ethan was doing his best to keep himself and Jess alive.

Standing still, waiting for the rocks to stop moving, she wiped a hand across her face to remove some of the rain.

Even on her dark glove, she could see the blood. Shit.

Come on Ray, hold it together.

Now was not the time for her body to fall apart.

She gritted her teeth and blinked her eyes hard to eliminate the dizziness. And slowly began to move once the rocks stilled. It took her more time than she liked to reach the caverns Dorian had mentioned. Once she was nearby, she started calling out for Jess and Ethan. She wasn't sure anyone could hear anything over the storm, but if there was a chance, she was willing to take it.

"Ethan! Jess!"

She called over and over, searching in one cavern and finding it empty, working her way back out, and climbing up to the next.

"Ethan! Can you hear me? Jess?"

Would the kids answer her? Weren't kids taught not to talk to strangers? Hell, maybe they were hiding from her, and she was making it worse.

A drop of blood splattered onto her shoes. Ray grabbed the side of a large boulder as dizziness assailed her.

Damn it, she wasn't going to become a third missing person Dorian had to search for.

Gritting her teeth against the nausea, she pushed away from the rock.

"Ethan." Her voice was much weaker this time.

"Mama?"

Ray swallowed. Had that been Jess, or was her mind playing tricks on her? Jesus, maybe this really was a tumor or something.

"Jess? Is that you?"

"Mama? Help."

That was no trick of her mind. No fucking tumor.

"Jess!" Ray forced every bit of power she could into her voice. "Keep yelling, sweetie. I'm going to help you. Can you sing the alphabet really loud?"

Ray let out a laugh of relief when a couple moments later a little voice started singing her ABCs.

"You're doing great, kiddo. Keep going."

Ray saw the girl a few moments later. She was sitting by a pile of rocks, not trying to shelter herself from the storm in any way. Ray made her way up to the girl slowly, careful not to jostle more rocks that could send debris falling on them both.

As soon as she got up to Jess, Ray realized why the girl was sitting in such a precarious location. Not because she was too young to realize the danger, but because Ethan was lying there on the ground, unconscious, one of his legs pinned under a pile of rocks.

"You're not my mommy." Jess looked highly disappointed at that news.

"Yeah, sweetie, I'm sorry. I'm Ray."

"Uncle Dorian's girlfriend."

Ray ripped off her glove with her teeth and felt for Ethan's pulse. It was there, strong and steady. Thank God. She looked over at Jess, who seemed to be waiting for some sort of response to her statement.

Getting into a discussion about the nuances of interpersonal relationships with a four-year-old in the middle of a storm probably wasn't a great idea. "Yeah. I'm his girlfriend. I'm here to get you back to your mom."

"Ethan's hurt bad."

"He's going to be okay."

Little Jess's huge green eyes filled with tears. "I've been trying to keep the rain off of him as much as I could while he was sleeping. I wasn't strong enough to move the rocks. And I didn't know my way home to go get help. And I'm afraid Skywalker is hurt."

"No, Skywalker made it back to Ethan's house. That's

how we knew you guys were in trouble. And you did the right thing staying here with him. He might've been scared without you."

Her lip wobbled, but she nodded. "This cave has a cut through to the other side. Ethan was trying to get us there when the rocks fell."

"How long has Ethan been sleeping?"

"He wakes up and talks to me but then goes back to sleep."

How long would it be before Dorian made his way back to this area? Ray couldn't leave the little boy here. With every minute of rain that fell, the rocks on the incline above them became more precarious. Not to mention, hypothermia was definitely an issue. Both kids had rain gear on, but they had been out in the elements for a long time.

"I'm going to move some of these rocks you couldn't lift, and we're going to take Ethan out through the other side of the cavern, okay?"

Jess nodded. "But you're hurt too." She pointed at Ray's face.

Ray winked at her. "Just a nosebleed, nothing to worry about. Let's focus on Ethan."

The little girl helped her move rocks as best she could, but after a few minutes, Ray told her to sit inside the cavern. She was too little, her hands too clumsy from the cold rain, to be of any real help.

The fact that the kid had stayed outside next to Ethan, when shelter was so close, was amazing in itself. Most kids would have gotten themselves dry and comfortable.

"You stay right here," she told Jess as the girl folded up against the cavern wall. "I'll be back inside with Ethan in a few minutes."

"Be careful of the rocks. I knew I had to protect Ethan from the rocks."

Ray reached over and tweaked Jess's nose. "I'm not going to let any rocks get your boy."

Ray fought through dizziness once again as she stood up, ignoring it and moving forward.

Ethan was moaning and stirring when she got back to him.

"Ethan? It's Ray, Uncle Dorian's friend. I'm going to get you out."

This damn rain wouldn't let up.

Ethan struggled to open his eyes. "Jess?"

"I set her inside the cave where she could be safe and out of the rain."

"I told her to go there," the kid muttered, sounding exactly like Finn.

"Well, evidently you were both too concerned with each other to leave each other's side. But now we've got to get you out of here. The rain is loosening more soil and rocks and there could be another landslide."

Maybe she shouldn't be saying this to a little kid. But hiding the truth from him certainly wasn't going to help him.

Ethan nodded. "I think my leg might be broken."

Ray began removing as many of the small and medium-sized rocks covering his leg as she could. The weight shifting around obviously hurt Ethan, but the kid stayed as stoic as possible against the pain.

"You look a lot like your dad."

"Not really. He's much bigger."

There was a small rumble above them and Ray glanced over her shoulder. A small pile of rocks rolled toward them.

Ray covered Ethan's face and chest with her own torso. "Incoming, buddy."

She gritted her teeth as the pebbles rained down on them, glad there weren't any much bigger than that. She needed to move faster. She shook the rest of the muddy debris off her back, then began digging at the rocks in earnest.

"You're young," she told him. "You've still got plenty of time to grow to your dad's fighting weight."

Ethan hissed as she moved one of the larger rocks closer to his leg. "Uncle Dorian too."

"I'll tell you one thing, your uncle Dorian is going to be pretty freaking proud that you got yourself and Jess to this cave. You almost made it."

Tears leaked out of the boy's eyes. "I—I . . ."

"I know it hurts, buddy. Hang in there."

She was getting to the big rock now. There was no way she'd be able to lift it. It would have to roll.

"Ethan, I am at the big rock. This is going to hurt."

"Wait! Have you seen Skywalker? The man gave him treats . . ." He faded out, breathing rapidly.

"Skywalker's fine. He's back at your house. Let's worry about you now. Ready? One . . . two . . . three."

She rolled the rock off his leg. Ethan's scream broke her heart, then ended as suddenly as it had begun when he passed out. She worked quickly to remove anything else on top of his leg while he couldn't feel any pain. It was definitely broken, but the boulder seemed to have missed most of his knee, and it didn't look like a compound fracture.

The kid wasn't very big, but a fireman's carry was the only way she was going to be able to get him into the cave and out the other side. Hopefully, Dorian would be nearby and be able to help.

Moving him as gingerly as she could, she hoisted Ethan over her shoulder and used her glutes to stand.

Damn kid might be young, but he was solid. He definitely would be following in his father's footsteps.

Little Jess was asleep where Ray had left her against the cave wall. Good, maybe she hadn't heard Ethan's agonizing scream.

"Hey, Jess. Wake up, sweetie. It's time to go." Ray couldn't lean down to help the little girl. It had been difficult enough to get Ethan on her shoulder the first time. She nudged Jess gently with her foot and the girl's eyes opened. She blinked up at Ray.

"I've got Ethan, sweetie, but we need to go."

"Is he okay?" Jess got up, and they began walking deeper into the cavern toward the other opening.

"I think he's going to be fine, but we need to get him home. He won't be able to walk." She grabbed for Jess's hand with her empty one. "Hopefully, Uncle Dorian will be outside and can help us get Ethan back into town."

If not, Ray would just have to gut it out. There was no way Ethan would be able to walk over this terrain with his leg in such bad shape.

Ray swallowed a curse when she saw the low opening at the other end of the cavern. By the time she navigated it, having to get down on her knees and ease her way through with Ethan still on her shoulder, she was breathing heavily.

"You're bleeding again, Ms. Ray."

Ray willed strength into her legs, forcing them upright again once she'd made it through the opening. It was definitely harder this time.

"I'm okay. Do you see Uncle Dorian anywhere around?"
I need you, D.

She had serious doubts about her own ability to get Ethan back down the hill alone.

"I don't see him, but maybe the man would be willing to help us if we could find him."

"What man?" Hadn't Ethan said something about a man also? "What man, Jess? There was someone out here with you guys?"

Jess nodded. "He helped us when Skywalker ran away. But I don't know where he went."

"Did you recognize him? Was he one of Uncle Dorian or Mr. Finn's friends?"

The little girl shook her head. "No. I'm not supposed to talk to strangers, but he helped us with Skywalker. He was sort of quiet."

"I think the little one is talking about me, Wraith."

Phantom stepped out from behind the tree, his handgun pointing straight at her.

22

R ay couldn't reach for her own weapon and get Ethan off her shoulder at the same time.

"Keep your hands out where I can see them."

"Mason, what are you doing here? Whatever you want, it has nothing to do with these kids." She wrapped her arm over Jess's shoulder and pushed the girl behind her.

"It didn't have to involve these kids. *You* involved them when you came after me," he said.

Phantom was dressed for the weather. He had planned this operation from the beginning.

"I didn't come after you, Mason. I've got no beef with you at all."

He shook his head slowly. "You shouldn't have killed my dogs, Wraith. They were all I had left. And now, I'm going to have to hurt what you and Ghost love to make up for it." He gestured to Ethan and Jess peeking out from behind her legs.

"I didn't kill your dogs. They were already dead when Dorian and I got there. I'm really sorry about them—"

"I saw you!" Phantom's voice switched from calm to

screaming; Jess burried her face in Ray's thigh and whimpered.

"How? How could you have seen me kill them if I didn't do it?" She knew that sentence didn't make a lot of sense, but the best she could hope for was to make him realize that the reality he thought was true, wasn't. Dorian struggled with the same thing sometimes.

"I swear I didn't kill your dogs, Mason. I don't know who did, but I can help you find out. We can punish them together."

"Knew you would say that. But I saw you. Eyes don't lie." Phantom took a step closer, and she took a step back. "Why is your nose bleeding?"

Ray didn't know, but it wasn't good. She was dizzy. Ethan felt almost unbearably heavy, and he shouldn't be. She should be able to carry his weight, more even, for much longer than this. Even watching Phantom now, he looked blurry, like her eyes couldn't quite track him correctly.

She didn't know what the fuck was going on with her body, but she had to get these kids somewhere safe.

Now.

Mason shook his head. "My nose sometimes bleeds. It was getting better. Why did you have to go and kill them, Wraith? I never had any problem with you."

Ray struggled to focus on his face. "I promise it wasn't me. Maybe it was someone who looks like me."

Phantom looked like he wanted to believe it. This was her chance. If she dove to the right, she might be able to get her gun from her side holster before Mason could get them back in his line of sight.

"It was you. You and Ghost. I never did anything to either of you. I was just trying to survive."

Ray took a slight step to her right. "I'm telling you, it

wasn't us. We were looking for you to try to help you. We have the same enemy."

Unless Mason was a pathological liar or had completely broken from reality. Either was not only possible, but probable. In which case, they didn't have the same enemy. Phantom *was* the enemy.

The word *enemy* was the completely wrong thing to say. His nostrils flared and eyes narrowed. She was out of time.

Grabbing Jess's hand, she dove as hard as she could to the right into the cover of some bushes and trees, turning in midair so she could take the brunt of the fall, protecting Ethan and his broken leg.

She kipped up, weapon in hand, almost automatically. She kept a watch out for Phantom as she spoke.

"Stay with Ethan," she told a crying Jess. Ray hated to leave her like this, but survival was the most important thing.

Ray dashed back into the open, hoping to catch Phantom unaware, but he was waiting for her. She didn't stop her forward progress, instead using her momentum to plow into him. Both of their weapons went flying.

Ray got one good uppercut into Mason's jaw before rolling away.

"Killing those kids won't bring your dogs back." She twisted around to face him. "You think I did it? Fine. Then you take it out on me."

Mason tilted his head as he got up, studying her. Both weapons were closer to him.

"You can't beat me hand-to-hand," he said evenly.

He was right. Especially not in the shape she was in. They'd all had their specialties; hers had been the crossbow. Phantom had excelled at knife work and close-quarters fighting.

She would try. Maybe she'd get lucky and incapacitate him. Maybe he wouldn't go after the kids.

She pounced, hoping for the briefest element of surprise.

She should've known better. Phantom sidestepped her aggressive attack, spinning around and catching her midback with a sidekick. She grunted, the only sound she allowed herself through the searing pain in her lower ribs. Definitely cracked.

The momentum threw her to the ground, and she rolled. A half second later, Mason's booted foot stomped on the ground where her head had been.

Ray leapt up, swallowing a moan as the motion torqued her midsection. She landed on her feet and immediately spun with a kick of her own, catching Phantom the slightest bit off guard and knocking him back a few feet.

He came at her again.

It was all she could do to keep up. To block the most damaging blows and stay on her feet.

But she wasn't doing any damage herself, merely prolonging the inevitable outcome of this battle.

Taking a blow to the jaw that spun her around and into a tree a couple seconds later reinforced that point.

But there was a branch.

This was her only chance. Leaning against the tree, partly because she really needed the breather and partly to draw Phantom in closer, she reached around and grabbed the stick. Using it as a club would be her best option. And she would only get one swing.

"I expected more from you, Wraith."

She spun with the club, aiming for his head.

He ducked easily, obviously expecting it. A solid kick to her gut sent her staggering back. Before she could breathe around the agony, he had her by the hair, his fist crashing into her face. Between the storm, her wounds, and the weakness she'd been fighting all day, she could barely make his features out.

Keeping his grip on her hair, he pulled her face right up to his.

"You should've left me alone. I heard you were dead. Let's see if this time you stay that way."

She tried to break away as he reached down into his boot and pulled out a knife. He could've ended this at any time. He'd been playing with her.

All she could hope for now was that this wasn't all in vain. That Dorian would find the kids, and they'd make it out alive.

She made one more attempt to break Phantom's hold but failed. His laughing, mocking face was the last thing she saw as everything faded to black in a blur of pain.

DORIAN STEPPED up behind Phantom and snapped his neck before he could slide his knife into Ray.

The man fell dead to the ground in an instant, and Dorian didn't spare him another glance. Not when Ray was lying unconscious right in front of him.

Phantom had been smart; he had left Dorian a false set of tracks at the top of the hill. By the time Dorian had realized there was no way the kids had gone all the way up there, he'd almost been too late to help Ray.

He reached down and picked her up carefully, not sure of the extent of her injuries. Ray could take a hit, so her being unconscious for more than a few seconds had fear clawing at the back of his throat.

"Hang in there, Sunray," he whispered against her hair as he walked her back toward the cavern. He had to get her out of this rain. Get help up here immediately.

He passed by Jess huddled protectively over Ethan. The boy had a stick in his hand and was trying to get Jess to move behind him so he could protect her. The kid looked like he was barely hanging on to consciousness himself.

"You two okay?"

"Yes."

Ethan had barely gotten out the word before Jess took over talking. "No, he's not. His leg is broken, and he's hurt bad."

Dorian respected that the kids were keeping it together during a crisis. He gave Ethan a nod. "Your dad and help will be up here soon."

He carried Ray inside the cavern and set her down gently. Her nose was bleeding, but she was stirring a little. Fear released its icy grip on his heart. He rushed back outside to pick up Ethan and bring them inside too.

He grabbed the radio out of his pack. "Eagle, this is Ghost, come in, over."

"Go ahead, Ghost, over."

"I've got them, Finn. I think Ethan's leg is broken, but he's conscious and has a little nurse fretting over him."

There was silence for a moment, no doubt due to relief as Finn passed the news around.

"That's good to hear, Ghost. Give me your location and we'll be up with the stretcher."

Dorian stepped back out into the rain in hopes of shielding the kids from his next words. "We're going to need two stretchers and a body bag."

Finn's curse was low and ugly. "Are you okay?"

"Looks like we found the killer Ray and I have been

looking for. Ray took some hits taking him down. She's in bad shape."

"Are you guys secure?"

"Looks that way."

There were a couple more moments of silence. "Gavin and Aiden are already on their way up to you. They'll make sure the extended area is secure. Medical will be a little behind them."

"Thanks, Finn."

"Thank you, brother. And thank Ray for us."

"Will do."

He walked back into the cavern. Jess was staring at Ray with concern.

"I know it looks like a lot of blood, sweetheart, but Ray got into a fight with that man."

"And she was already bleeding when she got here," Jess said.

"She was?"

Jess nodded. "Her nose was bleeding."

That made two nosebleeds that he knew of. Plus the headaches.

He crouched down next to her as those blue eyes fluttered open.

"Dorian?" She started to sit up, but he put a hand on her shoulder.

"We're secure. You need to stay immobile until we're sure about your injuries."

"Phantom?"

"Handled. No longer a threat."

She nodded once. "He was convinced I'd killed his dogs. He said coming after the kids was his revenge."

Dorian turned to Ethan and Jess. "Did he hurt you? Are you sure you're okay?"

"He was the one who told us he saw Skywalker," Ethan said, face tight. "I never would have come up here otherwise."

Dorian nodded. "You can take that up with your dad."

"Is Ethan in trouble?" Jess asked, her little lip quivering. Kid didn't cry running from a killer, but Ethan getting in trouble? Now came the tears.

No doubt Phantom had used the dog as a means to lure the kids away.

"You and Ethan are both safe," Ray whispered. "That's the most important thing."

Dorian looked over at her. "It's more than just them safe, thanks to you, all of us are safe."

He sat down next to her and took her hand. She smiled weakly at him and closed her eyes.

Another drop of blood fell from her nose.

23

Ten days later, Dorian held Ray in his arms as they slept.

Ten days of everything he'd stopped hoping for when he'd thought Ray had died. Ten days of things that other couples had every day and took for granted.

Eating with each other. Laughing. Rolling their eyes at each other's annoying habits—he left books everywhere, she kept turning up the thermostat.

Learning each other.

Making love.

Ray had been almost frighteningly weak for a while, so Dorian hadn't wanted to touch her in that way. But for someone renowned for his control, he found he had absolutely none when it came to Grace Brandt rolling her lithe body atop his, those big blue eyes staring at him with need.

It was all he could do not to keep her body tucked under his constantly, making love to her slowly and gently. Over and over.

Where he could take care of her. Where he could help heal her. Not just her body, but her mind.

Where he could make her feel his love.

It was going to take time. The damage from her years with Crypt wouldn't go away overnight. There were different types of torture.

He'd lived through one. She'd lived through another.

But they'd both lived through it.

When Ray was still barely able to get out of bed after the first three days, he'd talked her into letting Annie come over and check her out.

He'd stayed in the room—at Ray's request—while Annie did a basic physical. At the end, the doctor had smiled at them both.

"The nosebleeds are a concern, but they're not terribly uncommon and seem to be tapering off, along with your headaches. That's a good sign."

Ray raised an eyebrow at him. "See?"

He put a hand over her face and pushed her back down onto the pillow as she giggled.

That sound. God, he just wanted to listen to Ray's light-hearted laughter for the rest of his life.

Annie's smile got bigger at the sound too. "She's had a pretty stressful few months. Her body was probably letting her know it needed a break." Annie looked at Ray. "But, just to be sure, why don't you come by the hospital next week? We can run some tests. I know ID might be an issue, so I can work around that if needed."

Ray grabbed his arm and used it to help her sit back up. "Thanks, Doc. ID is an issue, at least until we get everything completely taken care of."

Ray was concerned that her ID could be tied to some of the crimes she'd committed for Project Crypt. Since Grace Brandt was legally and technically dead, it was much better to keep it that way.

Annie patted her on the arm. "It's probably overly cautious anyway. You're young, you're healthy. It's getting better, not worse." She stage-whispered, "But maybe it will keep the menfolk from worrying too much."

Dorian rolled his eyes and got up to walk Annie to the door. "Thanks for coming. I owe you two bottles of wine now."

The quiet doctor smiled. "I'll look forward to it. And Dorian, make sure Ray comes in next week for those tests."

"I thought you said they're precautionary. That she's young and healthy."

Annie shrugged. "She is. But that should also mean no problems in the first place. Let's just rule stuff out."

"I'll make sure it happens." Even if he had to carry her there himself. He kissed Annie's cheek. "Thanks again."

"I couldn't be more happy to help. I promise."

But two days later, he'd found he couldn't wait that long for the tests. Ray had tried to hide it, but her headaches were near constant. When he'd found bloody tissues, evidence of more nosebleeds, he'd straight up bullied her into going to get the test done.

The fact that she didn't argue scared him even more.

God bless Annie Griffin. Dorian owed her an entire carton of wine for this. She'd personally run a CT scan and a number of other tests on Ray while Dorian had waited with absolutely zero of his normal patience for them to be through, then she promised the results within forty-eight hours.

And now it was time for the follow-up visit. He kissed Ray, waking her, scooting her out of bed with no decorum. She was looking pale, but not unhappy, as they made their way back to Annie's office.

"I can't imagine what tests like these cost."

Dorian wrapped an arm around her as they walked in from the parking lot. "The fact that Annie and Riley are doing it all themselves helps a lot. Also, the hospital in Oak Creek has a private donor who helps out in situations like this."

"Situations where ex-assassins are having mysterious headaches and nosebleeds? That happen a lot in your town?"

"Generally only two or three times a week, smart ass. Cade Conner is from here, and he lost a friend due to lack of medical care. He wants to make sure that doesn't happen to anyone else."

"Cade Conner, as in the award-winning country singer that even I know about?"

"He'd be the one. Born and bred in Oak Creek, though as O'Conner, not Conner. But Annie will use funds from that, and we'll make a generous donation to help replenish some of what was used."

Ray nodded. Both of them had money stashed away that they could access as needed. It wasn't like having a checking account, but anybody who worked black ops learned to make sure they had money available.

Walking into Annie's office, Dorian practiced some of the breathing techniques Dr. Diaz had taught him. At the time, he'd just learned them to humor her, but right now he needed them. He hadn't felt fear like this in six years.

Hell, he wasn't sure he'd felt fear like this when the Haqqani network had held him prisoner. Pain, despair, anger, resignation that his own death was imminent, and even desire for it? Yes to all those things.

But at that point, he'd thought the worst thing had already happened to him—losing Ray. To think about losing her now, when he'd just gotten her back, nearly dropped him to his knees.

"It's going to be okay, D." Ray slipped her hand in his.

More than anything in the world, he wanted to believe her. He knew she still had secrets. Knew there were things they would have to work out. But all that was secondary to surviving.

Survival was always the most important thing. It was the very first lesson they taught at Linear.

Everything else was secondary.

As they walked down the hall, Ray hummed a tune under her breath. They were almost to the office door before Dorian realized what song it was.

"Are you kidding me right now? 'Live Like You Were Dying'?"

She grinned up at him. "I think I could go a couple seconds on a bull named Fu Manchu."

God, this woman. He stopped right there and eased her back against the hospital wall, boxing her in with his body.

"You're it for me, Grace Ray Brandt. You've always been it for me. I love *every single piece of you*. The ones that make you Ray and the ones that make you Grace—I'm in love with them all. No matter what news we get in there, you will always be it for me."

"Dorian . . ."

"I mean it, Ray. I know there are still secrets between us, but from here on out, you and I are in this together."

A shadow crossed her face. "I love you too, but I need to tell you—"

The door to Annie's office opened. "There you guys are. Get in here."

Dorian leaned his forehead against Ray's. "We'll finish this talk later."

He took her hand, and they walked inside the office.

Annie sat down behind her desk. "I don't believe in beating around the bush with stuff like this, so I'm just going to get to it."

Dorian prayed. He prayed to the God he had always believed in but felt betrayed by in that enemy prison. He prayed with just a single word.

Please.

Please.

Please, God. *Please.*

Annie cleared her throat. "I found absolutely *nothing.* Nothing to suggest a tumor, nothing to suggest any sort of blocked vein or aneurysm. There is nothing, based on the tests I ran, to suggest you have any sort of life-threatening medical concern."

Dorian couldn't stop the huge breath of air from escaping his body in a rush, leaving him almost lightheaded.

Annie was saying other stuff, explaining other health issues that could be causing the problem, from allergies to altitude to stress. Dorian was barely listening because it didn't matter. Whatever was causing the problem, they had time—*sweet, sweet time*—to figure it out.

The two women were in the middle of a conversation when Dorian stood and plucked Ray straight out of her chair and into his arms.

She giggled, the sound like a rainbow for his ears.

"Thank you, Annie. I owe you an entire vineyard full of wine. But right now, I've got to get this one home."

"Why?" Ray whispered in his ear. "Does Fu Manchu need to see if I can make the ride longer than 2.7 seconds?"

He turned his head and caught her lips with his. "Hell, woman, I'm already going to last an embarrassingly short length of time as it is. Let's not start measuring it in seconds."

Annie, laughing, said goodbye as he set Ray on her feet and all but dragged her down the hallway and into the truck. Her wandering hands didn't help the situation as he drove home much faster than what was legal or safe.

Those clever fingers of hers were making their way up his thigh as she unbuckled her seatbelt and moved closer to him.

"I'm healthy as a horse, so are you going to stop treating me like you're afraid I'll break?" She nipped his ear; he nearly swerved off the road.

"They've asked Gavin to fill in while Sheriff Nelson is recovering from his stroke and the accident."

"I know. But what does that have to do with treating me like I'm breakable?"

He glanced over at her for a split second before returning his eyes to the road. "If you keep this up, and I pull over on the side of the road and bend you over the hood of the truck and fuck you till neither of us can see straight, he might feel bad about arresting one of his best friends for indecent exposure."

She laughed. "Potty mouth. I guess you better hurry up and get us home."

It took all his focus not to kill anyone as he drove. Once in his driveway, he barely remembered to put the truck in park and take the key out of the ignition before dragging Ray across the seat and out the driver's side door.

"Check the front door, I'll check the back." His voice was ragged. He wanted Ray more than he wanted his next breath, but he wasn't willing to risk her safety. Not for anything.

Once he checked the windows and back door and saw

they hadn't been tampered with, he made his way back to the front door.

She was standing on the front porch, her blue eyes tracking him. "Clear."

He walked up to her and wrapped an arm around her hips, lifting her and opening the front door at the same time. Once he had her inside the house, he couldn't wait any longer. He turned around, pushing her up against the door.

"Now, Grace. I've got to have you right damn now."

She didn't make any protest, just reached between them, unzipping his jeans and then her own.

He wanted to slow down, to make this last, because the way he was feeling, it really wasn't going to be much longer than 2.7 seconds. But he couldn't.

She ripped her lips away from his. "I want you to take me the way you would've on the truck. Take me like you know you can't hurt me. Like you know we've got forever." She cupped his cheeks with her hands. "Because we do."

There were so many things he wanted to say, but they would have to wait.

He carried her over to the couch, both of them stripping off clothes as they went.

She smiled at him as she folded herself over the arm of the couch. "I don't want gentle, soldier. I want to celebrate being alive."

He ran a hand from the top of her neck all the way down her spine. Frontward or backward, this woman was always going to take his breath away.

He reached down, grabbed her by the hips and flipped her over so she was facing him. "I will gladly take you in this position until we damn near get arrested even inside my own house. But right now, I need to see your eyes, and I need to see your face." He dropped his hand to her chest. "I need to feel your heart against mine."

She nodded. "I want to be close to you too."

He slid his hands down to her ass and lifted her up, then walked them both around to the front of the couch so he could sit, his breath coming out in a hiss as she slid herself on top of him. Her blue eyes pinned his as she slowly worked herself up and down his length.

This was it, their beginning. No more deadly threats from the outside, no more deadly threats from inside her body either.

Just the two of them and whatever the future held.

24

D orian was surprised three days later when Ray asked him if it would be okay for her to talk to Dr. Diaz for a couple hours.

He looked across his kitchen table at her where they were sharing grilled cheese sandwiches for lunch.

"Yes. I'll call her right now." He didn't hesitate to answer.

Ray talking to Dr. Diaz was the best idea he'd heard in *ever*. Annie may have cleared Ray in terms of her physical health, but it was obvious things still weighed on her emotionally. Dorian would've suggested talking to the psychiatrist earlier, but it had to be something she initiated.

"Not about you. I know she has patient–therapist confidentiality stuff, and I would never ask her to break that."

He held out a hand to stop her. "No, you can ask her anything about me. Talk about anything to do with me. I don't have secrets when it comes to you. I'll tell Dr. Diaz, sign whatever she needs."

"Dorian . . ."

He picked up their plates, leaning down to give her a kiss as he walked by. "We don't have to be at the same place at the same time. When you're ready to tell me what you have to tell me, you will."

He called Dr. Diaz right after lunch and was surprised at how willing she was to make room for Ray in her schedule. She was even willing to see Ray today.

Dorian didn't question it. He drove Ray over to the office and explained his position to Dr. Diaz, giving the doctor permission to talk about anything they'd discussed in their sessions.

He wasn't going to have any secrets from Ray.

He kissed Ray on the forehead, ignoring her pinched features. "First time is the hardest," he whispered. "But Sierra is the best."

He walked around town while Ray and Sierra talked. He'd spent all of the past two weeks with Ray, mostly in bed, but they'd also gone outside so she could practice with her crossbow pistol among the trees behind his house.

He loved to watch her shoot that thing. Loved the tricks she could do—shooting two quarrels at once to hit separate targets. Hitting targets based on sound alone. Drawing, loading, and shooting at a jaw-dropping pace.

He loved the peace on her face when she held that crossbow pistol. It was a part of her, and he could tell that having it in her hands beat back the pain that still clouded her eyes sometimes.

Maybe he'd take her out to another one of his cabins—his special one, the one deepest in the wilderness, where he'd never taken another living soul. He'd built it himself, from top to bottom, near a river that he used to provide both basic electricity and running water. A generator and solar power setup provided the rest. On a whim, he'd added a second room a couple of years ago, even though it hadn't made any sense.

Maybe he'd always known he'd bring Ray there at some point.

He'd take her there for a while and let her shoot as much as she wanted, not having to worry about anything else. He'd talk about it with her tonight after Zac and Annie's engagement party at the Eagle's Nest.

Dorian stopped in and had a cup of coffee at the Frontier Diner, chatting with a few people. Most asked how Ray was doing. She'd become a bit of a celebrity after rescuing the kids.

Phantom laid in the morgue as a John Doe since he hadn't carried any identification and his prints had brought up nothing. Only Dorian, Heath, and Ray knew him as Mason Wyndham, and none of them offered the information to Gavin as sheriff.

Having a name wouldn't have given Gavin any more details. Instead, it was filed as a botched kidnapping attempt that Ray and Dorian had fortunately stopped, killing the suspect in the process of protecting the children.

Yeah, Dorian definitely needed to get Ray away from everything. Let her have some time to herself. Hell, he'd even leave if she needed it.

Although he'd be back. That was for damn sure.

When Dorian got the text that Ray was finished, he made his way back to Dr. Diaz's office. He wasn't exactly sure what he'd expected to find, but the psychiatrist looking absolutely gutted was not it.

"Ray went down to use the bathroom. She'll be back in a few minutes."

Ray hadn't given the same permission for Dr. Diaz to share information with him, so he didn't want to ask. But the look on Sierra's face was bringing back those same terrified feelings he'd had in Annie's office.

"You okay there, Doc?" She'd heard him talk about some of the most hideous atrocities humans could do to each other, and she hadn't ever reacted like this.

She nodded but didn't say anything. Her mouth opened, but it was like she couldn't get the words out.

"Jesus, Sierra. Listen, I know you can't tell me, but do I need to do something? Is Ray in danger? I don't give a damn about legalities if we're talking about something that might cost her her life."

Had he misjudged? Maybe Ray was depressed, suicidal, and he'd totally missed it. Could he have been that oblivious?

Dr. Diaz finally pulled herself together enough to get words out. "No, she's not in danger. She's not going to hurt herself or someone else. You have to talk to her. She has to tell you."

Something eased inside him, but not all the way. "Okay."

Survival was the most important thing. He wasn't letting anything take Ray from him.

"She and I will work through it."

"I know you will." But the doctor's face said the opposite. "Excuse me, I've got to get outside for a few minutes."

She was past him and out the door before he could figure out anything else to say to her. When Ray came back to the office a few minutes later, he was relieved that she didn't seem nearly as distraught as Dr. Diaz.

But then again, Ray had a lot more experience keeping her feelings hidden. He pulled her into his arms, grateful when she didn't resist in any way. "Are you okay?"

She nodded against his chest. "I think so. Talking about feelings definitely isn't my strong suit, but Sierra was really patient and quick on the uptake. I never felt like she was having difficulty believing what I said. Even when it seemed a little farfetched."

"She's had years of practice with me. I'm glad you're okay. Dr. Diaz seemed a little rattled."

She leaned back, looking up at him. "I thought so too, but then I figured maybe that was how she reacted to everything."

Dorian had never seen Sierra that rattled. But Ray was his number one priority.

"Listen, whatever it is you've got to say, I can take it. *We* can take it. Together. Why don't we forget about going out with everyone tonight?"

"No, I want to. I need a night of normal and fun with the people you call your family. Then . . ."

"Then what?"

She shrugged and looked down. "Then maybe I can call them my family too, someday."

"Deal. And whatever it is we need to talk about, we'll start on it fresh tomorrow."

"What if it's bad?"

"It's in the past, and that's all that matters. I love you. We'll face it together."

25

Ray could do this.

Dorian was right. They needed to handle the situation together. Dr. Diaz had seemed pretty shook up when she'd told the woman about Dorian's sleeper mission to kill his Special Forces team. She'd already known about Project Crypt, although not by name, from her sessions with Dorian. It was only when Ray mentioned the sleeper missions that the doctor lost some of her composure. But Sierra had definitely encouraged Ray to tell Dorian the truth. Even though it would be hard, it was time.

Dorian had helped her deal with her past; she would help him deal with his.

He'd already gone on to the Eagle's Nest. She was meeting him there. After everything she'd gone over with Sierra today, she needed a little time on her own.

She also needed to make sure her nose didn't start bleeding in the middle of the shindig tonight.

She trusted Annie, believed the doctor when she said there was nothing showing up in any of the scans and tests, but the truth was Ray's head never stopped hurting now. It was a constant pain, one that occasionally became so bad she could barely hide it. The nosebleeds were coming more often too.

If this was allergies, then they must have some killer pollen around here or something.

She looked in the mirror as she finished putting on the last of her makeup and sighed. She was going to have to tell Dorian about that too. He would worry, but she wasn't doing either of them any favors by trying to take it all on herself.

But that would have to wait until tomorrow also. Tonight was about celebrating life and love.

She was on her way out the door when she got a text from Angela.

Are you okay?

Ray winced. She hadn't been keeping Angela in the loop as much as she should have. She'd let her know about Phantom so Angela would know she didn't need to worry about that anymore, but then she'd been too busy living her own life—enjoying time with Dorian—to do much more. It was selfish.

She texted back.

Yeah, I'm good. Just taking a break. I'm glad this is all finally over. About to go meet Dorian and his buddies for a little fun. Something new.

Ray walked out to her car when Angela didn't answer right away.

Including Shadow?

Okay, weird. *Yes. Why?*

No reason.

Angela was acting strange. Really strange. Maybe she was having a hard time adjusting to the fact that this was all over. Ray had Dorian, and the use of her legs, but Angela was pretty much alone, and when it was all said and done, she might've paid the highest price of all. Maybe Ray should see about bringing Angela to Oak Creek and getting her a job or something.

Ray started the car and drove the few miles toward town. She was really going to stay. She was going to make this work with Dorian. Maybe they couldn't have a traditional family, but that was okay. They would just be everyone's really cool aunt and uncle.

Marriage.

Jesus, Dorian hadn't so much as said the word, but they both knew that was where they were heading. It would've happened a long time ago if things hadn't gotten so ugly with Crypt.

But like Dorian said, the past was the past. They would start a new future together.

One she was pretty damn excited for.

She pulled up to the Eagle's Nest, a stupid smile still blanketing her face, when she got another text from Angela.

I wasn't being honest before. I'm already in Oak Creek. I need to show you something that will change everything.

What the hell? *Where are you?*

I'm sorry, Wraith. I should've told you I was here, but I didn't know how to explain.

Ray stared at her phone. *Where?*

I'm in my van in the back lot of the hospital.

That was only a couple of blocks from where Ray was parked. Angela had a van that allowed her to drive with her partial paralysis. *I'm coming to you. Stay where you are.*

And she damn well wasn't going in blind. Ray reached under the seat and found the SIG P226 handgun hidden there. She already had a knife strapped to her ankle in her boot.

She jogged quickly to where Angela had parked, then held back so she could observe the van for a couple minutes without being seen. No one seemed to be around. No one was casing the vehicle.

Another text came in.

I'm in the back.

Ray stayed in the shadows as she darted over. She tamped down her irritation at more cloak-and-dagger stuff. She was ready for this part of her life to be over. She wanted the new part to begin. The Dorian part.

But she would hear Angela out first.

She tapped on the door before opening. Angela sat in her motorized wheelchair at a small desk with a computer monitor. She had pictures of all the once-active Crypt agents on the screen.

It looked like Angela wasn't ready to let this go.

Ray climbed inside and closed the door behind her. She crouched down next to Angela's wheelchair and grabbed her hand, giving it a squeeze. "Hey. You doing okay?"

Angela stared down at where their hands touched. Ray couldn't blame her—it might've been the first time Ray had ever touched the other woman.

"I'm glad you're here," Ray continued. "I was thinking maybe Oak Creek could be a home for you too."

Angela shook her head. "I don't think so. There's still some stuff that needs to be done with Project Crypt. Things I'm afraid you're not going to like."

"Angela, I'm done. We got the killer, and as far as I'm concerned, I want to move on. Dorian and I want to start a life together."

"But do you know all the stuff Holloman and the rest of the leaders at Crypt did?"

Ray nodded. "I know about it all. I know about the

sleeper missions, and I know that after the first couple of years, Crypt wasn't sanctioned by the US government anymore. When I got out, I destroyed as much as I could. All the info and research. I couldn't take Holloman down, but I could make sure that that info didn't stay in the hands of a group that was working for their own gain, not for the good of the country."

"You destroyed it all."

Ray smiled. "Every single damn piece I could get my hands on."

"That had to have made Holloman so angry."

Ray wasn't going to lose any sleep over that. "I hope so."

"You have no respect for the years of labor and millions of dollars that went into that research. The brilliance behind it."

Oh shit. Angela was offended. She was a scientist—Ray should try to use a little more tact. "You're right. But I'm not sorry. I can't be. Even if there was good that could've come out of that research, I'm not sorry I destroyed it."

She wasn't sorry she'd destroyed it, but she was sorry it hurt Angela's feelings.

"Maybe if you hadn't done that, things would've been different." Angela stared at the screen, shaking her head. "Maybe Crypt would've left you alone. Maybe they would've left Ghost and Shadow alone. They wouldn't need them."

"What are you talking about?"

The entire world shifted in front of Ray's eyes as Angela stood up from her wheelchair.

"Angela? What the hell?"

"You made us start over almost completely from the beginning."

Everything snapped into place in Ray's mind with a horrible efficiency. "*You're* the killer."

Angela actually laughed. "Don't be an idiot. Even out of my wheelchair, I couldn't take out Project Crypt agents."

"But you were working with the killer this whole time?"

Angela smiled, and nothing about the small facial gesture was comforting. "Yes."

She'd never been on the same side as Ray. Angela had always had her own agenda.

"We had to start again after your little stunt." The woman paced inside the van as Ray struggled to wrap her head around it all. "Version 1.0 of our research was always meant to be temporary, but losing all the data was a setback we hadn't expected. Your fault, Ray. Never forget that it was your fault. Just like you assuming that I didn't have an important role in Project Crypt. I did. I always did."

Ray had heard enough. She grabbed Angela by the shoulder and spun her around, backing her up against the side of the van, forearm to her windpipe.

Ray got right up in her face. "Is there some reason you think I'm going to let you get away with this? Any reason I should let you leave this van alive at all?"

Angela whispered something Ray couldn't quite make out. She eased her arm off the other woman's throat just slightly.

"Forever rockets pink and orange cried."

Ray couldn't feel her own arms. They fell from Angela's throat. She tried to move them again, but no matter what she did, they stayed glued to her sides. Her legs were the same.

She couldn't move her head to follow Angela as she walked around Ray and sat back down in her wheelchair. Ray was left staring at the van wall in front of her where Angela had been standing.

The only thing she could feel was the panic bubbling up inside her.

"You destroyed our research, Wraith, so it's only fitting that you bring us the pieces we need to move on to Version 2.0." At her desk, Angela leaned forward. Ray could just see the woman out of the corner of her eye. "We need Shadow. Heath is *very* special, the key to it all. We didn't know he was alive until he showed up attached to Linear Tactical."

"I don't understand." She could barely get the words out of her stiff mouth.

"I know you don't. This is complex stuff. The brain is a pretty miraculous thing. The conditioning we did to your minds isn't like something you see in a movie. We couldn't just create a phrase and you'd kill *anyone*. Each of you was programmed for a specific target."

"Manuel Cuellar," she mumbled.

Angela gave a big nod. "That's right. You discovered he was your sleeper mission. I'll bet you wish you could remember what happened that week, don't you?" Angela had moved and was now whispering in Ray's ear. "I hear Cuellar was into some pretty deviant stuff. Do you think you might have liked some of it? Do you know we programmed you so you would beg him to do whatever he wanted? I wonder what you begged for, Ray."

Ray tried with all her might to move her body so she could shut Angela up, but she couldn't so much as twitch.

"Here's the kicker. We tried to reprogram the agents after they completed their missions, but it caused brain damage. Mental instability. To everyone but you and Shadow."

Angela came around, standing right in front of Ray. She prepared herself for a blow, although there was nothing she could actually do.

Instead, Angela reached over and wiped under Ray's

nose. She brought her fingers up so Ray could see the blood. "Lately, you've been showing signs of damage too. Although given the degree to which we've been overusing you, that really shouldn't be surprising."

Ray fought against the paralysis. Whatever the other woman was talking about, it wasn't good.

She willed everything she had into moving her hands. And they did, but not nearly enough. The effort left her gasping, her breath sawing in and out of her chest like she was running a sprint.

And it still wasn't enough.

Angela shook her head in amazement. "Seriously, would you look at that? Look at you fighting it. We chose you as the cleaner because we thought you were the most morally flexible. Hell, I lobbied for it. And now here you are, the most protective of all. I was wrong. I can admit it."

Angela reached around Ray for a tissue and wiped the blood, now even more pronounced, from her face.

"Your brain has been fighting it on a subconscious level. That's so interesting."

"What?"

"You're the cleaner, Ray. That's always been your sleeper mission. Dr. Holloman knew from the beginning that this version of our research had an end date. You were designated to make sure no one lived to talk about it."

Something broke inside her. Angela couldn't mean . . . "What?" she croaked again.

"It will be easier if I just show you.

A few seconds later, Angela held an electronic tablet in front of Ray's face. "You have no idea how long I've wanted to show you this."

All Ray could do was watch as her entire life crumbled before her eyes.

She was the killer.

Angela stood there and made Ray watch clip after clip of her killing people connected to Project Crypt. This wasn't doctored footage. Ray was the killer.

When she saw irrefutable proof of herself killing Phantom's dogs, right there on the porch where she'd found them with Dorian, she let out a little whimper.

Angela twisted the tablet around so she could see. "Oh, the dogs? Yeah, that's particularly rough, isn't it? Remember your blackout after we met in Reddington City? That was me taking you up to Phantom's house to kill the dogs—then I had to do a little embalming to keep their bodies from decomposing too quickly. So fucking elaborate."

She waved the screen back and forth. "But Phantom was really upset to see the footage of you killing them. I think he really struggled to accept it. But, eyes don't lie."

She turned the video off, thankfully before Ray could watch herself kill Holloman and his young children.

But Ray had killed everyone else. People she might not have considered her friends but certainly had no reason to harm.

"All we really had to do was let you be who you were deep inside." Angela walked back to the desk. "It was so entertaining that you decided not to call yourself Grace anymore. Especially since you gave us years more access to your brain by attempting to protect Dorian."

"What do you want?" Not moving her jaw wasn't so much of a hardship now, considering she couldn't stop grinding her teeth together.

"At first I needed you to try to flush out that hard drive from Neo. It has to be destroyed, so we'll be recovering that soon enough." Angela turned to her with a little smirk. "But more, we need Heath. So, you're going to go into the little party and bring him back out with you. Dorian too, if you want. I'm sure we can find some use for him. And I'd love to show him this video."

"I won't do it."

"Are you sure about that? *Plates dropped in gold and jumped amuck.*"

At Angela's strange words, Ray could move her body again and her hands immediately reached for the crossbow that was sitting next to the computer.

But not to hurt Angela. Her mind ran through the list of people she needed to kill right now. They played in a loop over and over, Dorian and Heath at the top of the list.

The remaining people having to do with Project Crypt.

Kill them. Kill them. Kill them.

Ray dropped the crossbow and covered her ears in an attempt to get the chant out, but it didn't help. The noise was coming from inside her head.

Her fingers itched to pick up the crossbow pistol once again and storm out of the van, to get inside the Eagle's Nest to kill Dorian and Heath. It was all she could think about.

Kill them. Kill them. Kill them.

It was taking every bit of her strength not to do it. Lightning shot up and down her spine, and Ray struggled to breathe through the pain.

"This is level two. And believe me, I'm impressed that you can fight it. If I switch you to level three, you won't recognize yourself in your own body. You'll go in there and kill Ghost and Shadow and anyone else who tries to get in your way." Angela tapped the tablet. "Just like you did the other times."

What was she supposed to do?

"Ray, don't overthink it. Bring your friends out. Survive

today. Live to fight another day. That's what you guys always say, right?"

The hell of it all was that Angela was right. That had always been her motto. Dorian's motto. Sometimes you just survived and lived to fight another day.

"Okay, I'll do it."

26

Ray wasn't sure she would walk back out of the bar alive, and even if she did, she wouldn't live long after that.

She needed a plan, but trying to come up with one when it was taking every ounce of her control to keep from killing two of the most important people in her life was proving difficult.

"Don't overthink it," Angela said again.

God, Ray really wanted to punch her in the teeth and break both her legs so she needed to be back in that wheelchair. Ray had already tried it, but evidently Angela's voodoo words were having none of that.

"Just go in there, ask them to come out here, and everybody lives to see another day."

Ray reached for the crossbow pistol, a moan of relief escaping her lips as some of the pain eased.

"See how it works? You don't fight your programming, and it doesn't hurt so much."

Ray made a fist. All she needed was to get in one good

punch and Angela would be unconscious, no chance of her bringing on level three.

But the moment Ray tried to swing her arm in Angela's direction, it was like a spike drove through her skull. Ray couldn't stop her cry of pain.

Angela gave an exaggerated wince. "Oh yeah, the base coding of all Crypt programming is to forbid harm to the handlers. Sorry, I forgot to mention that."

She definitely wasn't sorry.

Ray recovered, slipped on the harness for the crossbow so that it rested across her back under her jacket, and tucked the crossbow inside. It felt easy, familiar.

Of course it did. She was a killer. There was no doubt about that now.

Angela held out an earpiece. "So you and I can hear each other. And so we can immediately go to level three if we need to. And if we do, just know that Dorian will be the first person you'll kill. Remember that. You may not get anyone else before you die, but you'll definitely kill Dorian. And I won't be the only person who can trigger level three if needed."

Which meant there was already at least one other person inside.

Ray nodded and left without another word. The pain eased a little as she walked toward the bar, but she knew it would ramp back up when she resisted hurting Dorian and Heath.

What could she do?

Think, Ray.

She wasn't bringing them back out here to be placed at the mercy of Project Crypt, or whatever they were going to call themselves with Version 2.0.

Maybe she could do the one thing Angela hadn't

thought of: take herself out of play before she ever got inside.

She grabbed her knife out of her boot. Sliding it into her jugular would take less than a second and very little effort.

And it would be worth it. Maybe it would even let Dorian forgive her for what she'd done if he knew she'd at least ended the problem when she could.

She brought the blade up to her neck but froze, unable to push it into her skin. It fell to the ground from her suddenly numb fingers. She couldn't pick it back up. They'd thought of this.

"Let's go, Wraith." Angela's voice in her ear had Ray moving forward again.

Think.

She was out of time, and her feet were still carrying her forward almost without her permission.

The second she walked through the door, Dorian's eyes found hers.

Even though the band was playing and people were dancing and talking and carrying on, he immediately found her. He'd been waiting for her to arrive.

But as he looked at her, the smile on his face faded.

What's wrong, D? Do I look a mess? Do I look like someone who just discovered that she's a murderer? Do I look like someone sent to kill you?

He started to stand up from the table in the back, his friends around him, but she gave him a short shake of her head even as it sent a spike of agony down her spine once again.

Dorian's eyebrows furrowed deeper, but he sat back down.

He was still watching her as she glanced to the table a

couple over. Shadow was watching her also. The urge to grab her crossbow rippled up her arm.

To kill them both. It was like something wanted to crawl through her skin and do it.

Heath was talking to a pretty girl but was still looking at Ray.

Things about him came rushing to her mind. That he could speak eight different languages, that he had an IQ of over 140, that he could run at six miles an hour for five miles straight. None of these facts were things she'd consciously known about him—they were tidbits Crypt had programmed into her brain to make her a more effective killer.

He could read lips.

That was something she could use, and not the way Crypt had intended.

But she'd be damned if she would lead Shadow into a trap for Angela and her cohorts, especially if they thought Heath was *special*.

Get out. She mouthed the words directly at Heath.

He frowned and then pointed to himself.

She nodded; a wave of dizziness washed over her.

Get out. Crypt is after you. Trap outside. Avoid back lot.

Nausea crawled up her throat as she finished mouthing the words. She hoped Shadow understood because she wasn't going to be able to say it again.

"What are you doing, Ray?" Angela's voice rang in her ear again. "Why haven't you made contact yet?"

"Give me a goddamn second. It's crowded in here, and I'm trying to act normal."

And she was trying to figure out what the hell to do.

Out of the corner of her eye, she saw Heath stand and

head toward the bathroom. Hopefully, then on to the kitchen door and out.

That left Dorian. She couldn't get him out, but she could at least give him what he'd need the next time he saw her.

Permission to kill her.

A waitress hurried by, and Ray reached into the girl's apron pocket, grabbing a pen without the waitress realizing it in her haste. Ray scribbled some words on a napkin, then balled it up in her fist.

Her return to Dorian had started with an arrow and a note. Her departure from him would also. It was all she could do.

Ray turned so she was facing the bar. She didn't know who Angela's inside man was, but maybe a fake conversation would buy her some time with Angela. Make her think Ray was making progress in her task.

"Hey, Shadow," she said to no one. "Do you mind heading toward the back parking lot as soon as you can? I need to talk to you about something."

Agony ripped through her skull, and she fell forward, barely catching herself on the bar before she hit it. She couldn't stop her moan.

"Ray, this is your last warning. I know you're fighting it. Stop and do what you were told. You've gotten Shadow, now get Ghost."

Ray forced herself up, wiping at the blood dripping rapidly from her nose, and turned, looking around the bar.

There. The man at the end, sitting alone, that was Angela's insider. Everyone else was talking to someone, laughing. He was the only one alone.

Ray ripped the transmitter out of her ear and stomped on it.

The guy at the end of the bar narrowed his eyes,

confirming Ray's suspicions; he reached for the weapon under his jacket.

Who was he going to kill? Her? Dorian? Had Heath already gotten out?

The plan came to her. She knew what she was going to do, but she was only going to get one chance at this.

Her programming from Crypt was demanding a certain outcome from her, but it was also allowing her to access and process information she wouldn't normally have readily available . . . things that might help her be a more effective killer.

Like the location of the bar's fuse box.

She pulled her crossbow from its back holster, ignoring the concerned gasps around her.

Everything slowed. The man was aiming at Dorian, not her. Ray couldn't force her body to turn the crossbow at him, but Crypt wasn't aware of every skill she had.

She jabbed the napkin onto an arrow, loaded it on the crossbow, and turned toward Dorian, shifting so she had a clear line of sight with no one in between. His eyes stayed locked on hers as she pulled the trigger, and the arrow flew toward him.

He didn't flinch when it landed mere inches from his head in the wood of the booth seat behind him.

The absence of pain in her body from aiming the shot at Dorian gave her the time she needed.

She had two arrows loaded in under a second, using the little trick she'd been practicing at Dorian's house recently. She flicked her wrist and let both fly.

She knew they were going to hit their targets when agony knocked her to the ground.

A moment later, the electrical box shot up in flames, and power went out in the bar. It didn't take long before cell phone flashlights started popping on. Smoke and fire poured from the fuse box; a mass exodus began.

When a waitress discovered the dead body at the end of the bar with a bolt sticking out of its chest and screamed, a mass *panicked* exodus began.

That's what Ray needed. Noise. Dark. And she damn well had to get away from Dorian. If Angela had someone else planted in here who could say the words and kick her conditioning up to level three . . .

Well, she'd already seen what she would do.

She and Dorian weren't going to get their happily ever after after all. That was for fairy tales.

All Ray could do for him now was get away. She had no doubt Angela would follow through on her threat to show Dorian what Ray had done.

That should make it a little easier for him if they met again, and he had to put Ray down.

Another wave of agony swamped her as she dropped her crossbow on the bar. She had to get out now or she wouldn't be getting out at all.

She joined the crowd rushing toward the door and let herself be swept away with them. Every step away from Dorian—away from her mission—brought more pain. By the time she felt the cool air outside, she was staggering. There was no way she was going to be able to run.

She was almost blind with pain when an arm came around her. For a heart-swelling second, she thought it was Dorian—but it couldn't be, not if she wasn't feeling a stronger urge to kill him since he was close.

"You always did things the hard way, Wraith. I told Angela not to send you in, but she was convinced she could control you."

She couldn't be hearing right. Was this Dr. Holloman? "You're-you're dead."

"Technically, so are you. Yet here we are."

He steered her away from the crowd. She couldn't do anything but stumble along with him.

"There will be plenty of time for us to get Shadow—he's critical to Version 2.0. But Ghost . . . the only reason we were going to take him was because we knew he'd never *stop* hunting if we took you."

They were almost to a car. She needed to get away from Holloman—if he got her in the car, he'd have her. She'd never get away again.

She turned and stumbled away from him, back toward the crowd. Maybe if she could get people's attention, they could help her. Holloman wouldn't want to draw attention to himself.

Everything was spinning. She could barely focus on the building. It seemed so far away.

"Really, always the hard way with you, Grace." Holloman tsked in her ear. She felt a sharp prick at the back of her neck.

She only had seconds now. She kept walking.

At least she thought she was walking. She wasn't making any progress.

She wasn't going to make it.

She couldn't take the next step.

All she could do was stare back at where the people were. The people who were going to be her family. Hers and Dorian's.

"Nobody's coming for you now," Holloman whispered. "Ghost knows what you are. Angela already sent the file with the video footage to him. He'll wash his hands of you. Live the rest of his life like you were never part of it. That's what you wanted when you came to me, right? Your life for his? For Dorian to live and have a normal life? He'll get that now that you're not in it."

She tried to drag her foot a single step closer. As if that single step could change something. Could make this nightmare disappear.

But she couldn't and it didn't.

She gave up and let herself fall into the darkness.

This darkness wasn't ever going to let her go.

27

Dorian didn't get up from the table at the Eagle's Nest, even with the chaos all around him.

He'd watched Ray shoot the fuse box and that man at the end of the bar with the shot she'd been practicing all week. She'd hit both her targets perfectly.

Dorian wasn't sure he was ever going to be able to get up from this booth again.

Not after the video file he'd watched on his phone.

Ray was the killer.

He wouldn't have believed it. Would have gone to his grave believing the videos were doctored—and fought anyone who'd suggested otherwise. Would have stood by her, hid with her, done whatever they had to do to prove she was innocent.

It was her own admission that had sealed it for him.

I'm sorry. The next time you see me, shoot without hesitation.

A note attached to an arrow. The same way she'd come back into his life was the way she was going out. Fitting.

Ray. Was. The. Killer.

He was still sitting there a few minutes later when the

bar manager rigged some sort of generator and got power running again.

Gavin had already switched over to his role as sheriff, and now that everyone was out of the bar, he was inspecting the body. Dorian was far enough out of the way that nobody asked him to leave, probably on Gavin's order. Not to mention, it was probably in law enforcement's best interest to keep Dorian nearby.

After all, there was a quarrel sticking out of the victim. Dorian was sure Gavin would have some questions about that.

He wasn't exactly sure how long he sat there before Gavin joined him at the other side of the booth.

"Forensic team is here now. They'll be taking over."

Dorian nodded.

"Some people were talking about seeing a woman at the bar with a crossbow."

Dorian nodded again. He wasn't sure what he could say.

"Jesus, D, was she trying to kill you?" Gavin pointed to the hole in the booth by Dorian's head. The bolt was sitting on the table. "Were we wrong from the beginning?"

Gavin really meant had *Dorian* been wrong from the beginning. Everyone else had at least tried to insist Ray was dangerous. They'd only stopped on his request.

"No." Dorian stared at the arrow on the table. "The same thing is true as when she shot me in that storm. If she had wanted me dead, she wouldn't have missed."

"Like how she didn't miss that guy?" Gavin pointed to the dead man across the bar.

Yes, exactly. Dorian didn't say anything.

Gavin ran a hand over his eyes. "If it makes you feel any better, the guy had a gun in his hand."

That was a drop of good news in an ocean of bad. But at least it was a drop.

"Are you saying this was self-defense?"

Gavin let out a sigh. "Dead guy definitely looked like he was about to shoot. But his body wasn't pointed toward her, it was pointed toward you."

What did that mean? That Ray had been protecting him? That's why she'd shot the guy?

Fine, but even if that were true, it didn't change what he'd seen on that video.

She'd said she had something she had to tell him. That it was bad. But he'd never dreamed it was something like this.

"You want to show me what's on your phone that you keep watching? Somehow, I doubt it's the latest YouTube dance craze."

Dorian stared at Gavin. This man was like a brother to him in every way but blood. He'd stood by Dorian when nobody would have blamed him a single bit for walking away. But this was a line. Once Dorian made this choice, there was no coming back from it. If he showed this video to Gavin as the sheriff, Ray's life was effectively over.

It might already be over anyway. But Dorian still couldn't do it.

"As my friend, yes, I would show you this video. But as the sheriff . . . I wouldn't waste your time with some crazy dancing when you have an important case to work on."

Gavin nodded and didn't push it.

"Okay." He pointed to the napkin with Ray's note. "That looks pretty hard-core."

Dorian met his friend's eyes. "I don't have answers for you. Hell, Gav, I don't even have answers for myself right now."

"Do you know where she is?"

"No."

Gavin raised an eyebrow. "Would you tell me if you did?"

Dorian didn't answer, mostly because he honestly wasn't sure what the answer was.

Commotion at the door drew their attention. One of the lab techs had stopped someone from entering. "I'm sorry, ma'am, you can't come in right now. This is currently a crime scene."

"I heard Dorian Lindstrom was still here. I've got to talk to him," Dr. Diaz announced.

Gavin raised his eyebrow at Dorian.

"Ray asked to talk to Sierra this afternoon. I don't know what she said, but they were in there for a long damn time."

"Let her in, Rick," Gavin called out. "I'll make sure she stays out of your way."

Sierra Diaz was soft and a little plump. She tended to move slowly, with a lazy grace that made her seem calm and welcoming.

None of that was evident now as she rushed over to where Dorian and Gavin were sitting.

"I need to talk to Dorian alone."

Gavin raised an eyebrow. "You do realize that this is a murder investigation, our prime suspect is Dorian's girl-friend, and I'm the sheriff."

Sierra turned to Dorian. "This is stuff concerning your work in the past."

Dorian shrugged. "Gavin knows about Crypt. Not the name, but that I worked for them, and that they ended up not being on the right side of the law."

"If Ray threatened to harm anyone when she talked with you this afternoon, you know you had a legal obligation to notify law enforcement," Gavin said to Sierra.

Sierra's eyes were still on Dorian. "Ray and I didn't talk about her today. We talked about you."

Dorian shrugged. "That's fine. I gave you permission to talk about me. She didn't mention any plans about grabbing her trusty crossbow and shooting up a crowded bar?"

"No, nothing like that. When Ray left my office, she had absolutely no intent to harm anyone."

Dorian could still remember how shaken Sierra had looked when her session with Ray had finished. "Are you sure about that? You were pretty upset when I got there."

Sierra's lips pressed together in a tight line. "Did Ray talk to you?"

Dorian gave a bitter laugh. "She said she had something to tell me, and that it was bad." He tapped the screen of his phone. "I had no idea how bad it really was."

Gavin stood up. "You know what? I am going to give you two a little bit of time to talk alone. I think I'm needed over with the crime techs." He walked away a couple feet and looked over his shoulder. "I'm willing to treat this like self-defense for now. But the fact is, she walked in here with the crossbow. It was an engagement party. What sort of trouble was she looking for?"

Gavin didn't wait for an answer, just walked away.

Dorian turned his phone around so it was facing Sierra and played the file that had been sent to him. The color had leaked out of her face by the time the video was done.

"Pretty gruesome, isn't it?"

"Oh no . . ."

"She didn't mention any of this to you when you talked today? This wasn't the *really bad thing* she needed to tell me?"

"I can't believe she would do this. There was no indication whatsoever that she had this on her mind."

He shrugged. "You think it's doctored? I'd think that too, if it weren't for the fact that Ray herself admitted to what she'd done." He slid the note over to Sierra. "Ray's parting gift."

Sierra smoothed out the napkin on the table, then watched the video again. "I'm not saying Ray didn't kill these people. I'm only saying she didn't do it of her own free will."

"What do you mean?"

"Ray came to me today because she wanted my opinion on whether revealing some information to you might cause psychological harm."

Dorian rolled his eyes. "Believe me, finding out the woman I'm in love with is a serial killer, even one with good intentions, is definitely damaging to my psyche."

"She wasn't planning on telling you that."

He tapped the screen again. "*This* was not her bad news?"

"Ray was going to tell you what *your* sleeper mission was."

"The torture I went through short-circuited whatever brainwashing Crypt did to me, so I didn't have a sleeper mission."

"You were programmed to kill your entire Special Forces team."

"What?"

"That was the reason Ray was in Kabul that day. She'd found out about the sleeper missions—and specifically about yours. If you hadn't been captured that day in Afghanistan and subsequently tortured, breaking your programming? You would've killed all your friends."

Dorian had no idea how to process this. "I wouldn't have done it."

She shook her head and glanced at his phone again. "You wouldn't have had a choice," she said slowly. "And you wouldn't have had any recollection of it."

Dorian looked over at Gavin. He would've killed Gavin? Killed his friends? Zac? Finn and Aiden?

God, the thought was unbearable.

"Watch the footage again, Dorian. I know it's Ray, but really *look* at her."

He watched it again and finally understood what Sierra was suggesting.

"*Ray's not doing it consciously,*" he whispered, watching the footage again. And then again. Oh, thank God. "But she told me that we each only had one sleeper mission. Hers was seven years ago."

"That sort of coercive persuasion—*brainwashing*—would definitely have huge detrimental mental effects. But under the right circumstances, it could be possible."

"Huge detrimental mental effects like nosebleeds and blinding headaches?"

Sierra grimaced. "Exactly like that."

For the first time since Ray had walked into the bar, Dorian felt like he could actually take a breath. Ray was a killer, but she wasn't a murderer. She hadn't killed these people, or those dogs, of her own volition.

Except for when he'd found out Ray was alive, Dorian had never known such a profound sense of relief. He hadn't been sure he was going to be able to walk away from her even if she had killed those people in cold blood.

Now he didn't have to.

"She should've told me about my sleeper mission earlier."

He could almost see Sierra slip into psychiatrist mode. "You'd be taking this a whole lot harder if all you had to focus on right now was the fact that you could've potentially killed your team. Ray knew that. If you weren't so relieved to have a logical explanation for her actions on that video, you'd be all caught up in your head about what could have happened."

Dorian stood up. She was right. All his concerns about what he might've done to his team years ago were secondary to helping Ray out of whatever was going on *right damn now*.

Gavin caught him as he walked across the bar toward the door.

"You're looking a lot less like somebody kicked your puppy."

"We need to work this situation on the assumption that Ray is innocent."

"And is she?"

Dorian shrugged a shoulder. "Let's just say there are factors in play that aren't necessarily evidenced here. I think someone is setting Ray up. Have you seen Heath?"

Of anyone, Shadow was most likely to know what the hell was going on here. Did he know anything about the sleeper missions? Have one himself?

Gavin shook his head. "He was at the table next to mine. I think he left before this all went down."

Dorian had been so caught up in his reaction to the footage that he hadn't questioned the most important factor of all: why was he getting this video now? It could've been sent to him at any time. Seemed pretty suspicious that it would show up at the exact same time Ray pulled out a crossbow at a bar.

"I'm going to try to find Ray."

"D, I've got to keep some distance from you in this. Right now, she's the prime suspect in a murder investigation. I know I'm only sheriff temporarily, but I took an oath to uphold the law."

"I understand." But Dorian also wouldn't be turning Ray over to law enforcement—especially not for something she'd had no control over.

"Be careful, D. I have a feeling this is bigger than either of us."

Dorian did too. And Ray was right in the middle of it. He had to find her.

28

His team was waiting in the parking lot. Dorian didn't want to stop and talk to them. He wanted to find Ray. Every second he delayed was another second she was in this mess on her own.

He gave the guys a passing wave on the way to his truck, hoping that would be enough, but no such luck.

Zac jogged over. Finn and Aiden were right behind him. "D, wait up," Zac called out.

"Gavin's inside," Dorian said. "He can catch you up on details. I've got to go."

"After Ray?" Aiden asked. "Violet saw her in there tonight. Saw her *shoot* at you with her crossbow, D."

Dorian let out a sigh. "It wasn't what you think. Believe me, if Ray wanted me dead, I would be."

Finn crossed his arms over his massive chest. "How many times are we going to need to hear you say that before we're standing over your dead body saying, 'Oh, well, I guess Ray wanted him dead this time'?"

"You guys, Ray is in trouble. I've got to find her."

Zac shook his head. "We were thinking more along the lines of Ray *is* trouble and you should stay away from her."

Dorian pulled open his truck door. "This is not the time for a damn intervention."

Zac slammed his hand down on the hood. Dorian stopped moving. Everyone did. Zac had been their team leader in the Special Forces, and the man did not lose his temper. Ever.

"D, man. We've been through a lot together. You've asked us to let you know when we see you going off the rails. We're seeing it now, brother. This woman . . . she has you heading in a direction we're not sure we can follow."

Dorian met Zac's eyes. "Then this time, I head in that direction alone. I'm not leaving her behind."

He got in his truck and pulled away, not waiting for their response. For the first time, he didn't care about his team's response.

He was on his own. So be it.

Dorian couldn't find Ray anywhere. He started at his house. He didn't expect to find her there, and she wasn't. But all her stuff was still there. As far as he could tell, she hadn't taken a single thing. All her clothes still hung in the closet. Her handguns were still in his gun safe.

Her beloved crossbow was stored in a locked box in the closet.

So whatever she had used at the Eagle's Nest, it hadn't been her personal one.

He could *almost* understand her leaving all her clothes and personal items behind. But her crossbow? He couldn't think of any reason she'd do that. Not if she'd had any choice at all.

He left and drove out to the cabin where she'd been hiding, to be sure she hadn't gone there.

Nothing. Same for the cabin where he'd taken her for interrogation.

He knew it didn't prove anything. There were literally dozens of other shelters in the area she could be hiding in. Or she could be halfway out of the state by now.

Maybe not of her own accord.

It was time to start back where everything had spun out of control. Which was before Ray had walked into the bar tonight.

He needed someone to build him a time machine. At a little after two a.m., Dorian found himself pounding on the door of the man who could provide the next best thing.

Kendrick Foster blinked out at him from his cracked door.

"I need your help, Blaze."

The man rolled his eyes as he opened the door farther. "I know you're using my new codename to soften me up."

Dorian gave the man a half smile. Kendrick had lobbied for a codename when he'd moved here a few months ago— first helping with part of a human-trafficking ring, then helping catch a conman who'd plagued the town for years. Since Kendrick was half black, half Asian—*Blasian* by his own label—he had become Blaze.

And the computer genius that could help Dorian now.

"Ray is in trouble. I need you to work your computer sorcery and get us some information."

Kendrick wiped a hand over his face and opened the door enough for Dorian to follow him inside. "Are we talking about misdemeanor sorcery or Feds-showing-up-at-my-door-complete-with SWAT sorcery?"

"Probably somewhere in between." He explained what had happened at the Eagle's Nest. "I need to know if there's any sort of footage of Ray before she entered the building. It might not give me what I need, but hopefully it will provide something."

"Okay, how about you go dig your way into my kitchen and make coffee, and I'll drag out my cauldron and warm up my eye of newt."

Dorian nodded and walked toward the kitchen, stopping a split second before he walked through the doorway.

Someone was there.

He dropped low and spun around the doorway's edge, knowing the intruder would be aiming high.

When he saw who it was, he didn't put his weapon away.

"Shadow. What are you doing here?"

The man kept his hands up where they could be seen. "I followed you."

"Have you become my secret admirer, Heath? Never would've guessed it."

"Ray told me to get out of the bar. Told me I was in danger and there was a trap being set in the back parking lot."

"What?" Dorian lowered his weapon but didn't re-holster it. "Ray was on the opposite side of the bar. She never came near you. How exactly did she warn you about all this?"

"I can read lips. She mouthed it to me."

"I didn't know you could read lips."

Heath shrugged. "It's not something I announce. Honestly, I'm surprised Ray knew either."

"So, you left right before Ray caused a panic and killed a man. Interesting timing."

Heath winced. "Look. I didn't know what the fuck was going on. I had no reason not to trust Wraith, so I left. I kept clear of the back lot like she said but got myself in a position where I could observe."

"And?"

"And there was a van there. Multiple tangos scoping it out, obviously waiting for me to show up. When everyone started running out, they made themselves scarce."

Dorian finally holstered his Glock. "So she was telling the truth."

"Definitely. Saved my ass. I might have walked right into that ambush."

Dorian walked past Heath to the coffee pot and started some brewing. "What do you know about Crypt's use of sleeper missions? Brainwashing us agents?" He made sure he could see his friend's face when he said it.

There was not a bit of surprise.

Heath didn't try to deny it. "I knew it was a factor. What do *you* know about Crypt's use of sleeper missions?"

"Evidently, the mission I was programmed for was to kill the members of my Special Forces team. Zac, Finn, Aiden, Gavin . . . they'd all be dead now if I hadn't ended up in that enemy prison."

Now Heath was surprised. "You had sleeper missions too?"

"I thought you said you knew about them."

Heath shook his head, running his hand through his hair. "I knew *I* had sleeper missions, but I thought it was just me. I didn't know they'd done it to anyone else."

Dorian pulled his phone from his pocket. "Not just you and me."

He showed the clips of Ray's kills.

"Jesus," Heath muttered before watching it again.

Dorian understood the need. "At first, I thought she was the killer, and it completely blindsided me. But if you look at her with the idea of brainwashing . . ."

Heath nodded. "You can see it's not really Ray. It's her, but not *her*."

"Exactly."

"Get your ass in here, D. I've got something!" Kendrick yelled from the other room. "And bring the damned coffee."

"He's searching for any footage that might show what happened outside the Eagle's Nest before Ray came in."

Dorian poured some coffee and headed into Kendrick's office. He handed the man the cup and sat down next to him.

"Heath stopped by for the party." Dorian gestured over his shoulder with his thumb.

Kendrick took a sip. "More the merrier. The good news is this was significantly easier to crack than that hard drive you delivered. Here's your girl acting pretty weird in the parking lot. Security camera footage caught her."

They watched the screen as Ray walked stiffly into view. She was about twenty feet from the door when she stopped and grabbed a knife out of her boot and put it up to her neck.

"Oh shit," Heath whispered.

Ray had obviously planned to use it on herself. Dorian could see her muscles straining to slide the blade into her throat.

But at the last second, the knife dropped to the ground, almost like someone had taken it out of her hand and thrown it away. She didn't even pick it up.

"She's under duress," Heath said. "Did you see that?"

"I saw it." Dorian rubbed the back of his neck. Thank God she'd been under duress.

Kendrick took a sip of his coffee, studying the screen closer. "Duress?"

"Long story," Dorian told him. "The short of it is, long-term brainwashing."

Kendrick smiled and shook his head. "It never gets boring around here."

"She doesn't have that same blank look as the other videos," Heath pointed out. "She's resisting whatever is happening to her, but she has at least some control. She's aware."

When her fingers moved up to her ear, both he and Heath leaned forward. "There," they said at the same time.

"She has a transmitter in her ear." Kendrick zoomed in as tight as he could on the side of her head. The image was grainy, but they could see it.

"So someone was probably listening to what she was saying, and talking to her."

"Looks like it." Dorian turned to Kendrick. "Are there more cameras in the back lot? Can you give us a shot of the vehicles there?"

"Yeah, let me access it."

They watched that camera, running it backward until they eventually spotted Ray and tracked her back to a van.

"We've got her. Let me run this through my true voodoo programs and see if we can find this van's current location." He handed Dorian his empty coffee cup. "It will take a little time for the system to run."

Dorian took the cup. "While it's doing that, can you look at some video footage and make sure it's not doctored?"

"Sure." Kendrick rubbed his hands together. "Is it a sex tape?"

Dorian rolled his eyes. "You wish. And if it were, I definitely would not be giving it to you to see if it was doctored. It's sensitive, Blaze."

"Okay, sure."

Dorian handed him his phone and went to go get Kendrick another cup of coffee while the man watched. Dorian didn't want to see the video again.

When he came back, Kendrick had already transferred the file off his phone and over to his computer.

The only thing worse than watching Ray assassinate multiple people was watching her do it on a bigger screen.

To his credit, Kendrick wasn't squeamish. He was studying the video itself, not Ray's actions. "I'm running it through some different filters that would isolate the most common video manipulations—stuff like improper shadows or stretching of sizes. I don't see any myself, but that doesn't mean it's not there. Meanwhile, there's something else I want to run too."

Kendrick wasn't talking to either him or Heath, he was talking to his computer. Dorian looked over at Heath leaning against the wall, but the man just shrugged.

"How long have you known about the sleeper missions?" he asked Heath.

"Only recently." Heath's eyes fell away. "I've always known there was something else going on in my head besides just my own thoughts, but I didn't know Crypt had planted them there."

Dorian wasn't sure what that meant.

"Okay, it looks like the software isn't finding any sign of video manipulation," said Kendrick. "That doesn't mean it's a hundred percent gospel accurate, though."

Dorian rubbed the back of his neck. "If you had to say what percentage accurate it was, what would you say?"

Kendrick shrugged. "Ninety-nine point nine. Sorry, man."

"It's okay. I never actually thought it was doctored. Just thought it was worth a shot."

The sun was coming up, and Kendrick was on his second pot of coffee and still talking to his computer when he called Dorian and Heath back into the room.

"Okay. We've got good news, bad news, and Blaze-rules-all news. Bad news is the van we were tracking was found abandoned in Reddington City thirty minutes ago. Parked somewhere where we couldn't get another camera pickup to see where the passengers went. So dead end."

"Okay," Dorian said. "What's the good news?"

"Good news is that people can't wait to put stuff like a bar fire on social media. Couple that with the rumor there's a dead body, and everybody's got something to contribute."

"How exactly is that good news?" Heath asked.

"It's tied to the Blaze-rules-all news." Kendrick looked over his shoulder and grinned at them.

Dorian barely kept from rolling his eyes. "Don't leave us in suspense."

Kendrick turned back to the screen and began clicking. "This."

It was amateur footage of the bar as people were coming out. A girl interviewing her girlfriend about surviving the horrible ordeal. Then Kendrick paused the video in the middle of a high-pitched sentence and zoomed in on what was over the woman's shoulders.

Ray.

"Oh my God." Dorian sat down hard in the chair as Kendrick started the footage again, this time zoomed in on Ray.

Dorian's heart broke as she seemed to try to take a step back toward the bar, away from the man in the shadows behind her, but couldn't. Her fingers twitched down at her side like she wanted to reach out but couldn't move.

There was such a look of desperation on her face.

He wanted to grab her through the screen and pull her out. Protect her. Fight whatever—*whoever* held her.

Dorian was still staring at that picture when another popped up on Kendrick's second screen.

"Fuck," Heath muttered when, from this new angle, they saw who it was in the shadows. Dorian couldn't have agreed with the sentiment more.

He shook his head. "I thought Holloman was dead. Ray said someone killed him and his family. That's what kept her so actively involved in seeking the . . ."

He trailed off. She'd been actively involved in seeking the killer, when all the time the killer had been *her*.

They watched as Holloman caught Ray as she crumbled, draped her arm over his shoulder, and dragged her to a car, not the van.

"Holloman has her," Dorian whispered. She'd destroyed all his research. Holloman had to hate her. Would make her life a living hell.

Heath shook his head. "No offense, but this info hardly reaches *Blaze-rules-all* status."

"Oh ye of little faith." With a few more movements of his mouse and keypad, a map appeared on the screen with a blinking red light in the center of it.

"What's that?"

"That is the old Port of Umatilla in Oregon, on the Columbia River, about nine hours from here. The most inland port on the West Coast. Those big-ass freighter ships use it to get containers farther inland."

"Okay," Dorian said. "Why do we care?"

"The car your Holloman guy was driving was spotted in Umatilla and then again at a traffic camera less than a mile down this road. The vehicle wasn't ever spotted going through the next cam on that same road. And the only thing of any substance in that two-mile stretch is this, the old port. That's where your girl is."

Dorian reached over and kissed Kendrick's dark, bald head.

"Blaze rules all."

29

This was not a two-man job. Both Dorian and Shadow knew it as they discreetly pulled up the back way at the mostly empty port in Umatilla. Ever since a much more modern port had been built a few miles down in Morrow County, this one hadn't seen much traffic.

Kendrick had gotten them all available plans and maps of the port.

But it was still definitely more than a two-man job.

Dorian should've gone to the team, but after last night's conversation, he wasn't sure he had a team to turn to anymore. Not ones he could trust to take care of Ray just as much as he could trust them to take care of him.

And right now, Ray was the only thing that mattered.

"The situation is fubar, man," Heath said. "The only advantage we have is that they don't know we're here."

"We've worked under circumstances worse than this." And besides, it didn't matter. Disadvantaged or not, they were going in.

Kendrick was still supplying them with as much information as possible. He'd sent them in with thermal imaging cameras, which would allow Kendrick to at least let them know where people were in the massive container storage warehouse. They'd made the nine-hour drive in a little less than seven and had spent the past couple of hours waiting for night to fall so they could strike.

"You've got four warm bodies on the outside of the building, all walking counterclockwise. I'm going to assume those are guards." Kendrick's face looked out at them from Dorian's phone. "You've got three people in the southwest corner, second floor of the main warehouse. Looking at the plans, that's a conference room.

"You've got at least half a dozen more on the downstairs floors. Some of them are grouped together, some of them are wandering around. Again, I'm going to go with guards for one hundred points."

"Anything that looks like a holding cell?" Dorian asked. "Anyone off on their own?"

"Actually, yes. Let me check the building plans." Kendrick's face disappeared from the screen for a second. "There you are, sweetheart. Second floor, three doors down from that corner office. Someone sitting alone in the corner of a small office. I think that's your girl, D."

"Roger that. Let us know if anything changes."

Kendrick nodded. "That could happen quickly, and without much warning. Also, not trying to add to this suck-ass parade, but you've got a container ship that has a window to sail at dawn. It would be the perfect way to get someone out of the country."

Dorian nodded. "If we are still here at dawn, we've got bigger problems."

"You're pretty woefully outnumbered. Y'all be careful."

Hearing a southern accent come from the younger man's

mouth—Dorian happened to know Kendrick was from Boston and had attended Harvard—brought the smallest smile to Dorian's face. "We will."

Heath had already gotten out of the car and opened the trunk. Without a word, the two of them loaded up with weapons and ammunition, although they both knew that if this came down to anything but a stealth mission, they were screwed.

But they would damn well take the gear anyway.

Dorian pulled up the building plans on his phone again. "I think the best bet is for us to access the roof through the fire escape on the northwest corner. That seems to have the least amount of traffic."

Heath nodded. "And then rappel down to the office with the window." He tapped the screen indicating the one he meant, farther away from the corner where the people were currently located.

"That should at least get us in undetected. Hopefully. We'll assess and move in from there."

They grabbed the rope and equipment they would need to get to the window and began the half-mile jog to the warehouse. At least the sun had set and darkness was providing them some cover.

"Thank you, Heath," Dorian said as they approached. "I realize you don't have to be here."

"It's Grace. I would've done it for her anyway. And if she hadn't warned me last night at the bar, I might've been the one sitting as a prisoner inside that building."

They moved the rest of the way in silence, sticking to the shadows to provide them cover. They stayed low as they made it to the fire escape, weapons drawn as the guard went by. Neither of them was looking to kill anyone, but they wouldn't lose sleep if it became necessary.

The fact that the guard was carrying an assault rifle, definitely not standard issue for a civilian security guard, let them know Holloman and the people working for him weren't playing around.

Once the guard had passed, Dorian gave Heath a hoist up so he could grab the fire escape ladder and pull it down quietly. They both climbed quickly and silently to the roof, then over the top of the office they would infiltrate. They had the higher ground but were a lot more exposed up here. It wouldn't take much to be discovered. Dorian motioned to Heath that he would hold the rope and lower Heath down. It would allow Dorian to more effectively cover them if things went bad.

Of course, if things went bad while you were hanging over the edge of the building, there was only so much that could be done.

Heath nodded, they tied off the rope, and Heath began his climb down. The crack of the window breaking as Heath cut it with a special glass cutter couldn't be helped. Fortunately, this was still a port, and there were enough sounds in the night that this one didn't draw undue attention.

"I'm in."

The words barely carried to Dorian, but once he heard them, he grabbed the rope and made his way down to the window, aware that if someone spotted him, he could have a bullet in his spine before he knew they'd seen him.

Heath was covering the door with his weapon as Dorian swung through the opening he'd made.

"Back corner," Heath whispered. He could hear the shallow breathing before his eyes adjusted enough for him to see her.

Ray had her arms wrapped around her knees and was pushed as far back in the corner as she could get.

Dorian crouched in front of her. "Sunray?"

"Dorian?" Her voice was so small, so frightened. "Is that really you?

He knew oh so well what it was to question your own mind. To want something to be true so badly that you were sure it couldn't be. "I'm here, sweetheart."

"You have to kill me. The things I've done—"

"You didn't kill those people of your own volition. They were sleeper missions. Sierra told me about mine."

"I'm still dangerous," she whispered, pulling herself back from him.

"Shadow and I are going to get you out. Then we'll figure out a way of getting the stuff out of your head."

She sat up frantically, scrambling to work her way around Dorian. "No! Shadow has to leave. He's who they want, in order to rebuild the whole project. He has to leave. He has to go." She scratched at Dorian, trying to work her way around him.

Dorian tried to restrain her without hurting her in any way. "Ray, stop. You've got to stay quiet so the guards won't hear you, okay?"

Heath left his perch by the door and crouched down next to Dorian.

"Hey, Ray." He gave her the charming grin that had won him the affections of women the world over. "Nobody's going to catch me, honey. I'm way too good, you know that."

His words had the opposite effect of what either of them had expected. Ray's eyes got wider and her breath became more and more labored.

"You have to go. You have to go. You have to go." She said it like a chant over and over, not allowing herself to stop and get any air. She turned to face Dorian. "They put something in my head earlier today. I have to scream. I have to scream. I have to scream."

Both he and Heath realized what was going on at the same time. Ray was fighting whatever it was Crypt had put in her brain. She'd been programmed to notify Crypt if Shadow was near.

"You go. It's you triggering her," Dorian said. "I'll get her out."

"You'll need help."

"I need her not screaming her head off even more. Plus, she's right. We can't let them take you if they need you that much. Get out. Get far away from here."

Ray had sunk to the floor, rocking back and forth, her arms wrapped around her head. Heath looked like he was going to argue, but then nodded.

"Good luck."

He ran for the window, diving out and grabbing the rope. But Ray couldn't hold back anymore. She let out a scream that sounded like it was ripped from her throat.

Dorian immediately covered her lips with his, cutting off the sound.

But it was too late, the guards had already been notified. Ray rolled over on the floor, completely dazed, and he ran over to the window. Shadow had made it down the rope and was already sprinting toward the cover of the next building. He was going to make it.

But the guards who had been patrolling the perimeter of the building had already rounded the corner and would see the rope and broken window any second. Going back out that way wasn't an option.

He turned back to Ray, who was stirring, but not quite conscious. He reached over and hoisted her over his shoulder.

Weapon in hand, he opened the door, thankful to find the hallway empty. He ran in the direction of the stairwell. If he could make it down that, maybe they could get to the container storage area that took up most of the first floor. That would at least give him a place to hide while he figured out what to do.

He felt a tap on the small of his back.

"D, put me down. I'm okay. I won't scream. It was just something with Shadow."

He opened the stairway door, then turned and lowered Ray onto her feet. He studied her face, trying to ascertain if she was really in control.

She was.

His breath escaped him in sharp relief. "Hey, you. Good to have you back."

"I'm sorry."

"Nothing to be sorry for. Let's get the hell out of here."

He handed her the Sig in his hand and pulled out the second one he'd brought as backup. "Container storage space downstairs is our best bet. Multiple exit routes, lots of places to hide." They could hear commotion in the hallway behind them.

She nodded. "Let's go."

They ran down the stairs and out the door, barely making it into the larger storage area before the guards were on them.

It was better here. It would be difficult for the guards to tell whether they'd made it out or if they were still in the building. Dorian grabbed her hand, and they dashed behind one of the shipping containers. It was only a second later when guards streamed in from all directions.

"Nobody has seen them," one of the guards said. "How do we know they didn't escape out the window?"

Dorian and Ray kept themselves plastered out of sight as the guards talked.

"Dr. Holloman wants us to check everywhere," another guard responded.

"Fine. Let's get started."

Dorian pointed in the opposite direction the guards were approaching from. They could take the guards out, but that would be proof they'd gone this way if someone found the bodies or radioed to them.

They played a silent game of hide and seek, keeping on the move and out of sight even when two more guards joined in the search. It helped that they really didn't think anyone else was in here.

When the guards had made a final sweep, he and Ray still undetected, she looked over at him, her face only slightly less pinched.

"No one's in here. Let's get outside where we can be useful."

Dorian grabbed Ray's hand as they heard a different door open.

"Report."

Ray's eyes flew to his. That was Holloman.

"Dr. Holloman, Dr. Landry. We were just about to leave. There's no one in here."

"Are you sure?" Holloman asked.

"Yes sir," the guard responded. "We've done a thorough sweep and there's no indication that anyone was in here but us. We think they probably went out the window, since that's where the rope is."

"I see." Holloman's voice was calm and steady as ever. "Well, just in case the agents we trained to be the best in the world are a little better than the rent-a-guard squad here, you won't mind if we look ourselves?"

"No sir." The guard's voice was tight, obviously offended.

Dorian listened, ready to move based on whatever direction Holloman and Angela came for them. It shouldn't be too hard to keep away from them either.

"If you wouldn't mind, Angela," Holloman said.

They were coming from the northeast side.

"*Mirror bells mapped booklets red tables.*"

Dorian had no idea what the hell Angela was talking about. He turned to face Ray to see if she had any idea.

And found her pointing his Sig right in his face. He brought his hand up and grabbed her wrist, snatching the gun to the side, just as she fired.

His ears rang at the sound. If he had been a split second later, she would've killed him. He held on to her wrist, forcing it outward as she tried to bring the gun back toward his head.

"There you go, Mr. . . . What is your name?" Holloman said.

"Anders."

"Mr. Anders. See, the people we were searching for were here after all. Your assistance isn't needed anymore. As you can see, we've got someone on the inside."

Dorian looked at Ray but could find no sign of the woman he loved. Her features were pulled into that blank mask. She was straining hard against the hand that held her wrist with the gun, but she wasn't fighting with any other part of her body.

"Ghost," Holloman called out. "I'm assuming since our fair Wraith is not screaming her head off, you're here alone in your rescue attempt. That was a mistake. Wraith, finish him."

Now Ray fought. Dorian stumbled back, crashing into the container; she head butted him so hard, he saw stars.

He managed to hang on to her arm and wrench her wrist farther to the side; the gun flew out of her hand and skidded across the floor. She immediately reached for the gun in his other hand. He threw that one aside too. He wasn't going to use it on her, and he wasn't going to let it fall into her hands.

Fighting was his only option. Because even without a weapon, Ray was more than capable of ending a life.

She got in three or four good blows to both his head and his gut—the woman had always been lightning fast—before he started fighting in earnest. He didn't want to fight her. Every blow he landed killed something inside him. But if he was going to help Ray, he was going to have to win this battle first.

It was fighting Ray, but also not. The robot he was fighting had all of Ray's skills, speed, stamina, and strength. And was obviously well versed in the tactics Dorian used to fight, ready to easily anticipate his moves with counter-moves of her own. But there was something missing, that same something that had been missing when he'd watched the videos of her killing those other people.

Her *fire* was missing. The same something that hadn't been participating when she'd killed those people wasn't participating in this fight now.

Dorian blocked a kick, then spun, catching her mid-punch and pulling her back to his front in a bear hug.

"Come on, baby. Fight this with me. You can do it." He had no idea if she could understand what he was saying or not. When she reared back and head butted him again, he would have to go with *not*.

Her next combination of punches and kicks sent him flying out into the main corridor of the warehouse. He could feel the weapons trained on him from all over the room.

"Have your men stand down, Mr. Anders," Holloman said. Dorian was too busy dodging more blows to look at him.

He forced himself to go on the offensive, landing a series of blows of his own that at least slowed Ray's momentum down a little. A hard sidekick to her midsection had her doubling over and falling backward.

"Hold, Wraith," Holloman said.

Ray immediately stopped. They both were breathing heavily. Dorian didn't dare take his eyes off her in case this was some sort of trick.

Holloman looked over at Dorian. "You do understand that she'll just keep going, right? Until you kill her or she completes her mission? She won't remember that she did any of this." He gestured over at Angela, who was busy recording everything he said. "When we show her how she killed you, it's probably going to be pretty devastating."

"Timothy, look." Angela pointed at Ray.

Her fists clenched, and her eyes darted back and forth behind her closed eyelids. Dorian watched in horror as blood definitely not from any blow he'd given her began to drip from her nose.

Then her ear, as if her eardrum had burst.

"Whatever you're doing, stop it now, or I swear on all that is holy I will fucking end you."

Holloman tsked. "I'm not doing anything, Ghost."

"She's fighting it." Angela's voice was filled with awe. "That shouldn't even be possible."

"Well now, this just got interesting, didn't it?" Holloman turned back toward Ray. "Wraith, resume your attack."

Ray took a step toward Dorian, then stopped. Her entire body looked as if she had been struck by lightning: her arms flew out from her sides, fingers pointed stiffly at an unnatural angle, and her back bowed so tightly it seemed like her spine would snap.

Oh God. She was killing herself trying to stop.

"Ray!" Dorian screamed. "No. Fight me. It's okay, baby. Just fight me."

"Wraith," Holloman said, voice still too fucking calm, like always. "Kill Ghost. Do it now."

She took another step forward, a low moan of pain radiating from her body. She was still coming toward him, arms rising in a fighting stance, but she was obviously slowing herself down enough to give him the advantage.

Dorian slipped behind her and wrapped his arms around her in a tight bear hug again. This allowed her to fight him rather than having to fight herself.

Dorian looked at Holloman while holding Ray. "Let her out of this, and I'll let you keep me. You can redo all your conditioning. Get the research you need on what exactly the torture did to my brain with the programing. You'll still have her, and now you'll have me. This sick little game can happen on another day."

Holloman studied him. "A willing participant would make a difference in the research."

"You'll have it."

Angela shook her head. "This is not what we agreed, Timothy. Not what we need. We should stay the course with our research. Find Shadow and concentrate on him. He's the key."

"And you've always been obsessed with him. No, this is too good of a deal to pass up." Holloman turned back to Dorian. "Your *live to fight another day* stance might leave you with something to regret this time."

Ray thrashed in his arms, kicking back with her feet, and trying to head butt him again. "I'll take the chance."

"Mr. Anders, please restrain Ghost and take him to the ship container we designed for holding."

"Turn her off first."

"Wraith, stand down." Ray immediately stopped fighting against him. "We'll turn off the rest of her conditioning after you've surrendered yourself. And remember, we can always turn it back on."

Dorian let go of Ray and did something he didn't think he'd ever be able to tolerate again.

He allowed himself to be shackled and led into captivity under his enemy's control.

30

I t was Monday. Mondays were always the worst because the short guard with the scar over one eye came in. He liked to play with fire.

Specifically, he liked to burn Dorian with it.

Of course, Dorian had no idea if it was actually Monday or not. As far as he knew, inside this dark hellhole, which only got light when someone came in to hurt him, every day could be Monday. Or maybe the guard who seemed like he was here once a week really only came once a month.

Dorian definitely had no idea how long he'd been here. Chained. With no chance for escape.

And Grace was dead. She had died in that explosion a few weeks ago because he couldn't get to her in time.

He'd—

No.

Grace—*Ray*—was alive. He wasn't in that prison in Afghanistan.

He was in a shipping container in a port in Oregon.

Ray was alive.

Dorian fought back the panic that clawed at his gut at

the feel of restraints around his wrists and ankles again.

You will damn well keep it together, soldier. You're of no use to Ray or yourself if you're in some sort of damn coma.

Keep it together.

That was much easier said than done with the darkness pulling at him, ready to take him under whenever he stopped fighting.

But he wouldn't stop fighting. He had way too much to fight for now.

Helping Ray. Getting them out. Fixing what they'd done to her.

That didn't stop the demons from whispering in his ear, their insidious murmurings scratching along the deep recesses of his psyche.

How could he help Ray? He wasn't going to get out of this box whole. Once this ship set sail, he could be here for weeks.

He wouldn't survive.

Dorian reined his thoughts back in. He *would* survive. He would take it one minute at a time and do whatever he had to do. He'd done it in Afghanistan. He would do it now.

But he was pretty sure he'd lost the battle when he heard Zac Mackay's voice through the metal of the shipping container.

"We need to be prepared that walking him out of here might not be a viable option."

"Roger that." That was Gavin's voice. Now Dorian knew he was hallucinating. "Then we bring him out whatever way we have to. And Ray also. If he was willing to risk his life to save her, we're not leaving her behind."

Okay, had Dorian really lost it? There was no way the team could be here. Even if Shadow had called them right away, convinced them somehow that helping Dorian and

Ray was the right thing to do, there was no way they could've gotten here this quickly.

Yet a few moments later, Dorian blinked against the light pouring into the container as the door pushed open and his team entered.

"It's D, he's restrained." Gavin walked toward him slowly as Zac and Finn both covered the exit with their weapons. "D, it's Gavin, man. Can you talk to me?"

"Are you asking if they cut out my tongue?"

Gavin chuckled. "Are you mobile?"

Could he move on his own, that's what they were asking. It was a fair question, given how they'd seen him in the past after he'd been restrained.

"Affirmative. Both mentally and physically mobile." Treatment for whatever hits he'd taken from Ray could wait.

Gavin reached down and began cutting through the zip ties around Dorian's wrists and ankles. "I'm glad to see you're doing so well, brother. I know this isn't your favorite place to be."

"How did you get here so fast? Shadow just left here a couple hours ago."

Gavin reached out his hand to help Dorian off the floor of the shipping container. "Not Shadow. Kendrick called us right after you guys left. We borrowed one of Cade's jets and flew. This wasn't a two-man job."

Dorian nodded. "Thank you for coming."

Gavin shrugged and slapped Dorian on the shoulder. "We're family. Family fights, but we don't turn our backs on each other when we're needed."

"I know you don't understand about Ray—"

Zac turned to him. "We don't have to understand about Ray. We understand that *you* love her and that there are larger forces working against her."

Gavin nodded. "Sometimes justice and the law aren't exactly the same. I forgot that for a minute, and I'm sorry. Now, let's get you guys out of here."

"I'm afraid it's not that simple."

Finn looked at them over his shoulder. "You're going have to explain it on the way. This location isn't secure."

Dorian nodded. They handed him a weapon and moved out.

They were already on the cargo ship. Compared to some barges, this one was on the smaller side, but there were still dozens of containers all around them.

"Kendrick already has a pretty good idea where Ray is being held," Zac said. "She's still off ship. It looks like Holloman is keeping her close by."

"Yeah, there's something you guys need to know," Dorian said. Telling them that Ray could go nuclear with only a sentence wasn't going to be easy.

They stopped before rounding the corner that held the rope they'd used to get from the dock onto the ship, since the bridgeway was monitored. Aiden was there, standing guard, and gave them a nod. "Good to see you, D."

"Thanks, Shamrock. I need to borrow a little of your luck."

Aiden scratched the recent scar on the side of his face. The scar he had gotten saving his woman. "You can have as much as you want."

They began working their way one by one across the rope. When Aiden brought up the rear, Dorian gave the guys the bad news. They needed to know what they were up against.

"There's something you need to know about Ray. The reason Holloman is keeping her so close is because she's the best weapon they could use against us. Against me. He says one voodoo phrase, and she turns into an assassin. She'll do everything in her power to kill us. Or at least me."

Gavin reached into his pack and pulled out a pair of headphones. "Then we make sure we get these on her before there's any voodoo. Blaze assures me she won't be able to hear anything with these on."

That kid was a genius. If Ray couldn't hear anything, she definitely couldn't be triggered. "Blaze rules all," he muttered before turning to the guys. "If we go busting in there guns blazing, they could trigger her before we eliminate them. I can't take the chance."

"We need some sort of distraction," Zac said.

They all turned, weapons trained as another voice joined them. "What you need to distract them is something they want more than you and Ray combined."

Shadow was back.

"Kendrick let me know where to find you guys."

"I thought you'd left. Ray's gonna be pissed to find out you're back here." Dorian reached out to shake Heath's hand.

"Believe me, there's very little I want more than to keep my brain, and whatever is in it, out of Holloman's hands. So we'll have to make sure I'm not taken."

Gavin nodded. "That office where they're holding Ray has two doors. If Heath can draw their attention to the front of the room, one of us can go in the back door and get the headphones to Ray."

Dorian shook his head. "No, I'll get the headphones to Ray."

She was going to be in bad shape in every possible way: physically, mentally, emotionally . . . At this point he was praying they weren't too late.

"D," Zac said. "Just because you're mobile doesn't mean

you're one hundred percent. Are you sure you don't want one of us to do it?"

"It needs to be me."

"We'll make an exit route for you. It's going to be tight. The ship is scheduled to leave soon," Aiden said.

Finn reached over and squeezed Dorian's shoulder. "We're going to get your girl out."

"Thank you for coming. All of you guys. I know we're family, but this might be beyond even that.

Zac shook his head. "You got left in hell once before. That's not going to happen again."

The other men murmured their agreement.

"Okay, let's do this." Zac had been their Special Forces team leader back in the day, and he picked that role back up easily now. "Everybody knows where they're supposed to be. Dorian, once you have Ray, we'll all meet at the southwest corner of the property. We've got a getaway vehicle for you there. Once we're all clear, we'll get local law enforcement involved."

The team scattered to their preassigned locations, leaving Dorian and Heath.

"I'm going in two minutes," Heath said. "Holloman is going to be interested in what I have to say, but wary. You're going to need to time this right."

"I will." Dorian held his hand out to shake, and Heath took it. "Thank you for coming back."

"Let's get her out, then you can thank me. I'll give you ninety more seconds to get into the place."

Dorian didn't waste any more time. He turned and ran down the hallway. When he rounded the corner, a guard was standing in front of the door. Dorian didn't hesitate. Before the man could make a sound, Dorian swung around with his foot and slammed the guard's face into the wall.

Then, like he'd done with Phantom, Dorian snapped the man's neck.

"Sorry, friend." Dorian wasn't talking to the guard. He couldn't take a chance that the man would regain consciousness and warn his friends about the rescue attempt.

He was talking to Mason. The man had been set up, sent to kill Ray because of the dogs. He'd died trying to avenge the death of the most important beings in his life.

Dorian cracked open the door just in time to hear Angela's surprised gasp as Heath entered the door in front of them.

The guard immediately pulled up his weapon, but Holloman stopped him. "Do not engage!" It was the closest Dorian had ever heard the man to panic. Evidently, Shadow really did have something in his brain Holloman wanted.

"I want to know what you did to me," Shadow said. "I want to know what's inside my head and how to make it stop."

"I can help you, of course," Holloman said. "But you'll need to put that weapon down."

"Timothy, this has to be a trap," Angela said. "He's probably here to rescue Wraith and Ghost."

Holloman laughed. "You might be right, Angela, but look at him. He wants answers."

This was Dorian's chance. Holloman was definitely focused on Shadow. Dorian slid the door open silently, his heart breaking when he saw Ray in the back corner, in a cage. Clearly, they didn't trust her not to fight their mind control.

That's my girl.

Keeping low, Dorian slipped through the door. Shadow was still talking about whatever it was inside his head.

And Shadow wasn't making it up. As much as Holloman wanted answers, Heath did too.

Dorian was almost to the cage before Ray lifted her head up from her knees. As soon as she saw Dorian, her spine stiffened, panic flooding into her eyes. Dorian brought his finger up to his mouth, fighting his own panic at the state she was in. She looked like death.

He could tell she was at the end of her rope. And both of them knew she wouldn't survive another round of fighting. She couldn't fight him, herself, *and* whatever it was they'd done to her brain.

Dorian took a few more silent steps, and he was to her. She was now shaking her head frantically back and forth, her eyes glossy and unfocused. He wasn't sure she was going to understand what to do with the headphones.

Dorian crouched down by the cage and tried to hand them to her. Ray covered her head with her hands and began rocking back and forth. But at least she was silent.

Shadow began talking louder, almost yelling, to keep the attention focused on him. It wasn't going to work much longer.

Dorian focused his attention on Ray. He reached through the bars and touched her ankle, sliding his fingers under the legs of her pants so he could touch her skin. He stayed there, touching her, as she stopped rocking and her fingers unwrapped from her knees and slid down to clutch his. He squeezed them and she opened her eyes.

He held out the headphones.

"Trust me," he mouthed. Neither of them read lips like Heath, but surely she could make this out.

She took the headphones and slipped them over her ears.

He squeezed her leg once more, then stood up, coming

up right behind the guard who still had his gun pointed at Shadow.

"You done?" Dorian asked Shadow as he clocked the guard in the back of the head. The man crumpled. "Or did you have more monologing you wanted to do?"

"*Bowls and robes slept along the beach*," Angela called out. She turned to Dorian, a smile on her face. "We don't need weapons. Wraith will break out of that cage to kill you."

"Not today she won't."

Angela looked over at Ray and let out a shriek of fury when she saw the headphones. Ray was watching everything but obviously couldn't hear any of it.

Dorian turned his gun on Angela, pointing it right between her eyes. "I want the phrase that releases Ray completely, or I swear I'll be taking both you and her with me, and every single thing that was done to me in that Afghani prison, I will do to you. When you give up your secret after the first ten minutes—because believe me, bitch, you *will*—I'll still have forty and a half more days of torture to go."

The color leached out of Angela's face. She looked over at Holloman, who nodded.

"*Rocks of pistons never run hotels.*"

Heath pulled out his backup weapon and pointed both guns straight into Holloman's and Angela's faces. "Go ahead and test it out. If either of them so much as breathes too loudly, there will be two fewer evil scientists in the world."

The keys to the cage were on the coffee table. Dorian grabbed them and knelt down to open it. Ray's blue eyes stared out at him, but they were cloudy, defeated.

She flinched as he reached toward her, still huddled in the back corner of the cage. He couldn't reach her, and it didn't look like she'd be coming toward him anytime soon.

Everything in his brain rebelled against it, but Dorian climbed into the cage with her.

God, he would climb into any cage for this woman.

Gently sliding his hand into her hair at the back of her neck, he eased her closer. He slid the headphone off one ear enough so that she'd be able to hear only him, in case Holloman or Angela tried something.

He whispered the words into her ear.

"Dorian?" she whispered, like she couldn't quite figure out where she was or what was happening.

"Grace?"

She made a face. "Don't call me that."

It was her.

"Leave these on."

She nodded, and he slid the headphone back over her ear.

"I've got her," Dorian said to Heath. "Let's go."

Dorian helped Ray out of the cage. She was barely able to stand. It didn't matter. He would carry her as long as he needed to.

He led her toward the back door, but when he looked over his shoulder, Heath was still standing there with Angela and Holloman.

"You go," Heath said. "Get her out. Get her help. I've got to get some answers. I can't live like this anymore."

"Shadow . . ." Dorian didn't want to leave him behind. Not in a situation where Holloman had the upper hand.

But then, all hell broke loose outside. Gunfire from all directions. Ray still had her hand resting calmly in his, unable to hear any of it.

Dorian looked back at Shadow. He had lowered his weapons, but it looked like he had no intention of moving.

Holloman pulled up a gun from his own waist, but with

Ray in this position, Dorian couldn't get a shot off. He was about to watch his friend die.

Holloman spun and shot Angela in the head. The woman collapsed to the ground with a surprised look on her face.

Holloman turned to Shadow. "Now, if you want answers, I'm the only one who has them."

Heath had brought his own weapon up as Holloman had fired. Frustration was clear on his face. He wanted to kill Holloman, but couldn't.

Holloman smiled. "That's right, Shadow. You're going to have to let me go. I'm sure we can meet again another day. Oh, and by the way, we might've accidentally sent a copy of Wraith's greatest-hits video to law enforcement. They may be here looking for her."

Not two seconds later, the scream of distant sirens filtered through the gunfire.

No one in the room could doubt what it cost Heath to re-holster his weapon, but he did it.

"Get the fuck out of here before I decide I can live with the voices in my head. I'll be coming for you, Holloman."

Heath joined Dorian and Ray, and they rushed out the back door as Holloman slipped out the front.

They ran.

They were barely down one hall, the sound of gunfire obvious from outside and in some rooms behind them, when Ray stumbled.

Dorian didn't slow; he scooped her into his arms.

When they got to the stairwell, Aiden and Finn were waiting to provide them cover.

"She okay?" Finn asked.

At some point Ray had completely passed out.

"Physically, I think so, but I've got to get her out of here.

Holloman sent the video of Ray committing crimes. Assassinations. It's pretty damning."

Gavin nodded. "We've already seen it. We've got a vehicle and bug-out bag ready for you guys. You take off with her. We'll take care of these guys and give law enforcement a story with enough truth that they can believe it. But that video, man . . ."

Dorian nodded. There wasn't going to be an easy way to explain it. "Just getting her out of here is enough."

Gavin put his arms around Dorian and Ray. "Take care of her. Take care of yourself. We'll see you when we see you, brother."

The sirens were getting closer. "Finn will get you to the car. Time for me to go be a sheriff."

Gavin ran in one direction, and Dorian followed Finn in the other.

Shadow had disappeared somewhere during it all.

The car was parked on a dirt road about a mile away. Finn hugged Dorian, then immediately turned to run back to the action.

Dorian laid Ray gently down in the back seat of the late-model Honda. He tried to remove her headphones, but she immediately got restless, so he put them back over her ears. He kissed her forehead, then got behind the wheel.

The bag in the passenger seat contained everything they needed. Cash. IDs for both of them. Gear and clothes for anything they'd need in the wilderness.

Dorian started the car and pulled out. He had no idea where he was going.

It didn't matter where they went. All that mattered was that he and Ray were together.

The rest they would figure out.

EPILOGUE

our Months Later

F Grace Brandt, international terrorist and covert
agent, died that day at the Port of Umatilla, when
Acting Sheriff Gavin Zimmerman shot her. Unfortunately,
her body fell into the Columbia River and was washed away,
never to be recovered.

But three of Zimmerman's closest friends, all respected
former special forces soldiers, witnessed the fact that Grace
had drawn on Gavin, and he'd been forced to kill her. And
that she had definitely been dead before she hit the water.

There was no word or trace of Project Crypt, of course.
All the crimes pointed directly to Grace without even a
breath of some secret conspiracy. The Feds solved a bunch
of cases they hadn't known were open.

That day Grace Brandt died, but Ray Lindstrom was
born.

It was four months later and Dorian still hadn't gotten
used to Ray's black hair.

But those eyes, those beautiful blue eyes, still brought
him to his knees.

It hadn't been an easy four months. Not for her or him.

Ray still struggled every day with what she'd done. The people she'd killed. They'd at least been able to confirm that she hadn't killed Holloman's wife and young children. Bastard hadn't even had a family. Holloman and Angela had set that all up—a method of pulling Ray back in if she threatened to walk.

On some days, the fact that she had killed Phantom's dogs seemed to eat at her the most. They'd made a huge donation in Mason Wyndham's name to the shelter where he'd gotten them.

It didn't change what she'd done, but it was something.

"Are you going to do anything today or just sit around and be lazy?" he called out to her.

Ray lounged on a large rock outside of the cabin they'd inhabited for the past two months. Dorian had wanted to take her somewhere warm—a beach, or an island—but in the end, they'd come back to his cabin in Wyoming. The one he'd never taken anyone to.

The one, he realized, he'd been preparing for the two of them all the years he'd been building it. He'd just never known it would be their permanent home.

The team had come and helped them finish it.

The first thing they'd done was set up a perimeter warning system. If anything larger than a bobcat crossed over the three-hundred-meter perimeter they'd set up, they would immediately receive a warning.

No one would be sneaking up on them unawares.

With the guys' help, Dorian had added two more rooms to the cabin in a little over a week. They'd updated all the plumbing, put in a more powerful generator, and loaded them up with supplies and furniture.

Including Dorian's favorite reading chair from the other cabin.

How many hours had he sat in that chair already, reading, with Ray curled up in his lap? Both of them content to just be with each other?

Sometimes, on the really bad days, she wore the headphones. No one could say words that would take away all her choices if she couldn't hear them. But she'd been wearing them less and less.

The last thing the team had done before they'd left was to stand as witnesses as Kendrick—a newly ordained minister thanks to the internet—married Dorian and Ray. The union wasn't officially filed with the state, but neither of them cared.

Ray hadn't wanted to do it at first, arguing that Dorian might want to have children someday. Ones she'd never be able to provide.

He'd looked her in the eye and told her the only thing he could. The only thing that mattered. "You and me. Always. Everything else is secondary."

Ray Lindstrom became Mrs. Ray Lindstrom, Dorian Lindstrom's other half. He wouldn't have had it any other way.

Shadow had shown up once since, promising to keep them updated on his hunt for Holloman. He still had more questions than he did answers, figuring out what was so *special* about him, and who exactly was behind Project Crypt's reboot. It couldn't be just Holloman.

But that was on Heath. Dorian was glad to no longer be a part of that fight and was determined it would never touch his bride again either.

"Storm and I are going to sit around and do what we're best at: being lazy." The bride in question smiled up at him.

Yep, still took his breath away.

He laughed and walked down to the rock, scooping her up, then lay down on it himself, settling her on top of him.

She wiggled to get closer, and he smacked her on the ass. "Keep that up and we'll traumatize poor Storm right here on this rock."

"Wouldn't be the first time." Her laugh was a little rusty, but it was there. And he was going to keep doing every single thing he could to bring it back.

The best part about living through the trauma he'd lived through? He knew how to help someone else live through it too. And Ray was going to live through it.

Her body was still tired. She slept nearly twelve hours a night and still didn't do much in terms of physical activity at all. But she seemed to be getting stronger, not weaker. No more headaches, no more nosebleeds—all that had ended once Ray no longer had to fight Crypt's conditioning.

So they would take every day as it came.

Oak Creek and the people there who cared about Dorian and Ray would welcome them back with open arms whenever they were ready. After all, they didn't know her as Grace Brandt anyway.

And if Ray was never ready to go back, that was okay with Dorian too.

Not every forever included a white picket fence. But their forever included each other and that was all Dorian needed.

ACKNOWLEDGMENTS

This was possibly the most difficult book I've ever written. Readers have loved Dorian from the beginning—wanting his story ASAP.

But half way through the book I truly struggled:

Was Ray really the woman for Dorian?

Would readers respond to their story?

Maybe readers wanted someone more sweet and innocent for their precious D.

Someone who could have babies.

Someone who wasn't so broken. Dorian himself was broken enough.

Sigh.

It got bad enough that I even stopped the book half way through and restarted it with an entirely new heroine.

Ray just sat back and waited and let me try whatever I needed to. Because she knew the truth: she was Dorian Lindstrom's soulmate.

Nobody else was going to work for him except her.

After about a week I realized that truth too. And the rest

of the book pretty much wrote itself. Dorian and Ray had a story to tell.

A love so powerful, nothing could keep them apart.

I hope in the end it was as special to you as it was to me.

But getting that all worked out in my head took the support of a lot of real life people. They deserve my thanks:

As always, my husband and kids for putting up with my craziness. Especially this time. I know I say that every time.

To my Bat Signal tribe: Ladies, your friendship and encouragement continues to mean everything to me. To the newbies: Patricia & Terri...so glad we've all found each other.

To my Alpha Readers, who took this story on before it was polished and looked for the potential underneath: Kaitlin S., Susan G., Jessica N., Denise H., Andra T., Judy W., Jacquelyn N., Mary L., and Sharon C. Thank you so much for your encouragement and suggestions! You made a huge difference!

To my editors and proofreaders: Elizabeth Nover, Marci Mathers, Stephanie Scott, and Aly Birkl. Once again, thank you for your patience, consistency, and hard work. I depend on you so much and you never let me down.

And finally, as always, to my readers... I can't believe we're already at book 5 in the Linear Tactical series! Thank you for reading these books and taking these characters into your heart. Because of you, there's many more to come!

With gratitude,

Janie

ALSO BY JANIE CROUCH

Battle Tested

ABOUT THE AUTHOR

"Passion that leaps right off the page." - Romantic Times Book Reviews

USA TODAY bestselling author Janie Crouch writes what she loves to read: passionate romantic suspense. She is a winner and/or finalist of multiple romance literary awards including the Golden Quill Award for Best Romantic Suspense, the National Reader's Choice Award, and the coveted RITA© Award by the Romance Writers of America.

Janie recently relocated with her husband and their four teenagers to Germany (due to her husband's job as support for the U.S. Military), after living in Virginia for nearly 20 years. When she's not listening to the voices in her head—and even when she is—she enjoys engaging in all sorts of crazy adventures (200-mile relay races; Ironman Triathlons, treks to Mt. Everest Base Camp) traveling, and movies of all kinds.

Her favorite quote: "Life is a daring adventure or nothing." ~ Helen Keller.

facebook.com/janiecrouch

twitter.com/janiecrouch

instagram.com/janiecrouch

Printed in the USA
CPSIA information can be obtained
at www.ICGtesting.com
LVHW092106270624
783940LV00006B/429

9 781950 802005